WARNING AT DAWN

The man came in on his knees, inching forward a little bit at a time. He was one of Zim's legion of flunkies, glorified servants who ran errands and carried messages for him from various parts of the palace. They were all required to enter into his presence this way.

The man had made it about fifteen feet inside the room when Zim finally shouted at him: "OK, get up, you ass!"

The man immediately obeyed and began tiptoeing across the room toward the mountain of pillows. With a trembling hand he proffered a note on a silver tray up to Zim.

A hush came over the room. This was not considered pleasant news, and the man who had delivered it was in desperate fear of his life at the moment. It was not unknown for Zim to kill the messenger when the news was bad.

Zim read the note silently. "Who sent this?" he asked.

The man at the base of the pillows quavered a bit.

"Your guest in Room Six," he replied with a shaky voice.

Zim considered this, then reread the note.

It contained only two words: *They're coming.*

CHOPPER OPS

Mack Maloney

B

BERKLEY BOOKS, NEW YORK

CHOPPER OPS

A Berkley Book / published by arrangement with
the author

PRINTING HISTORY
Berkley edition / October 1999

The Penguin Putnam Inc. World Wide Web site address is
http://www.penguinputnam.com

ISBN: 0-425-17116-7

BERKLEY®
Berkley Books are published by The Berkley Publishing Group,
a division of Penguin Putnam Inc.,
375 Hudson Street, New York, New York 10014.
BERKLEY and the "B" logo
are trademarks belonging to Penguin Putnam Inc.

PRINTED IN THE UNITED STATES OF AMERICA

10 9 8 7 6 5 4 3 2 1

For my good friend
Bob Bloomer

PART ONE
SEVEN
GHOSTS

1

Western Saudi Arabia
February 9, 1991
0200 hours

The American air base at Al-Khadi was a very secret place.

Located deep in the western Saudi desert, it appeared on no maps. The only road leading to it was 173 miles long, winding and unmarked. Barely a dozen people in the Saudi military knew the air base existed, and still they weren't privy to its location. Even the U.S. Army engineers who built the place back in 1989 weren't sure exactly where it was. They had been trucked to the site blindfolded when construction began. When they finished, they left the same way.

Air operations at Al-Khadi took place only at night. Extremely strict blackout restrictions were always in effect then. No lights. No radios. No electronic gear of any kind was permitted to be turned on unless absolutely necessary. Even the lighting of a match was forbidden without proper authorization.

Only one runway was open at Al-Khadi this fateful night. The rest of the base was shut up tight. The weather had something to do with this. An unusual desert fog had settled over the base earlier in the evening; it was so thick by midnight it resembled a snowstorm. The Saudis called this cold and wet phenomena *el-fadeh-al*, "unwanted visitor from the west." Traditionally, it was an omen of bad luck.

A single airplane stood waiting in this murk, its four propellers turning and blowing waves of cold mist behind them. An eerie growl from the plane's muffled engines washed across the desert floor, bouncing off the mountains that surrounded the air base. The ground crew moved like spirits under the plane's wings and fuselage, emerging, then disappearing within the swirl of fog.

This particular aircraft had many names. Stout of body and thick in the nose, it was a variant of the ubiquitous C-130 Hercules cargo plane. Its official serial listing was AC-130/SO-21D. Since operating out of Al-Khadi, its radio call sign had invariably been "Alpha One Blue." Its aircrew called the big plane "The Space Hog." But the unusual aircraft was most readily known by the name of the secret unit to which it was attached: ArcLight 4.

The air war against Iraq had been going on for nearly a month now. Allied bombers were continuously pounding targets inside Iraq and occupied Kuwait. The ground assault to retake Kuwait would begin in just two weeks. In anticipation of this, the big ArcLight 4 airplane was about to take off on its thirteenth mission in as many days.

ArcLight 4 was not a bomber—not a conventional one anyway. It was actually a combination spy plane and weapons platform. Its bulbous nose was stuffed with surveillance gear—infrared TV cameras, NightScopes, powerful electronic eavesdropping equipment. Its thick fuselage was packed with weaponry. Three M-134 7.62-mm miniguns were mounted in portholes on the aircraft's left side. Essentially modern Gatling guns, these six-barreled weapons could each fire one hundred rounds *a second*—an incredible rate. The aircraft also carried a 105-mm light howitzer, capable of firing a variety of ordnance including armor-piercing and high-explosive shells.

The aircraft delivered its fierce barrage by going into an orbit above a target, tipping on its left wing, and firing all four weapons at once. Such a fusillade could perforate an area the size of a football field in less than ten seconds. Mobile targets, troop concentrations, and such things as missile launchers and heavy guns were usually vaporized in even less time. Sustained firing by the gunship's combined weaponry most often resulted in craters that seemed more at home on the moon.

The plane's crew was a combination of sorts too. It was made up of U.S. Army Green Berets, U.S. Air Force officers, and Defense Intelligence Agency specialists. There were thirteen in all, and the delineation of duties was simple. The Green Berets handled the weapons, the DIA men ran the snooping equipment, and the Air Force guys flew the airplane. Each man on board had the highest security clearance possible.

On paper, the plane's mission this night was the same as the previous twelve. Get airborne, turn on its snooping equipment, try to ascertain special targets—SCUD sites, biological or nerve-gas weapons depots, suspected nuclear storage facilities—and then go in and hit them with the airplane's awesome weaponry.

So far in the war, ArcLight 4 had destroyed a half-dozen such targets in some very out-of-the-way places. The fuzzy border between Iraq and Iran had been one of them. Enclaves of pro-Saddam guerrillas hiding valuable equipment in the rugged hills of east Jordan had been another. One flight a week before had brought the secret airplane all the way up to the Turkish-Russian border to stop a column of arms smugglers heading for Saddam's beleaguered troops. It was no surprise that the airplane carried no markings, no country insignia, no outward indication as to who it belonged to. After all, the airplane's modus operandi was to go places and do things no other Allied airplane could possibly do.

That was why its crew, its operations, and the airplane itself officially did not exist.

In many ways, it was a ghost.

By 0235 hours, the plane was ready to go. It rolled out onto Runway East One, the only airstrip open. The base control tower turned on the double set of dull blue lights lining the runway, but only long enough for the big airplane to get itself positioned. Then they were switched off again. The pilots would have to rely on their NightVision goggles for the actual takeoff.

Waiting now at the end of the runway, the airplane's crew ran one last diagnostic check. All of the airplane's vitals—its engines, its fuel supply, its communications and backup gear—were in order. Its weapons systems were all lit green. Its tons of eavesdropping equipment were functioning in the high range as well.

This mission tonight had the makings of a fairly easy one. The crew's orders called for it to sweep up Iraq's western border, cross over the top of Saddam's domain, and then fly back down its eastern fringe. Total flying time, just under six hours. A Sunday drive compared to the fifteen-hour marathon flights the crew was used to doing.

That was why it was so odd then that after the strange airplane took off and disappeared into the cold misty night, it was never heard from again.

2

Bethesda, Maryland
Ten years later

The phone call came just after 1 A.M.

It roused Gene Smitz out of his recurring dream about playing first base in the 1986 World Series. It was raining outside and in that first groggy moment, Smitz thought the ringing was the sound of raindrops hitting his window. But there was no rain *that* hard, his sleepy brain told him. Yanking himself out of his dream just as Mookie Wilson's dribbler was heading right for him, Smitz reached over and answered the phone.

The voice on the other end was a whisper, echoing and distant. That was how Smitz knew it was from his office.

"You are needed at Bethesda Naval Hospital," the voice said. "Second floor, Room 333. It's best you don't delay."

The cab driver had no problem with that. When Smitz said he needed to get to Bethesda Hospital as quickly as possible, the Sudanese cabbie drove the twenty-two

miles in eighteen minutes. The ride was so wild it gave
Smitz at least one strange thought: Was his life *so* ironic
that he would be killed in a taxi rushing to a hospital?

They came close—the streets had turned slick in the
chilly spring downpour. But somehow he arrived at Bethesda in one piece. And while he didn't know why he
was being summoned to the Navy hospital, at least he
was sure it didn't pertain to any member of his family.
The Office would not have called him for that.

No, this was a work-related thing.

Smitz jumped from the cab, threw the driver a twenty,
and hurried inside. He was a slight, thin man, not quite
wiry, and just twenty-five years old. His overgrown haircut and tortoise-shell glasses gave him a perpetual
college-boy look. This was why the hospital security
guards double-checked his ID badge before letting him
into the private-area wing of the vast hospital. Smitz just
didn't look like a CIA guy. An accountant, maybe. A
junior ad executive, possibly. But not CIA. His eyes just
didn't have it.

Once in, he took the stairs two at a time up to the
third floor. He reached Room 333, and the small mystery
was solved. A trio of CIA officers was waiting outside.
They were his supervisors, three in succession, right up
the ladder. This meant only one person could be behind
the door: George Jacobs. The Old Man. The chief of the
CIA's Special Foreign Operations Section. Smitz's big
boss.

"What happened to him?" Smitz asked the three men
outside.

Only one of his supervisors replied. His name was
Larry Stone. He was a Grade-A prick, and an angry,
bitter man. He resented the fact that Smitz was nearly
as high on the pecking order as he at nearly half his age.

"He wants to see you," Stone told him. The words
came in icy tones.

Smitz began to open the door, and Stone caught his
arm.

"And listen, Harvard boy, it's his heart," Stone said.

"So if he has something to tell you, don't delay in letting him do it."

Smitz nodded curtly and went through the door.

The room was small, spare, white. There were no windows. No other doors. There was a bed at the far end. It was surrounded by a jungle of tubes and hoses. Green ones, white ones, blue ones. A disturbing-looking red one. Then there were the machines. Pumping. Breathing. Beeping. Beneath it all, wrapped in a single pale blue blanket, was the boss.

A shock of white hair, ruddy complexion. A big man who looked ten years younger than his sixty-five years, Jacobs managed a smile when he saw Smitz walk in.

"Sorry to get you out of bed, Smitty."

"What happened, Chief?" Smitz asked, trying not to stare at the gaggle of life-support machinery.

Jacobs laughed. "Old football injury kicking up."

"Chief, I'm sorry . . . I . . ."

Jacobs waved away Smitz's concerns.

"I don't have any regrets," he said. "Except I didn't make as much money as I wanted. You know how the government pays. But maybe where I'm going, they pay better."

Jacobs laughed. Smitz tried to.

"We have some business, though, Smitty, you and me," Jacobs went on.

Smitz turned to the nurse sitting next to Jacobs's bed and gave her a nod. She left quickly. Then Jacobs pointed to his briefcase on the table nearby.

"Red folder, white envelope inside," he said. "Everyone I know is inheriting my problems—and here's a real stinker for you. Sorry I can't leave you with something better. Believe me, if I had my way, I'd just let this one slide. But they are making me do it."

Smitz took the folder out of the briefcase. It was indeed red and sealed several times in red tape. One page was sticking out, and Smitz saw it was a letter with the Presidential seal on it.

"This is a Level Six program, Smitty," Jacobs said.

"Way high on the scale. And it's a real pain-in-the-ass job. But it's something that has to be done and now it's your baby. Read the briefing papers when you can, will you?"

Smitz stared into Jacobs's eyes. He didn't look that sick. And despite the spaghetti jumble of tubes and hoses, none of them seemed to be connected to him.

"I'll handle it until you get back on your feet, Chief," Smitz told him. "Don't worry."

Jacobs just laughed at that too.

"Just remember two things about this job, Smitty," he said. "First, it's a very screwed-up program. Stitched together, interservice bullshit. The personnel are still being assembled. The training is just beginning. The equipment is still somewhere in the pipeline. But something has to happen eventually. The problem might get visible. So, do what you can, OK?"

"Will do, Chief . . ."

Jacobs reached up and shook Smitz's hand.

"Thanks, Smitty . . ."

Smitz hesitated.

"How about the other thing, Chief?" he asked Jacobs. "The second point about this program?"

Jacobs had to think a moment.

"Oh, right," he finally said. "The other thing is, you might find yourself doing a lot of flying for this one."

"OK. So?"

Jacobs motioned for him to get a little closer.

"If you do," Jacobs said in a whisper, "try like hell to stay out of the helicopters."

Smitz left the room, brushed by his supervisors, and retreated to a nearby waiting area. It was deserted, safe enough for him to read the file.

He bought a cup of bad coffee from a nearby vending machine and sat down to read.

The file was barely an inch thick. The first bunch of pages contained a slew of PALs—Presidential Action Letters. They were addressed individually to the personnel ordered to work the program. Most of these people were military. Many of them were Marine Corps. Four were from Army Aviation. Four more were from the Navy SEALs' medical personnel section. Four letters still had their addressee lines blank. Smitz groaned. Jacobs didn't have to warn him about this. From experience he knew that any program involving interservice "cooperation" seemed cursed from the start.

It got worse. The next page displayed the PS2, the personnel selection sequence, which was a fancy way of documenting in graph form both how and why the civilian and military personnel selected for the program had been chosen. But the PS2 sheet was nearly blank; its graph lines were limp and flaccid. Many names had been scratched out; still others were of personnel not even contacted yet. With the exception of the Marines, it was as if someone was simply picking names out of a hat, instead of trying to collect a cohesive group of individuals whose talents would interact for the greater good. This didn't make any sense to Smitz. He could only hope someone up top understood it.

The next part of the file contained a series of satellite photos with map grids superimposed on them. Most were identified as being from the Persian Gulf region, specifically Iraq. They showed what appeared to be sites of recent combat damage. Villages, convoys, oil-storage facilities—all of them torn up, burned, or flattened. In many photos, bodies were in evidence. Smitz's first thought was that the photos had been taken during the Gulf War, nearly ten years before. But each of the pictures carried a date much later than 1991. The most recent one was marked with a date from just a few months ago.

Only two photos depicted places located outside the Persian Gulf region. One of these showed an enormous black hole in a field near a town in Bosnia identified as Crztia. The caption for the second photo said it was taken near Dishu Bur, Somalia. It showed a large portion of slum-like neighborhood simply vaporized.

The third document in the file was actually an envelope containing the Action Paper, essentially the background on why this particular program had been put together. Smitz took a deep gulp of the putrid coffee and opened it.

He expected to find reams of pages explaining what the program involved and what he was supposed to do. Instead, he found just four meager information sheets. The first showed a very blurry photocopy image of what Smitz recognized to be a C-130 cargo plane. It had no markings or insignia, however, seemed bigger than a normal C-130, and appeared to be painted a light shade of camouflage gray. There was a caption attached to the bottom of the photocopy, but most of it had been inked out. The only thing Smitz could make out were a few words directly underneath the airplane's image. They read: "ArcLight 4. Last known radio call sign: Alpha One Blue."

The second sheet had three other photographs attached, none of which had captions. The first showed an aerial photograph of a small airfield Smitz guessed was somewhere in the Caribbean. He'd been in that area enough times to recognize the fauna and the water color. The place looked tiny, with one short airstrip and a few buildings. It also appeared to be deserted. The second and third photos showed the same place, just as empty, taken through a Starscope camera at night.

The third page told Smitz what he should bring for the environment he was going to. Pack light summer wear and nothing else. An index card stapled to the fourth page said Smitz was to report to Andrews Air Force Base within twenty-four hours to get transport to his new assignment. Once he was on-site, further information on the program would be waiting for him.

And that was it. No more photos, no more background. Nothing.

Smitz closed the file and resealed it. Two things began bothering him immediately. First, this seemed to be a big project for someone like him who was still pretty low in rank in his section. Rarely did his assignments take him away from Washington, D.C., or its close environs. This one, though, seemed to indicate he'd be going somewhere hot and humid and be there for a long period of time.

But secondly, never had he read an action report with such a paucity of information. Usually a project folder was *too* thick with paperwork. This one was abnormally thin. Something had to be missing here. Perhaps there was more information in another file in Jacobs's briefcase. Smitz threw the coffee cup away and walked back down the hallway to Jacobs's room.

Only Stone was waiting outside the door now. The other two supervisors had left. Smitz tried to push by him, but the man stopped him.

"You're too late," Stone told him. "He's gone."

"Gone? Gone where?" Smitz asked. "Another room? Another floor?"

"Gone as in 'dead,' " Stone told him coldly. "Ten minutes ago."

Smitz thought he was kidding.

"But I only *left* here ten minutes ago," he said.

Stone didn't blink. "Take a look for yourself," he said.

Smitz went through the door and stopped after two steps. Jacobs *was* gone, as were the tubes and the machines. Only the unmade bed remained.

Stone was right behind him. He handed him a small white card with an address on it.

"This is where you can send flowers," he said.

Smitz looked at the card and then back at Stone, then at the empty room again.

Then without another word, he turned on his heel, went out the door, and took a cab home.

3

It was precisely 0700 hours when the sleek silver-and-blue jet fighter began its takeoff run.

Engines screeching, the jet roared down the runway, parting an ocean of early morning fog. Exactly eight seconds into his takeoff roll, the pilot yanked back on the stick. A stream of fire exploded from the aircraft's tailpipes. Suddenly the fighter was airborne.

It immediately went on its tail, its needle nose pointing straight up into the cloudless sky. The jet accelerated so quickly, it was soon nothing more than a silver speck, twisting its way heavenward. With one last flash of sunlight off its wings, it disappeared from view altogether.

The airplane's official name was the YF-17 Cobra. It was an unusual, one-of-a-kind airplane with an interesting lineage. Back in the early 1970's, the Cobra had lost a fly-off for the Air Force's new-generation fighter, a competition eventually won by the F-16 Fighting Falcon. The Cobra was hardly a bust, though. Its design was so impressive, the Navy tinkered with it and created the F/A-18 Hornet, currently the Fleet's premier fighter-attack plane. Hundreds of Hornets had been built over the years. Yet only one Cobra had ever flown—and this was it.

In the world of military aviation, the phrase goes: If it looks good, it flies good. With its sharp nose, short wings, and twin tails, the YF-17 looked good and flew good. *Real* good. But for all its elegance, this particular airplane was essentially a flying clown. There was an air show today at Fallon. More than a quarter of a million people were expected to attend. The YF-17 was one of many airplanes performing; in fact, it was due to go on first. That was why the pilot was taking this practice run so early in the day. He had ten minutes to run through his routine, a pre-show quickie that would allow him to get familiar with the terrain over which he would be performing.

The main attraction of the day would be a performance by the Navy's Aerial Demonstration Team, better known as the Blue Angels. The eight blue-and-gold F-18's were tucked away inside a secure hangar, one of many at the sprawling high-desert air base. Their scheduled takeoff time was still nearly six hours away.

There was also a dizzying assortment of military aircraft on static display to entertain the crowds. Mammoth C-5's, grandfatherly B-52's, a few hard-luck B-1's. Also sleek F-16's, tiger-sharked F-14's, bulked-up F-15E's. Even an F-22 Raptor prototype.

But of them all, no doubt the oddest airplane was the Cobra.

It appeared again about a minute later, streaking in from the west. Flying no more than two hundred feet off the deck, the Cobra twisted wildly as a long plume of red, white, and blue smoke streamed out of its tail. The patriotic cloud thus laid, the pilot put the aircraft on its tail a second time and once again rocketed back up into the deep blue desert sky.

When the Air Force decided to put the YF-17 out on the air show circuit, it realized it needed a pilot who was more than the typical ice-water-cool flyboy type. More than someone who could quickly adapt to the airplane's unique controls and master its nuances, the Air Force needed someone who didn't mind being a high-tech carnival act, who could handle the rigors of the road and long hours of solitary practicing. Someone who, for want of a better word, had a flair for "showmanship."

So the computer at the Air Force's Personnel Assignment Center at the Pentagon was given the task of finding just such a pilot. As the story went, it took exactly twenty-two seconds for the computer to spit out the file of the man now at the controls of the YF-17.

He was Major John Thomas Norton IV. Most people knew him as "Jazz."

From the start it appeared to be a great match. At thirty-four, Norton was an outstanding pilot, near the top of the Air Force's performance chart. He'd flown F-15's for the 16th Fighter Squadron in Langley, Virginia, then F-117 Stealths out of Holliman in New Mexico. He'd seen action in the Gulf War and over Kosovo, and at present was on the very short list for space-shuttle training. If that didn't come through, his superiors fully expected him to be assigned to flying black projects out of Groom Lake, the infamous Area 51 or some other secret location.

But what the computer might not have known was that the business of show flying was already in Norton's genes. True, Jazz's father had flown F-4's in Vietnam and his grandfather had driven Mustangs in World War II. But Jazz's *great*-grandfather had spent the 1920's as a barnstorming pilot. He'd been a minor celebrity, famous for doing everything from wing-walking to intentionally flying rickety biplanes nose-first into the sides of old barns.

The question then was this: If the Air Force had realized that Great Gramps had made a living crashing his airplane for the delight of hundreds, would they still have made Jazz Norton the prime choice to fly the YF-17 when the air show assignment came up?

No one knew the answer—least of all Norton himself. And in the six months he'd been on the circuit, no one had bothered to ask.

Norton was twisting in the cockpit of the YF-17 now, inverted, looking over his shoulder at the ground below and sucking his oxygen mask like a madman.

He was a handsome fellow. His sandy hair and tanned face accentuated his movie-idol looks, these inherited from his mother's side of the family. At five-ten, he was taller than your average fighter pilot. But with his broad shoulders, rock-hard jaw, and steely eyes, he *looked* like a fighter jock.

The bright Nevada sun was lifting large clouds of steam off the whole base now, and the visibility on the ground was almost down to zero. This would make Norton's practice run a little more difficult—and dangerous. For most pilots this would be the beginning of palm-sweating time, and breathing heavy was a natural side effect.

But this was not why Norton was sucking in oxygen so greedily. He was simply hungover—the lasting effects of a night's worth of carousing in nearby Reno. Every pilot knew there was nothing like a lot of pure "O" to remedy a hangover. Jazz was simply taking the cure.

He flipped the Cobra back upright and then began a long twisting dive down. He checked the oxygen-enrichment needle on his environment panel, and turned it all the way up to 100 percent. A series of deep breaths and he felt his head slowly start to clear.

Despite the fact that getting the YF-17 gig had knocked him out of an assignment of flying *really* cool stuff at Groom Lake, Norton enjoyed his air show job. He knew all the secrets of the Cobra by now, and under the hood it was a real hot rod. The manufacturer had rebuilt the plane's power plants shortly before it went out on the air show circuit, and that had enabled the thing to go really fast. In return for tweaking the engines,

the airplane's service reps asked Norton to beat the pants
off any F-16 he might meet out on the road—unofficially, of course. There were some long memories in the
fighter plane game. Norton promised he'd do everything
he could.

He brought the Cobra back down to two hundred feet
now, and leveled off above the steamy runway again.
This time down he would practice what he called the
TSK—the Ten-Second Killer.

He could perform it in his sleep by now. On the count
of one . . . begin wagging the wings back and forth. Two
. . . three . . . hit the smoke-release lever. The mist down
here was like a forest fire now; Norton was carving
through it like a shark through water. At five seconds,
level off. Hold for six . . . seven . . . OK, kill smoke.
Hold for eight . . . nine . . . OK, increase throttle.

Ten! Mark! Go!

He took another massive gulp of oxygen and yanked
back on the stick. He was soon sitting feet up again,
eyes straight ahead and climbing back up to the stars.

He'd kill this hangover yet.

Among the early arrivals at Fallon were two men in a
Ford Bronco.

The vehicle was painted black, inside and out. Even
its windows were opaque. Though its license plate said
it was from California, this type of truck was not exactly
unknown around Fallon, or any other U.S. military air
base for that matter.

It was a Spook-mobile—and these guys were Spooks.
Members of U.S. Intelligence. Real-life men-in-black.
CIA. DIA. NSA. NRS. Whoever. It didn't matter. They
were Spooks. Pure and simple.

The truck was a dead giveaway.

The Bronco was parked next to the main runway,
away from several knots of early-bird civilians. The two
men were leaning against its hood, sunglasses on, binoculars at the ready.

They'd watched the Cobra's spectacular takeoff, and

followed it up until they could no longer see it. They
had watched its two approaches, flashing through the
thick fog, twisting this way and that, spewing out its
colored exhaust fumes before disappearing again.

They couldn't help but be impressed.

"Well, they were right," one of the Spooks said as
the jet left the Earth's grip again. "He *can* fly the hell
out of that thing."

"I don't think we've seen anything yet," his partner
replied.

Suddenly the airplane appeared again. This time it
materialized at the north end of the base and began another eye-blistering transit of the main runway. Roaring
through the last of the dissipating fog at full power, it
rolled wing over wing a dozen times before twisting up
and away and ascending into the heavens once again.
Between the noise and the speed and the shallow altitude, it was a rather frightening display.

"I don't know about this," the first Spook said to the
second. "Should he really be flying like that?"

The second man calmly lit a cigarette and threw the
match on the asphalt of the fuel-soaked taxi area.

"Ain't you ever been to an air show before?" he
asked. "They all fly that way."

They climbed back into the Bronco and began driving
slowly to a more populated part of the base. They kept
the airplane in sight the whole way, watching it continue
its bewildering set of aerial tricks. One time, the plane
came across the runway, again at mind-numbing speed—
upside down. Another time it went by tumbling nose
over end—once, twice, three times before recovering
Mach 1 speed and disappearing again.

"This guy appears to be a little fucking nuts," the
first Spook said. "Are you sure this is wise what we are
doing?"

"Look, we're just hired hands," the second man re-
plied. "Let whoever sent us out here worry about that.
Besides, maybe he's still drunk. He had quite a time in
Reno last night."

The plane came by again. This time it was standing on its tail and barely inching its way forward in a kind of waddling motion. Just when it appeared the jet would fall out of the sky it was going so slow, the engine was lit and it rocketed away again.

The first Spook took the binoculars and tried to follow the plane as it ascended again. "Did you know his mother was an extra in Hollywood?"

"No kidding?"

"She appeared in eleven movies from 1962 to 1978. Since deceased."

"Bummer. His father is dead too, I think."

"Right. He has no brothers, no sisters, no cousins. Six steady girlfriends in the past ten years but no wife. He has no real family at all. Maybe that's why he doesn't mind flying so crazy."

The Cobra reappeared over the main runway and now went into a series of mind-bending turns. It made six quick circles before pulling up and leaving the area with yet another ear-splitting scream.

The two men in the Bronco were dizzy by now, and stopped watching the airplane altogether. They began driving faster towards the main airplane parking area of the base.

At the same time the YF-17 appeared once again, twisting crazily as if out of control, the last spectacular stunt. The Cobra's engines were roaring and fire spouting from its tailpipes. Then, as if it was suddenly transformed, the jet leveled out, reduced airspeed, and came in for a textbook landing.

In all, its flight had lasted less than seven minutes.

"From what I can understand," the first Spook said, "this guy's whole family has made its living flying airplanes. I'm not sure he's going to like what we have to tell him."

The man in the passenger seat just shrugged. "Well, like I said, it doesn't matter," he said. "He has no choice."

*   *   *

The Bronco was waiting when the Cobra taxied up to its hard stand.

Norton had already popped the canopy. Now, as he took one last gulp of oxygen, he finally killed the airplane's big twin engines and jerked the plane to a stop.

His ground crew appeared and a ladder was fitted to the side of the Cobra. A young airman came up and helped Norton unstrap. This ritual took about fifteen seconds. When it was over, Norton stood up, stretched, and then started down the ladder, taking a glance at the Bronco, parked nearby.

Black truck. Black windows. Even the tire rims were painted black. Norton had seen such vehicles before.

Spooks? he thought. *Here to see the show?*

That seemed unlikely.

The two men were walking towards him before he reached the bottom of the ladder. They were both wearing brand-new jeans, Western-style white shirts, black boots, and baseball caps.

Yep, Norton thought. These guys were definitely Spooks.

They *always* dressed the same.

He met the pair at the bottom of the ladder. Neither one struck him as someone who had seen any military service.

"Enjoy the show?" he asked them good-naturedly.

Both men ignored the question.

"You Norton?" one asked instead.

Norton yanked off his helmet and smoothed back his ruffled hair. "I am," he replied.

Both men flashed their ID badges. Norton thought he saw something like CIA-DIS. Or was it NSA-CIS? He didn't know, and in the end, it didn't make much difference. They were just Spooks.

"We have to have a little talk," the first man told Norton.

Norton shrugged. "Here? Now?"

"Here, now," the second guy said.

Norton now gave them a good once-over. What would

these two want with him? He had already tip-top security clearance; it was a requirement for his job. Then it hit him: They were here to clear him for his long-pending job at Area 51.

What else could it be?

"OK, then," he said. "Talk . . ."

"Where did you learn to fly like that?" the first Spook asked.

Norton just shrugged again. "It comes naturally," he said, adding with a pause, "After about five thousand hours in the air."

"You can fly anything with your eyes closed," the second guy said. "Day or night. Through unfriendly skies. That's what we heard."

"Yeah? Who told you that?" Norton asked.

The Spooks ignored this question as well and moved in a little closer. The first guy lowered his voice.

"Look, we've got a question to ask you," he began. "Now we don't know whether you like this traveling-carnival thing or not. But depending on your answer, you can be out of this three-ring circus and into something very heavy inside a minute."

"I'm listening," Norton replied. "Ask away."

The first Spook took a deep breath.

"Ever fly a helicopter?" he asked.

4

St. Louis International Airport
One week later

The airport had been closed for two hours.

All scheduled flights had been notified of the shut-
down days in advance. Many had been canceled or diverted to other airports nearby.

Roads leading in and out of the sprawling airport had
been blocked off for ninety minutes. Dozens of St. Louis
city policemen were manning these detours, miserable
in a driving rain. Closer in to the airport itself, the secondary terminals as well as all the parking lots were
being guarded by Missouri state troopers. The main terminal itself was crawling with Secret Service. By 1625
hours—4:25 in the afternoon on this dreary day—everything was set.

The President's plane arrived on schedule, exactly five
minutes later.

Air Force One landed smoothly, its wheels hitting the
rain-swept runway with hardly any skidding. The pilots
immediately threw the engines into reverse, and the huge

airplane began slowing down. It was met at the far end of the runway by a caravan of security trucks. One had its four-way flashes blinking; it began moving towards the main terminal. The giant Presidential 747 slowly followed.

The heavy rain had forced a small greeting ceremony indoors. Some five hundred people—political types and their families mostly—were now crammed into one corner of the terminal, separated from the unloading ramp by a phalanx of Secret Service agents. Relegated to the far corner of the terminal building was a tight knot of media types. TV and newspaper people, they'd spent the afternoon grumbling about the poor position so hastily assigned to them.

Air Force One finally jolted to a stop in front of the terminal platform. Outside, the rain came harder and the wind more fierce. A small army of aides burst from the airplane's main door and trooped down the rampway. Finally the President himself emerged. He walked into the terminal building, waved to the assembled locals, posed for a picture with an elderly supporter, and then was whisked away. Down the causeway and out to the rainy street, where he was put into a pre-positioned limousine, which roared off behind a huge motorcycle escort. A fund-raising speech in downtown St. Louis awaited him.

Two minutes after the Presidential plane touched down, a similar-looking 747 landed. This plane was painted in standard Air Force gray. Its radio call sign was "Phone Booth." It was crammed with sophisticated communications and emergency medical equipment, including a fully equipped mobile surgical room. This plane's passenger hold was also carrying two Presidential security doubles, a gaggle of mid-level Presidential aides, and a handful of reporters.

Five minutes after that, an Air Force C-141 Starlifter landed. Painted white and converted into a passenger carrier, this plane was hauling, among other things, a backup team of Secret Service agents and a dozen low-

level White House staff members. It joined "Phone
Booth" at the end of the runway, and together they tax-
ied to a spot about one hundred yards away from where
Air Force One was parked.

Twenty minutes after this, another airplane entered the
St. Louis landing pattern. This aircraft was a noisy,
smoky, thirty-five-year-old C-130 Hercules cargo plane.
It was painted in faded green camouflage, and the
plane's propeller engines were extremely loud in com-
parison to the relatively quiet jets that had landed before
it. In the airborne Presidential entourage, this C-130 was
the runt, the caboose. The Number 4. Its cargo hold held
nothing more exotic than a pair of backup Presidential
limousines, some Presidential suitcases, and the various
pets of the Presidential entourage.

No surprise its radio call sign was "Doghouse."

The pilot of this aircraft was Major Bobby Delaney.
Mid-thirties, narrow but solidly built, with a shock of
rusty hair, he'd been in the Air Force fifteen years, the
last eighteen months of which he'd spent flying the Doghouse.

Earlier in his career, he'd drawn some good duty, including a DFC for his performance flying F-15's during
the Gulf War. But since that time, he'd watched many
of his colleagues leave the military to take jobs with the
airlines or driving private business jets. Many were now
making over six figures in salary.

Delaney hated his present job, and not just because of
the shitty service pay he was drawing. This duty was
long days and long nights, with many hours of boredom
in between. Not two months into his assignment, he'd
made an informal request to be re-designated. But his
superiors had informed him that resigning Presidential
duty so early would be considered extremely imprudent.

So Delaney was stuck, for at least another eighteen
months anyway, hauling around two bulletproof cars and
a half-dozen poodles and cats. He was serving his

country by flying what was essentially a cross between an airborne tow truck and a kennel.

Next to his divorce eight years before, nothing had been quite so miserable.

The flight to St. Louis had been a routine if bumpy affair.

A storm system over southern Ohio had forced a fifty-mile diversion over Kentucky. By the time Delaney's plane entered St. Louis ATC coverage, the three previous airplanes in the Presidential entourage had already been unloaded.

It was dark and raining even harder when Delaney finally landed the four-prop beast on an auxiliary airstrip at the airport. The unloading of the backup limos—always a laborious process—began soon afterwards. A team of Secret Service agents had to inspect each limo before it was unstrapped from its tethers in the back of the airplane. After this, each limo was rolled down the plane's cargo ramp, then inspected yet again. During all this inspection, Delaney and his four-man crew were required to stay in the C-130's cramped cockpit, thumbs-in-asses, until the all-clear was given. With the rain and the gathering darkness, this time-intensive drill stretched into two hours, nearly as long as the flight from Andrews Air Force Base had taken in the first place.

By the time the crew was finally released, Delaney was hungry, thirsty, and feeling like he'd just dug ditches for fifteen hours. It was all he could do to drag himself up to the airport's messy food shop and order a massive cup of black coffee.

"Hey, Slick," he heard a voice behind him say. "Brazil called. They're running out of beans."

Delaney spun around to see a face he hadn't set eyes on since the last days of the Gulf War.

"Jazz? Jazz Norton?" he whispered. "You've got to be shitting me. . . ."

It *was* Jazz. He'd been waiting at the other end of the coffee shop for the last six hours.

They shook hands heartily. Delaney had flown with
Norton during Desert Storm.

Norton signaled for a cup of coffee. "How you been,
Slick?" he asked.

Delaney didn't reply. He just kept staring at Norton.
His old friend was wearing a black nylon jacket, white
Western-style shirt, brand-new jeans and boots, and a
baseball cap. He couldn't recall seeing Norton dressed
quite that way before.

"Jessuzz, man," Delaney asked him. "Are you still
in the service?"

"Yeah, still am," Norton mumbled.

The coffee arrived and they found an isolated table in
the corner of the shop.

Delaney was still a bit in shock.

"What are you doing here, Jazz?" he asked. "Is this
just a happy accident?"

Norton chose to ignore the question. "You're still flying around with the President, I see," he said instead.

Delaney took a gulp of his coffee. "Almost a year
and a half," he answered. "With another year and a half
to go."

"Must be nice duty," Norton said, dumping five tea-
spoons of sugar into his own coffee.

"Best I've ever done," Delaney said. "Warm bed
every night. Lots of travel. See a lot of interesting shit.
Meet a lot of interesting people. I've become fascinated
with the Presidents. Reading a lot about them. You
know—who they were, what they did . . ."

"You hate it *that* much?" Norton interrupted him.

"Do I ever," Delaney replied without missing a beat.
"I'd rather go to downtown Baghdad every night than
be someone's chauffeur's chauffeur."

Norton stopped in mid-sip.

"Be careful what you wish for, old buddy," he said.

Delaney studied his old friend again. It was as if he
hadn't aged a day in the last nine years.

"So, Jazz, what's up?" he pressed Norton. "My gut
tells me this isn't just a co-inky-dinky that you're here."

"Well, I can tell you," Norton replied. "But then I'll have to kill you."

Delaney just shook his head. The clothes were giving Norton away.

"Man, I can't believe this," he said finally. "You've gone Spook? *Really?*"

Norton just shrugged and sipped his coffee again.

"But you always hated those guys, Jazz," Delaney said. "I've seen you sleep through intelligence briefings."

"Things change," Norton replied.

Delaney could only shake his head. "Jazz Norton— philosopher *and* Spook. This is too much. . . ."

Norton leaned a bit closer over the table and lowered his voice a bit.

"OK, here's the straight jack," he said. "I got privy to your desire to drop out of this Presidential car caravan stuff. I passed that information on to some new acquaintances of mine."

"Other Spooks?"

"Yep."

"What kind? From where?"

Norton just shook his head. "You've never heard of them."

"Hmmm, CIA, huh?" Delaney said. "OK, go on."

"Well, when I first met them they wanted to know if I was into changing my surroundings," Norton said. "Like immediately, and in a very radical manner."

"Cool . . ."

"Don't be too hasty," Norton cautioned him. "I heard them out, and they gave me an hour to think about it. I did, and then went back and told them no. Then they said too bad, and sprung a letter from your boss himself."

Delaney had to think a moment.

"My boss? You mean the President?" Delaney asked.

"Yep," Norton replied. "It was a Presidential Action Letter and it had my name all over it."

"What did it say?"

"It said my commander in chief was ordering me to join this . . . well, little enterprise that's been cooked up. And that I really had no choice in the matter."

"Christ, Jazz," Delaney said. "This sounds deep."

Norton grinned a moment. "Let's just say that some people in the Agency are never at a loss for dreaming up wacky stuff."

He paused a moment.

"But truth is, something's come up and for whatever reason they picked me to be involved."

Delaney took just his second sip of his coffee since they'd sat down. It was already cold.

"So, Jazz, you've had a big career change," he said. "What's that have to do with me?"

"Well," Norton said. "When I climbed on board I got to pick who I wanted to go down the yellow brick road with. . . ."

"And you picked me?" Delaney asked with a kind of half-gasp. "Why?"

Norton sat back and relaxed a bit.

"During Desert Storm, you were the best in our outfit," he told Delaney matter-of-factly.

"That's bullshit," Delaney shot back. "*You* were the top man. You were the squadron gunslinger, for Christ's sake. We followed *you* in—not the other way around."

"OK," Norton replied. "I was good at getting to the target and getting the weapons onto it. But you were better at getting us the hell home."

Delaney started to protest—but stopped. It was true, he couldn't argue. Whenever the unit went out and things got hairy—be it bad weather, nighttime, Gomer flak, or all three—they all turned to him and he always led the way home. Truth was, he didn't know how he did it most of the time. He'd just pointed his jet south, followed his nose, and brought the pack home, which, despite all their navigation and homing equipment, was still a difficult thing to do at times.

"OK," Delaney said at last. "I'm a hound dog. So what?"

Norton leaned in closer again.

"So my new friends say we might need someone who's good at getting home again."

"You are using that as the royal 'we,' I hope?"

"Not necessarily," Norton replied.

Delaney sat back and thought a moment. "Man, you're giving me the creeps. Are you saying you want me to get mixed up in whatever bad spy novel you've found yourself in?"

"Yep," was Norton's succinct reply.

Delaney finally drained his cup.

"Well, as much as I hate doping around some White House asshole's cat, I'm also smart enough not to volunteer for anything," he said.

Norton just shook his head. "This isn't a volunteering situation."

"What do you mean?" Delaney asked.

"Well, like I said, when I jumped on board, they asked me who I wanted with me and I told them you," Norton replied.

"So?"

"So you know that letter I got from your boss, the President himself?"

Delaney nodded.

Norton reached into his jacket pocket, took out an envelope, and placed it on the table in front of Delaney. It was red and was sealed with red tape.

"Well," Norton said, "he wrote one for you too."

5

Thule, Greenland
Next day

At noon on what was the warmest day of the year so
far in Thule, Greenland, it was thirty-four degrees below
zero and the wind was howling at forty-five knots.

This *was* typical weather for the isolated U.S. Air
Force base this time of year. It was located just a few
hundred miles from the North Pole, and anything above
fifty below and below fifty knots windspeed was considered downright balmy.

That didn't mean the weather was enjoyable, though.
Just about everyone who wasn't on duty at the frigid
base was either asleep or at the Exchange Club, a combination PX, restaurant, barbershop, and bar.

In the past, at any given time as many as two thousand
Air Force personnel could have been found at Thule.
But a lessening of Cold War jitters had reduced the
base's profile to little more than a pinprick in the snow.
It was once a stopping-off point for massive B-52 bomb-
ers on nuclear-alert exercises, interceptors keeping an

eye on Soviet recon planes, or perhaps something more exotic like the occasional U-2 spy plane dropping in for some gas. Now Thule was a place only the unluckiest of pilots found themselves diverted to.

Among the reduced number of inhabitants these days, the talk always concerned the weather, the snow, the cold. By far the most exciting thing that had happened at the base in years was a recent rash of UFO reports. Bright lights had been seen zipping back and forth across the horizon. Some red, some bright blue, they were said to be doing some fantastic things in the sky, especially over the mountains to the north.

The base commander finally had to issue a directive informing all base personnel that officially nothing unusual was flying anywhere near the base and that it was best that the UFO talk dry up and everyone go back to concentrating on their mission—which was staying warm. The UFO reports faded after that, which was too bad.

At this point in its long service life, an alien invasion of Thule would have livened things up considerably.

The unofficial name of the Base Exchange saloon was the Ice Cube, usually written as Ice³. Sitting at the end of its crowded bar at the moment were two men who'd been in town for only a week. They were the commanders of a massive KC-10 aerial tanker attached to the 157th Air National Guard refueling wing out of Portsmouth, New Hampshire.

Their airplane had wound up in Thule after making a routine training flight eight days before. A bad engine had forced them to stay grounded. Then the weather got worse and the orders came down that no unnecessary flight operations would be permitted until the weather broke. Between getting the bum engine fixed and the snow, seven interminable days had passed by.

So here the crew had sat, cold, drunk, and bored, waiting for a receiver valve for their engine and a break in the "summer weather."

The nickname of their KC-10 was "The Pegasus." It had a reputation of sorts around the Eastern Seaboard of the United States. Its crew was known as the best in the aerial refueling game. They were held in high esteem by fighter pilots who on occasion found themselves flying on dark nights over the North Atlantic with the weather getting bad and their fuel tanks getting low. Many times the Pegasus would take off from Portsmouth, find the lonely fighter, fill its tanks, and get it home safely.

The commander of the KC-10 was Major Jimmy Gillis. He was a tall, lanky, handsome man of fifty-three. His copilot was Captain Marty Ricco, stout, muscular, two years younger than Gillis. Both men were married and lived in New Hampshire; both had two kids. They'd been piloting the Pegasus for nearly twelve years together. Their crew of seven had been with them for almost as long. They were a tight group. Besides seeing service during the Gulf War, they'd participated in countless exercises over the North Atlantic, plus three European TDYs in support of NATO Bosnia air patrols. Together the crew had experienced many high points.

Being stuck in frozen Thule was not one of them.

By 1930 hours, Gillis and Ricco had finished their third beer of the evening. Their enlisted guys were playing video games nearby. Country music was blasting from the PA system. The TV above the bar was showing some Alpine games—a cruel joke—but Gillis and Ricco found their eyes glued to the screen. So bored were they that even an hours-long program about skiing, skating, and bobsledding could capture their attention.

So neither they nor anyone else at the bar noticed the plane that landed on the base's main runway at precisely 1935 hours. It was the first aircraft to come into the base in three days, and it was, in a sense, an unusual one.

The airplane was a C-14 Jetstar, a bird usually reserved for flying big brass around. It was the military equivalent of a Learjet. Small, powerful, two jet engines, a rather luxurious interior.

The Jetstar set down quietly and discharged two passengers. Its pilots were told to do a "hot" gas-up—that is, take on fuel while their engines were still turning. If all went as the two passengers hoped, neither they nor the Jetstar would be staying in Thule very long.

Dressed in heavy parkas, the passengers made their way over to the Ice Cube, and after a battle with the wind and blowing snow, managed to open its inner door. Finally waddling inside, they quickly closed the door behind them and headed towards the bar.

No one in the place paid them any attention, least of all Gillis and Ricco. It was only after the two men reached the end of the bar that Ricco bothered to look up. Both men pulled back their hoods and wiped the ice and snow from their faces. Ricco stared up at them and then nudged Gillis.

"You believe in ghosts, Jimmy?"

Gillis looked up at the two men staring down at them.

"You got to be kidding me," he breathed.

He recognized the visitors right away. It was Norton and Delaney.

"Well, if it isn't the Mutt and Jeff of refueling business," Delaney cracked.

Ricco quickly stood up and was immediately brow-to-chin with Norton.

"Let's see, when was the last time we met?" Ricco hissed, glaring up at the fighter pilot. "Oh, yeah. It was, like, twenty miles from Saddamville. And we were getting our asses shot off. . . ."

Norton didn't blink. Instead he just smiled.

"Good to see you again too, Marty," he said.

Gillis was on his feet now. He towered over both Norton and Delaney.

"Weren't they going to court-martial you guys?" Gillis asked the two pilots bitterly. "If not, they should have."

Norton never lost his smile—but he knew Gillis was right.

It was the sixteenth day of the air war over Iraq. An F-15 from Norton and Delaney's sister squadron had been shot down by ground fire and Iraqi troops were closing in on the pilot. Norton and Delaney were the only Allied airplanes in the area. They were needed to keep the Iraqi soldiers at bay until an Army rescue team could reach the scene and extract the pilot.

The problem was, both of their fighters were running very low on gas. There was no way they could loiter over the area where the pilot was hiding and still have enough fuel to reach a friendly base. But there was no way they were going to let a fellow American fall into the hands of the Iraqis either, especially since at that time, Saddam had been urging his troops to *cook* and *eat* any downed American pilot they found. Both Norton and Delaney simply refused to leave the scene.

So there was only one other option. Norton radioed upstairs for the nearest aerial tanker—and it was the Pegasus who answered the call.

In doing so, Norton broke a slew of regulations, most notably calling for a refueler to enter a hot zone with more than twenty thousand gallons of JP-8 jet fuel in its belly.

But the Pegasus responded—and fueled both him and Delaney at an altitude so perilously low, both fighter pilots *should* have been court-martialed, and given the express train to Leavenworth.

As it turned out, the refueling went well. Norton and Delaney held off the Gomers long enough for the Army SAR chopper to arrive and pull out the downed pilot in one piece. A confrontation back at Riyadh came to blows—it was the seven guys from the Pegasus against Norton and Delaney. But the two sides were separated, and eventually flew off in opposite directions, never to cross paths again.

Until now.

"Let me guess," Ricco asked the fighter pilots.

"They got you two shoveling snow off the runways, is that it?"

"Nope," Norton replied. "Actually, we're delivery boys these days. We have a message for you two."

Gillis and Ricco were totally confused now. This meant Norton had them right where he wanted them.

"And all the bullshit aside," Norton added, "you guys should have been given a medal that night. It took guts what you did. Not many people would have done it."

"So what . . ."

"So, we have new orders for you," Delaney told them.

Gillis and Ricco just looked at each other. Was this a joke? Why would these two random a-holes they'd encountered briefly many years before track them down to Thule?

Norton handed them both a letter. Each was wrapped in red tape. Each was marked with the Presidential seal.

"See you soon, guys," Norton told them. "And don't forget to bring your suntan lotion."

With that, he and Delaney went out the door and disappeared back into the snowy gale.

6

Central Iraq
Next day

The village of El Quas-ri was no more.

The place had stood on the same spot in Qaarta region of Iraq for more than four thousand years, existing more than two millennia before Christ walked the earth. The fountain in the main square had drawn water since the reign of Ebbenazzar III. The fields nearby had produced onions and rice since 2300 B.C.

It was strange then how quickly the end came. For centuries, the elders in the village had passed down stories of Qel, the mythical flying beast. This winged monster would periodically visit the other villages in the Qaarta region and destroy them with great spits of fire from its mouth and great gusts of wind from its wings. But it had never descended on El Quas-ri because its people had always remained faithful to God and had lived honest lives.

But on its last day, neither faith nor honesty could save the people of this ancient place.

*   *   *

It was late afternoon when their world came to an end.

Most of the village's 250 people were gathered in the town square, a tragically ironic twist as it turned out. The occasion for the crowd was the appearance of a new Toyota truck recently purchased by Amhed Amhed, the son of the village police chief. The truck—a two-door, sixteen-cubic-foot beauty—was the most modern vehicle ever to be driven in the village. It was painted white with silver lines across its hood and doors and very shiny hubcaps. To the people of El Quas-ri, it looked incredibly stylish.

Ahmed Ahmed was very proud of it. He'd ordered the truck seven months before, and had kept his fellow villagers updated with each passing day on the status of its delivery. They'd staged a celebration a week before when Ahmed finally left for Basra to claim the vehicle. When word got around that Ahmed had returned with the truck, many of the villagers dropped what they were doing and immediately rushed to the town square. That was why the crowd had formed.

There they had found Ahmed telling all who would listen everything about the vehicle. Its engine, its chassis, its transmission, its spiffy interior. Ahmed related his journey to the port city of Basra, what he was doing when he first saw the truck, and his brush with an Iraqi Army major who had taken an immediate liking to the vehicle as well. The major—a brutish man with a huge scar running down his right cheek—had held him up for two hours, questioning him about the truck, how he had ordered it, how he had raised the money to buy it. In the end, Ahmed had been forced to pay the Army officer the equivalent of twenty American dollars in order to let him leave with the truck.

But Ahmed had anticipated this. He'd taken an extra fifty dollars to Basra with him to be used as the bribe money he knew he would need if he hoped to bring the truck back to El Quas-ri. From his point of view, the twenty dollars he'd paid to the Army major had been a bargain. In reality, he was actually thirty dollars ahead of the game.

The villagers especially liked this aspect of Ahmed's adventure to Basra. They were very proud of him. He was the clever son of a clever man.

Only good things could befall someone so smart.

Ahmed was telling his story for the fifth time when the late dusk suddenly turned back to bright sunshine.

It came at first as a flash of light hitting the middle of the village square, stunning the villagers. The fire came next—scorching, searing, deadly. A rain of metal, razor-sharp and white-hot, came down on them, seemingly from every direction.

The children were consumed first, which was strange as they were the smallest targets. But the fire—which was actually the combined fusillade from three miniguns and a 105-mm howitzer—tore into them with sickening ferocity. Then the stream of shells ripped through the elders and the women who had gathered a short distance away from the Toyota. Finally, the fire reached the younger men of the village clustered around the rear bumper of Ahmed's new truck. Many of them were literally cut in half.

The flying monster then flew off to the east, banked, and reappeared over the village. This time it spat fire into the houses, the huts, and workshops, killing anyone who had not been present in the square. Forty-three more people, plus seventy-one homes, were decimated in this manner. The bodies were quickly reduced to bone fragments, blood, and sinew. The homes were reduced to dust, some smaller than the finest grains of sand.

It was over in a matter of seconds—thirty-three to be exact. In that short time, 228 people lay dead or dying, and nothing over the height of twelve inches was left standing in the village.

Only a few of those two dozen who were wounded but still alive saw the huge helicopter appear over the village ten minutes later. It landed, and a man in a green

Iraqi Army uniform was the first to step off. He was a major. He had a huge scar running down his right cheek.

As he supervised the killing of the wounded, the helicopter crew hooked the Toyota truck onto a thick cable hanging beneath their heavy-lift aircraft, preparing to fly it away. In the brutally quick, massive attack, the Toyota was the only thing that had not been harmed. Indeed, it wasn't even scratched, so accurate had been the fire from the sky.

This was a good thing for the Army major with the scarred face.

He had admired the white truck with the silver stripes from the second he saw it on the dock at Basra.

And now, it was his.

7

It was a place that did not show up on any tourist maps—yet it looked like somewhere just about any tourist in south Florida would want to visit.

It was called Seven Ghosts Key by some. It was an island located about forty-five miles south of Key West, deep in the Florida Straits.

Five miles long and a half mile wide, it was covered with palm trees—some real, some not—and various other kinds of tropical fauna. It was surrounded by very light blue water. A huge coral reef dominated its northern side. A white sandy beach stretched along its southern end.

The center of the island boasted what appeared to be a small airfield, one capable of handling civilian aircraft like Piper Cubs, Cherokees, and so on. Close to this was a dock with facilities for a few dozen sport-fishing boats and yachts, with gasoline pumps, a repair shack, and bait barrels also on hand.

The main part of the resort was a cluster of six buildings located next to the airport. Three were obviously hangars—though to the trained eye they might have appeared a bit too large to handle only private airplanes. Two more buildings looked like motels—brightly colored one-story framed structures with lots of windows. The fifth building looked like a warehouse. The sixth was a restaurant. It was of vintage 1950's design, its roof and gutters adorned with ancient-looking patio lights that were turned on both night and day. Its expansive deck looked out over the calm waters to the north of the key.

The only vehicles ever seen on the island were powder-pink jeeps. Their sole purpose seemed to be for transporting fishermen from the docks to the restaurant and back, yet rarely did any of these vehicles move from their parking lot behind the boat slips. The pristine beach on the south side also appeared very inviting, with its pearl sand, its field of beach umbrellas, and the waves gently lapping against its straight-as-a-razor shoreline. Yet rarely could any visitors be spotted there, or anywhere on the island for that matter.

This was because Seven Ghosts Key was not what it seemed. First of all, its runway was actually two miles long—four fifths of it invisible, hidden by cleverly painted camouflage and intricately placed fauna. The restaurant, while serving as a mess hall as well, was crammed with millions of dollars of military communications equipment. What appeared to be an air-conditioner vent-house on its roof actually contained a Hawk antiaircraft missile battery. One of the large hangars boasted facilities big enough to house more than a hundred people. A second held enough weaponry to outfit a small army. The third actually served to store aircraft, many of which had never been seen by a civilian eye. The pink jeeps all carried Uzi machine guns or M-16CGS NightVision-equipped rifles. And the "motels" held even more mysterious things inside.

No, Seven Ghosts Key was not what it seemed.

It was, in fact, another very secret place.

*   *   *

When Marty Ricco woke up, the sun was shining in his face. He hadn't felt such warmth in months.

Where the hell was he? Certainly not in Thule anymore . . .

He sat bolt upright, wiped the sleep from his eyes, and it slowly came back to him. He was still on the airliner. The same one he'd climbed aboard in Bangor, Maine, the night before, per his new orders. It was an old, battered, noisy turboprop of a type he didn't think existed anymore. They'd been hopscotching in it since midnight, setting down at least four times for refueling or bad weather or both. Somewhere along the way, Ricco had fallen into a fitful sleep. Now he was awake and the very hot sun was shining in his face.

He looked about the cabin. Gillis was sprawled over three seats across the aisle from him, sleeping restlessly. The ancient airliner had room for about fifty people. Yet from what Ricco could see, he and Gillis were still the only passengers on board.

He sat all the way up now. Where the hell had they been flying to this whole time? He looked out the window and found himself staring down at a lot of bright blue water. And at this, a smile began to spread across his face. It was a strange sensation; he was by habit a dour man. But now, though it seemed his facial muscles had to break through six months of ice to accomplish the feat, it finally happened. His first real smile in half a year.

But it would not last very long because a moment later the old airplane began shuddering madly. Its engines screaming in protest, it began to fall out of the sky. Panic ripped through Ricco. That clear blue water was coming up at him very fast. He looked over at Gillis, who was still sleeping. Then he looked back out the window and saw the water getting closer . . . closer . . . *closer.*

Ricco lunged across the aisle to shake Gillis awake. There was no way he was going to die alone like this. But just as he began jostling his partner, there was a sudden thump and guttural screech. Ricco put his nose back up to the window and saw they were down and rolling along a runway .

Awakened by Ricco's panic and the landing, Gillis did a long stretch and yawned.

"We here finally?" he asked sleepily.

"Yeah," Ricco replied, trying to sound calm as he caught his breath. "You missed a great flight. . . ."

It took a while, but the airliner finally rolled to a stop next to a stairway that had been placed out on the runway. Ricco looked out the window again. They were at a small air base of some sort. One runway, a few buildings. Lots of palm trees. A nice place.

He and Gillis gathered their duffel bags and made their way forward. The plane's access door opened and they stepped out into the morning sunshine. It was already blistering hot even though the sun was just barely above the horizon.

"We in the Caribbean?" Ricco asked Gillis.

Gillis yawned. "Good guess, I'd say."

They walked down the stairway and dropped their bags on the tarmac. That was when the airplane started pulling away. This surprised them; they'd just assumed the pilots were getting off too. But this was not the case. The pilots had never even slowed down their engines. Ricco tried yelling up to them, but the airplane had already backed up and was taxiing away. It turned back onto the runway and quickly took off again. In all, it had spent no more than a minute on the ground.

"What the fuck is this?" Gillis roared. "They're just leaving us here?"

"Where are those a-holes Delaney and Norton, that's what I want to know?" Ricco asked, looking around desperately.

But they could see no one. The base looked absolutely deserted. Had they been dropped at the right place? Were they supposed to wait here for someone? Or was this part of some elaborate hoax?

"If those two assholes are scamming us, I'll kill them," Gillis declared.

They stood there, next to the stairway, for five minutes, trying to fathom their strange situation. The sun got higher and the wind blew hotter, but still they could not see a living soul anywhere. They were both wearing their heavy thermo-wear arctic flight suits and they were beginning to broil in them.

"Let's get out of the sun at least," Ricco finally said.

They began walking. The first building they reached was the restaurant. They stopped at the front door and listened. Voices . . . They could hear a group of people talking inside. Or at least they thought they could. Gillis tried the door, but it was it locked. They both pounded on it for almost a minute, but no one answered. Then they listened again, but the voices had gone away.

Next, they walked to the boat slips, but no one was there either. Then they walked back to the section of the base where the three hangars were located. The stink of aviation fuel was thick there. But all three buildings were locked up tight as well.

"OK, I give up. Where the hell is everybody?" Ricco cursed.

"Still asleep?" Gillis replied wearily. "Like I want to be?"

They finally reached the pair of motel-type buildings. With their long sloping roofs and logwood ranch construction, the buildings looked like they'd be more at home out West somewhere, maybe in Arizona or Montana. They seemed very out-of-place here in the Caribbean.

Both pilots were drenched in sweat by this time. They were tired, hungry, more than a little confused by their long flight to nowhere. Ricco took a deep breath and tried the front door of the first building.

It was unlocked.

"Hallelujah," he grumbled. "At least we can get out of this heat."

They walked into the one-story building and were surprised to find it was dark inside—and very spare. It appeared to be a barracks of some kind, or more accurately, a cross between a boot camp and a prison. There were two dozen bunks lined up perfectly along one wall; that was the extent of the building's contents. There were many windows, but just one door at each end of the building. Everything looked old, yet smelled of freshly cut wood. In many ways, the outside of the building didn't match up at all with the inside.

"What the hell is this place?" Ricco asked. "A movie set?"

Gillis just dropped his bag and groaned.

"I don't care," he said. "If it's a place to lay my head, then it's home."

Not counting the bumpy ride down there, neither of them had slept much in the forty-eight hours since receiving their new orders. The odd surroundings were doing nothing to dispel the sleepy notions. So Gillis walked over to the first bunk and collapsed on top of it. Ricco selected the bunk next to him and did the same.

They were both quiet for a few minutes, drifting in and out of sleep. Finally Gillis broke the silence.

"Hell, you know, there's a chance we might be looking at something pretty good here," he sighed. "A couple weeks in the sun wouldn't hurt me any."

"Same here," Ricco replied sleepily.

Yet no sooner had they both drifted off again when they were awakened by a huge crash. This was followed by a flash of light so bright, it blinded them both. Then they heard shouting, and the sound of glass breaking and doors being kicked in.

"Jessuz! *What the fuck?*" Gillis yelled, nearly falling off his bunk.

Suddenly the building was full of armed men. They were coming through the doors, through the windows, falling from the ceiling. They were soldiers, in full combat gear, from shielded Fritz helmets to gas masks to ammo belts and flash grenades. They were running up and down the room, expertly "clearing it" as if they'd done it a hundred times before. In seconds, many very nasty-looking machine guns were pointing at Ricco and Gillis.

The two pilots were terrified. Several soldiers picked them up and hurled them to the floor, their gun barrels jammed to the backs of the pilots' necks. Both pilots were certain now that they had landed somewhere other than the U.S. and that they were about to be shot to death. Ricco cried out. On his lips was one last curse for Norton and Delaney.

"Those fuckers!"

But then someone blew a whistle and everything froze. The soldiers all stopped in their tracks. There was suddenly no more noise. No more shouting. No more footsteps.

Nothing, just the wind outside.

Then one man pushed his way through the crowd of soldiers surrounding Ricco and Gillis. This man was Asian, short but rugged and sturdy-looking. He was wearing the desert camouflage uniform of a U.S. Marine Corps captain.

He took his helmet off and glared down at Ricco and Gillis.

"Who the hell are you two? We're in the middle of an exercise here!"

With shaking hands, Ricco and Gillis quickly pulled out their Presidential Action Letters and showed them to the young officer. The captain hastily read them and then nodded to his men.

"OK, let's call this a false start," he said calmly. "Reset everything and we'll do it again in ten minutes."

At this, the soldiers all lowered their weapons and began to empty the building. Those who had burst through the windows went out the same way. Those who had come down from the ceiling, climbed back up and disappeared through the roof. Still others drifted out the front door.

The Asian officer then looked at Gillis and Ricco's PALs again and helped them to their feet.

"So, you're the aerial refueling team," he said. "The Air National Guard guys . . ."

Ricco and Gillis nodded with relief.

The officer handed the letters back to them.

"Well, this is the combat-simulation building," he told them. "And it's off-limits to just about everyone. I believe you're bunking in next door."

He gave them a quick once-over and added: "I think you can grab a shower and new pants over there as well."

With that, the young captain walked briskly out of the building, barking orders to his men as he went. And just like that, Ricco and Gillis were alone again. They both looked at each other and realized they'd been so scared, they'd wet their pants.

"Oh, man," Ricco groaned, inspecting his damp crotch. "What the fuck have we gotten ourselves into?"

8

Jazz Norton was in big trouble.

Four MiG-29 Fulcrums aligned in perfect combat formation were breaking through the low clouds right in front of him.

Their wings seemed to sag, there were so many weapons hanging beneath them. Each MiG was bearing at least four Aphid air-to-air missiles, plus a huge cannon in its nose. All four were painted in brown-and-tan desert camouflage. To Norton's tired eyes, the color scheme looked particularly sinister against the background of dreadful lemon sky.

The MiGs were projected just five miles off the nose of his attack helicopter. His threat-warning screen began blinking furiously when the four dots representing the dangerous MiGs showed up. A loud screech went through his headphones. The MiGs had spotted him! Their radars were now keying in on his chopper, arming their air-to-air missiles as a prelude to firing at him.

Other panels on Norton's control board began blinking. A TV readout of his ground-threat-warning status was buzzing madly. It was displaying no less than six

SA-6 SAM sites going hot on the ground below, as well as a dozen separate radar-guided antiaircraft batteries hidden in the hills all around him. Their gunners had spotted his copter, too. Like the Fulcrums, they were preparing to fire at him.

His target-acquisition screen was also blinking. It was displaying an odd collection of buildings in a hidden valley surrounded by high desert cliffs just ahead. Many helicopters were whirring above this place, which, to Norton's eyes, looked like a rambling ranch of some sort. There were six buildings in all. Soldiers were running through the streets between them. There was a T-72 tank sitting at one end of the compound. A large red circle on his acquisition screen was completely covering it.

The display warning was blinking: *Time to Fire: 8 seconds . . . 7 seconds . . . 6 seconds . . .*

Norton grabbed his control stick and started squeezing it very tightly.

Damn . . . what now?

He hastily scanned the copter's control systems. What the hell was he supposed to do again? Was it add power and dive? Or cut back and flip over? The T-72 was his main target—it seemed to constitute the greatest threat at the moment. But should he postpone firing at the tank and take out the nearest AA battery first? Or should he continue on to his main target and hope the AA gunners were not accurate with their first shots? And what about the Fulcrums? Could they shoot him before he could shoot the tank?

Norton didn't know the answers to these questions or the few million others racing through his brain. So he just jammed the stick forward and increased throttle, not waiting for the copter's computer to reply. He was going in on the tank.

But suddenly a SAM warning buzzer went off in his ear. One of the SA-6 surface-to-air missiles had been fired at him. Damn! He'd forgotten all about them! More out of self-preservation than anything else, Norton leaned even further on the controls, plunging two hundred feet in three seconds and miraculously dodging the SAM streaking up towards him.

He somehow recovered flight at 250 feet and realigned himself with the tank. But was he now too low to fire his antitank missiles? Should he pull up and go around again? Should he fire at that AA gun sitting on the eastern edge of the town first, then try for the tank?

While all this was bouncing around Norton's skull, yet another cockpit buzzer went off. It was his fuel warning light—he was past his bingo point. He now did not have enough fuel to get back to base. Another buzzer went off. A stream of AA was heading right for him. Then another buzzer began screaming.

Norton looked up just in time to see the Aphid AA missile coming right at him. The Fulcrum that had fired it at him was already pulling up and away.

The missile hit the copter a second later. Norton saw yellow flame first. Then orange. Then deep red.

Then everything just went black. . . .

"OK . . . end simulation!"

The lights came back on, and Norton took a long, deep troubled breath. He was bathed in sweat and the insides of the helicopter simulator were beginning to smell rank again. He looked at his hands. They were trembling. His lips were cut and bleeding, sliced by his own teeth. His knees felt made of water. He'd been through 127 simulations in three days, and at last it was taking a toll on him. Like a recurring nightmare, he always faced the same scenario. He had to ice a tank before either AA or SAMs or Fulcrums iced him—and always, he failed to deliver and survive. Either the Fulcrums got him or the ground fire did. It seemed impossible to beat both threats at the same time.

Such was the fate of a fighter jock being made to fly a chopper.

The past dozen days had been the strangest in his life. From Fallon to here, to St. Louis, to Thule, and back here again. The cruelest joke was, he wasn't even sure where "here" was. Not exactly anyway. He knew he was on an island, and the island was somewhere off the southern tip of Florida. And he knew this island was run by the CIA as a secret training site for operations to be undertaken elsewhere. But other than his trip to St. Louis to pick up Delaney, and their quick hop to the top of the world to recruit Gillis and Ricco, he'd spent just about all of his waking hours locked inside this smelly Tin Can, drowning in his own sweat, trying to learn how to fly an attack helicopter without ever leaving the ground—and losing every time.

It was called UIT—ultra-intensive training. So far, for him, it had been a bust.

The Tin Can was the nickname for the HSM—or Helicopter Simulator Module. It was in the subbasement of Hangar 2, the huge barn located right next door to the smaller warehouse building that housed his quarters. A short tunnel connected both structures, thus negating the need for him to actually go outside and see the sun or breathe the air, unless he was going to chow, which was usually at night and which he always ate alone. Indeed, much of the island's training facility was located underground. Built inside old bomb shelters, he had been told.

The helicopter simulator was aptly nicknamed. It was a huge white barrel set up on six monstrous spider legs. It had 360-degree three-dimensional TV screens inside, and with loads of surround-sound effects and laser-light manipulation, it didn't take long for the mind to accept that you were actually flying something and that people were actually throwing bad stuff up at you.

When he wasn't being blasted out of virtual reality, Norton was usually asleep in his quarters. There really was little else to do. The security on the island was so tight at the moment, he was prohibited from speaking to anyone other than the Tin Can techs. He hadn't seen or talked to Delaney since getting back from Thule. And the CIA operations officer in charge of the mission—a pup of a guy named Gene Smitz—had spoken to him on just two occasions, both times to remind him about the importance of security and to see if his living arrangements were up to snuff.

On that last score at least, Norton could not complain. His billet was comfortable enough. It had a bed, a chair, a small fridge, a microwave, plenty of coffee and fruit. There was a separate shower and a toilet. There were boxes of magazines for him to read, a TV, and a VCR with plenty of videos for him to watch. Still, he hated being cooped up inside the small windowless room. It was in essence a luxurious prison cell.

The only thing he hated more was being strapped inside the Tin Can.

No surprise that more than once in the past twelve days he'd asked himself one question: *What the hell have I gotten myself into?*

Still, he didn't know the answer.

He finally unstrapped himself and squeezed out of the simulator. He was stressed to the point of being woozy. How could his brain be so fooled? He was here, in one piece, safe and sound. Yet every time he crawled out of the Can, he felt like he'd flown a combat mission—for real. And had been blown out of the sky—for real. A crude sign above the door said it all: *Everything but the pain*, someone had written. That was the truth. . . .

The worst part was, if history was any judge, once he was out of the Can, he would be permitted a quick bathroom break, a chance to grab a Coke or a cup of coffee, and then be thrown right back into the simulator to do it all over again. For the 128th time.

But as it turned out, this recess would be different.

Usually he found a technician waiting for him outside the simulator door; the small, glass-enclosed control room from which the Can's activities were monitored was down a staircase ten feet away. This time, though, the first face he saw belonged to Delaney. The slightly ragged-looking pilot was inside the control room, speaking with the six CIA geeks who ran the Tin Can.

Norton hadn't seen Delaney since returning from Greenland. Though they lived in billets in the same building, their schedules ran exactly opposite. Whenever Norton wasn't doing his time inside the Tin Can, Delaney was, and vice versa.

But now here Delaney was, dressed in a flight-simulator suit just like Norton, and looking quite stern and official. Yet he was carrying what appeared to be a small Styrofoam beer cooler.

"I have orders to bring Major Norton up to the Big Room," Norton heard Delaney telling the simulator techs. "Smitz told me to tell you that you can dispense with the major's post-simulation briefing as well. He's through for the day. And so am I."

Like every bullshit artist, it wasn't what Delaney was saying, it was how he was saying it. The pointy-head techs listened in silence, then did a group shrug and went about the business of shutting down the Tin Can. Delaney finally turned towards Norton, pointed to the cooler, and pantomimed drinking a beer. Norton gave him a thumbs-up, signed the Tin Can log book, and bade the techs good-bye.

Then he joined Delaney, ran up three sets of stairs, and left Hangar 2 a free man.

"I owe you one, buddy," he told Delaney, walking out into the sunshine for the first time in days.

"Only if we don't get caught," Delaney replied. "I can think of about a dozen regulations we're breaking here."

Norton was sure of that. In his indoctrination—which took place in the days after he was recruited at Fallon and before he went up to St. Louis to collect Delaney—he'd been told everything that was about to happen to him was top secret and that he should not discuss it with anyone, not even other members of the project team. This was peculiar. Norton had been involved in secret ops before, and never had there been a ban on the individual members discussing the situation. But apparently none of those ops had been as secret as this. It was strange, though. This weird place. The way they were drawn together. The way they were recruited. Was the CIA just getting better? Or was there another reason the clamp was so tight?

He didn't know.

Since Delaney had been brought in, there had not been the opportunity for them to have a conversation. So did that mean they couldn't discuss their shared experience now? Would it be against the rules? Would anyone be listening in if they did?

They began walking down the long camouflaged runway. They were quiet at first. The afternoon was upon them. The base seemed deserted—as usual. Yet voices were on the wind.

In just a few moments, Norton was sweating again. The sun was that hot.

"If I didn't get a break from that Tin Can soon, I was going to flip," he finally told Delaney.

"Join the club," his colleague replied. "I've been spending so much time inside that thing, I'm having nightmares. It's like people are whispering to me when I'm trying to go to sleep. Think the Spooks might be programming that in? You know, filtering suggestive stuff to us subconsciously?"

"If these people can build all this and get away with it," Norton told him. "I'd say they are capable of anything."

Delaney gave out a long moan. "Just what I need, something to make me even more paranoid. This place really gives me the creeps."

Norton couldn't disagree with him. Seven Ghosts Key *was* a very odd place. There were at least a couple hundred people on site. Yet the island always managed to looked deserted due to its surfeit of subterranean facilities. As a result, the feeling of isolation was almost overwhelming. There were no other islands to been seen in any direction. No airplanes ever seemed to fly overhead. No boats ever seemed to be sailing on the horizon. Yet

the island was located close to one of the busiest mari-
time areas in the world.

Even the origin of its name was weird. When he first
arrived here, Norton had been told by one of the CIA
officers that the island's facilities had been built in the
late 1950's to launch raids on Cuba, which was just over
the horizon. At that time, the island was known simply
as Green Rock Key. Then, sometime in the mid-sixties,
something very strange happened. One dark and stormy
night, as the story went, seven CIA employees assigned
here simply disappeared. They went to sleep one night,
but in the morning their bunks were empty and unmade.
The island was searched thoroughly, as were the waters
surrounding it. No boats were missing, no aircraft had
landed or taken off during the night. Yet no trace of the
seven individuals was ever found.

Hence the name change.

Under the circumstances, it was a little bit of history
that Norton could have done without.

After five minutes of walking in the brutal sun, he and
Delaney finally reached their destination: the fake yacht
club at the southern tip of the island. Here sat a dozen
aging yachts and fishing boats, vessels on hand to help
maintain the illusion that this place was little more than
a private rich man's fishing club.

Some of the yachts were so old, though, they were
probably antiques. It was obvious none of them had been
out to sea in decades. They had no engines, no sails.
They were simply props.

He and Delaney climbed aboard one called *Free Time*.
It was an elderly charter boat, a forty-four-footer with a
huge open deck and sixteen fishing chairs set up on its
stern. Norton and Delaney settled into the two seats closest to the shade, and Delaney dipped into his cooler. A
six-pack of tall Budweisers was buried under a small
mountain of ice inside.

"Where did you manage to get that?" Norton asked
him.

"The mess hall guys have a private stash in the meat freezer," Delaney said, passing Norton a brew. "I told one of them I'd take him for a ride in the Tin Can some night. He's nuts about flying in that thing. Says he'll get us as much booze as we want, just as long as we give him a spin around the block every once and a while."

Norton just shook his head. He had not seen a beer or any alcohol since being on the island, nor did it ever dawn on him to look for any. Delaney, on the other hand, had been here less time than he had, and yet he'd managed to secure a six-pack and a future supply.

That was Slick. . . .

"Skoll!" Delaney said, tapping cans with Norton. Both took a long deep slurp of the cold beer. It felt like gold running down Norton's throat. For the first time since coming to this place, he actually felt his muscles start to relax.

"So," Delaney said with a burp. "Have you figured it out yet?"

"Figured out what?" Norton asked in reply.

"What the hell are we doing here?"

Norton swigged his beer again, then wiped the cool can across his hot forehead.

"You're asking the wrong person," he replied. "They keep telling me we'll all be briefed soon. But all I've been doing is playing in the Can. . . ."

Norton let his words drift away. This was true. Though he'd been on the island for nearly two weeks, he still had no idea exactly why the CIA had brought him and the others here. Again, the security surrounding the project was that tight.

"Well, I guess we'll know soon enough." Delaney sighed. "Then we'll probably be complaining that we know too much."

They sat and drank for a few moments in silence. A light breeze blew in on them, reducing the temperature a few degrees to about a hundred or so.

Delaney broke the silence again.

"So, what kind of a chopper have you been flying in the Tin Can?"

Norton bit his lip for a moment. Was he really supposed to be talking about this?

He sipped his beer. *What the hell . . . why not?*

"Well, because the simulator is rigged for an attack chopper, I just assumed it was an Apache," he answered finally.

Delaney nodded. The AH-1 Apache was the U.S. military's premier attack copter, and hands down the best aircraft of its kind in the world. It was a frightening aerial weapon, small, quick, heavily armed, survivable.

"But those simulators ain't no Apaches," Delaney said. "They handle too big. Fly too big. And the control panel is ass-backwards. It's like I'm reading right to left, instead of the other way around."

Once again, Norton had to agree. The setup as presented in the Tin Can *was* cockeyed. In any aircraft he'd ever flown, the layout of the instruments had a rationale behind it. Fuel gauges were all grouped in one spot, environmental controls in another, electrical supply in another, and so on. The controls were allocated in such a way that the pilot could review them quickly and the eye was naturally drawn to their location after just a few hours of experience. But the controls in the simulator seemed to be for a helicopter whose cockpit panel had been thrown together slapdash, with logical placement no more than an afterthought. Fuel gauge here, auxiliary fuel gauge way over there. Ammo supply here, firing sequence button way up here. Many things about the control layout seemed foreign and didn't make sense to him. Plus many of the controls weren't even marked.

"And how about the weapons regimen?" Norton asked Delaney. "My ship is set up as a two-man tandem. Is yours?"

Delaney replied, "Absolutely . . ."

"But the way I'm set up, it looks like I'm flying the pig *and* shooting the guns."

Delaney took a huge gulp of beer.

"Same here," he said. "I'm doing the driving and the shooting and the gunner is doing diddly."

"Weird . . ."

"Very weird . . ."

They finished their first beer in silence.

"You won't believe how fast they have my ship going," Delaney said finally. "That thing flies so freaking fast, it almost makes sense they have a fighter jock at the wheel. I guess that's why we're here."

"Yeah, well, I get scared when something starts to make sense around here," Norton said.

Delaney coaxed the last few drops of beer from his can. Norton wiped his sweaty forehead once more.

The slightly cooling breeze blew off the water again. The beer was having its first effects on Norton. For a moment it actually seemed like they were just two guys, enjoying a hot afternoon, drinking beer, and fishing off the end of a huge boat.

If only . . . he mused.

Delaney reached into his cooler, took out two more beers, and handed one to Norton.

"Did you know Mutt and Jeff arrived yesterday?" he asked Norton.

"No kidding?"

"I heard they've been crybabying to Smitz ever since," Delaney said.

"They really don't want to be heroes, do they?"

"Can't blame them, I guess," Delaney answered. "I mean look where it got *us*."

Norton bit his lip again. That was another thing troubling him. His decision to turn the CIA on to Gillis and Ricco had been preying on his mind.

At the time, it seemed like the right thing to do. The Spooks said this mission needed good air-to-air refueling guys, and when Norton was asked for the best, he gave them Gillis and Ricco.

But *had* he done the right thing? Or had he just been grandstanding? Caught up a little too much in the cloak-and-dagger excitement of those first few days. How could he justify involving the two tanker pilots in a mission he knew nothing about? What witches' brew had he gotten them into? With its reputation for screwing things up, could he really trust the CIA? Or any Spook, for that matter? Had he just been swept up in it because *he* wanted to be a hero? Because he wanted to do something more exciting than fly the Cobra at air shows?

He didn't know. And that was the problem. Gillis and Ricco weren't regular military; they were National Guard guys. Weekend warriors. They probably had wives and kids and homes, things he and Delaney did not. What if Gillis and Ricco got killed on this mission? What if by Norton's recommendation he'd brought Gillis and Ricco into something that would end up causing their wives to be widows and their kids to be fatherless?

He took another long sip of beer. Delaney was blabbing away about the weather or something, but Norton could not hear him. His ears were ringing too much. And his shoulders were suddenly feeling very heavy.

These disturbing thoughts were eventually knocked away by a sharp jab to his rib cage, courtesy of Delaney. The pilot was indicating that Norton should look at something off to their left. Norton did, and immediately saw what Delaney had spotted.

It was a group of Marines, about twenty of them, or one quarter of the complement known to be on the island. They were crawling through a grove of palm trees about fifty feet away from the yacht. The Marines were dressed in heavy combat gear and carrying enormous weapons. They were almost invisible.

Norton had seen the Marines training several times since arriving on the island, in those first hours before his marathon sessions in the Can had commenced in earnest. Each time, the Marines were in the process of surrounding and attacking Motel Six, which was the name given to the island's first motel-like structure. (The second motel-like structure, the one where many billets were located, had been named "Motel Hell.") Now it appeared the Marines were preparing to attack the structure once again.

Norton and Delaney watched with bemused interest as this first group of Marines got into position. Then they became aware of a second group of Marines inching their way up towards Motel Six from the opposite side of the runway. And a third group was in the process of scaling the structure's rear wall. Then, someone blew a whistle, a flash grenade went off, and the Marine assault was on. In seconds jarheads were swarming all over the structure, kicking in doors, going through windows, dropping down through holes in the roof. Norton and Delaney could hear shouting, heavy footsteps, the sizzle and pop of more flash grenades going off.

"Hey, man, this is better than the movies!" Delaney declared with a noisy slurp of his beer. "I just wish they would attack something else for a change. This particular act is getting boring."

The Marines apparently did mock assaults on Motel Six as many times a day as Norton and Delaney found themselves stuck inside the Tin Can. In other words, endlessly.

"Let's see," Delaney said. "We can call this mystery number two hundred and seventy-three. What the hell are these guys practicing for?"

Norton just shrugged. "Again, it's probably something we don't want to know."

The mock assault was over in a matter of minutes. Then the Marines started filing out again. Some of them passed right by the boat dock where Norton and Delaney sat, now drinking their third set of beers. Their blackened faces stared in at them. They looked exhausted, hot, sweaty—and most of all, thirsty.

Delaney raised his beer in a mock toast to the Marines.

"Semper fi, guys!" he called out to them. "Keep up the good work!"

The Marines growled at them, but kept moving.

"Can I tell you something, partner?" Norton said to Delaney.

"Sure . . ."

Norton watched the Marines disappear back into the palm groves.

"Something tells me we should be *real* nice to those guys," he said.

Before Delaney could reply, they heard someone walking down the gangplank towards their boat. Delaney quickly went to hide the beer. Not that he was afraid drinking on duty was against regulations. He simply didn't have enough to share with a third party. But this person had no interest in drinking. It was a guy named Raoul. He was one of several CIA flunkies on the island.

"I've been looking all over for you two," he said, out of breath but with relief.

"Why? Where's the fire?" Delaney asked him.

"The fire is in the Big Room," Raoul told them in cracked English. "The time has come—that's why Smitz wanted me to track you down."

"Time has come for what?" Delaney asked him, now chugging his beer in full view.

"For the briefing," Raoul said. "The big one. The one to explain whatever the hell we are all doing here."

"The 'mother of all briefings,' " Norton said, "It's finally time."

"Yeah, cool," Delaney said draining his beer. "And we get to go drunk."

9

The Big Room was another name for the main dining area inside the restaurant on Seven Ghosts Key.

It was an odd place inside an odd place. Back when the restaurant was built, prior to the Bay of Pigs invasion, someone thought it would be clever to paint folksy native murals on the walls as one more piece in the mosaic of the island's cover story.

The result was a collection of very dated and crude paintings. A huge marlin jumping at the end of a fishing line. A crimson tropical sunset. A garish voodoo ceremony. Children playing in the surf. The murals gave the place a certain campy look, but were also weird and unsettling. One was particularly eerie. It showed three jumbo black women carrying pots on their heads on their way to market. The way the mural had been painted, they seemed to be laughing at anyone who came through the front door.

The far wall of the room contained no murals. Instead it was dominated by a huge curtain, behind which was a gigantic TV screen. Communications gear of all shapes and sizes surrounded this screen. Radio transmitters, fax machines, scramble-cable printers, a secure Internet hookup—they looked like planets orbiting a rectangular star.

Usually found next to all this high-priced stuff was the chow table. It was well-stocked by the CIA-run kitchen located in the basement of the restaurant. The line of hot dishes was always substantial here, the coffee always fresh, the Cokes always ice-cold. Spooks had to eat too, and considering the location and the circumstances, the fare on Seven Ghosts Key was very good. But there was no hot food steaming today. No bucket full of icy Coke. Not even any coffee brewing.

Instead the buffet table was closed, the coffee machine stood mute, and there were three guys who looked very much like doctors sitting on folding chairs. In front of them was a smaller table with three black bags containing huge hypodermic needles opened up for all to see. And instead of plastic coffee mugs, there was a line of paper cups, each with several pills inside. None of this looked particularly inviting.

The first thing Delaney spotted as he and Norton walked in was the hypodermic needles. He almost passed out on the spot.

"Man, this is not going to be good," he whispered. "Not for me. Not for anyone."

They avoided the table of needles, and took seats in the last of five rows of chairs set up facing the big screen. The air-conditioning was working full blast, and it was actually chilly inside the room. Norton felt his sweat turn to ice; he wished he'd been able to finish one more beer. Delaney simply slumped in his chair and began a long series of burps.

More of the base's invisible occupants drifted in. A few of the tech support people. The guys who ran the simulators. The security team. The CO of the Marine contingent, Captain Chou Koo—who everyone called "Joe Cool"—arrived with a flourish. Four members of the U.S. Army Aviation Corps wandered in next, distinctive in the bright green fatigues. Behind them were four Navy SEAL medics, the tiny Red Cross patches over their left breast pockets identifying their function. What the SEALs' role was in all this Norton didn't have a clue. But like the Army pilots, they had certainly managed to keep themselves well hidden until now.

Behind the SEALs came a man Norton had seen his first day on the island and not since. He was a tall, powerful-looking individual, early forties, with a slightly Nordic look about him. He was wearing a black flight suit and a pair of Keds sneakers, the same outfit Norton had seen him in the first time. His baseball cap had a patch above its bill that read: *Angels Do It Forever.*

Norton elbowed Delaney when this character walked in.

"Who is that guy?" he asked his colleague. "He seems familiar."

Delaney burped once. "He looks like a pilot. But I haven't the foggiest."

Smitz came in next. The young CIA case officer arrived, as always, briefcase and omnipresent IBM NoteBook in hand. He nodded to Norton and Delaney, who returned his greeting with mock salutes. Others stood and shook his hand. Still others ignored him completely. Accompanying Smitz was a middle-aged CIA officer Norton knew only as Rooney. Norton had figured out that where Smitz was the one actually running the mystery operation, Rooney was the guy in charge of Seven Ghosts Key itself. Following them in were a half-dozen civilian types, unknown to Norton and Delaney, but undoubtedly CIA as well.

The last ones to arrive were Gillis and Ricco. They walked into the Big Room like aggrieved parties walking into court. Slightly flustered and confused, looking this way and that, checking out every door and window as if they were already plotting out an escape route. It was clear they wanted no part of whatever was about to happen here.

They were about to take seats when they spotted Norton and Delaney. Their demeanor changed instantly.

Gone were the twin baffled looks. Both faces now turned red. They began walking over to Norton and Delaney. It was clear they wanted to talk.

"Oh, boy," Delaney slurred. "Here we go . . ."

"You two assholes are dead meat," Gillis growled at them upon arrival.

Neither Norton or Delaney moved a muscle. They remained seated and simply looked up at the two National Guard pilots.

"What's your problem?" Delaney asked them calmly.

"You dickheads twisted something to get us assigned here. *That's* the problem," Ricco said through gritted teeth. "Now we're stuck out in the middle of nowhere, without a clue as to what the deal is."

"Hey, join the club," Delaney said dismissively.

Gillis, the taller of the two, leaned in closer to them.

"We know this is some kind of weirdo practical joke of yours," he said angrily. "And I swear, when I get the chance, I'll kill both of you twice."

Delaney just laughed at him. Norton didn't. His shoulders were still feeling a bit heavy.

"I was asked to recommend a solid refueling crew for this mission," Norton told them. "And you were the first choice. That's the story, straight and square. Besides, I've got better things to do than play practical jokes on you two lugnuts."

"We're going to be away from home for two fucking months," Ricco said, seething now with each syllable. "Do you know that? We got homes, families, things to do—not like you two cowboys."

Norton just glared up at Ricco. Oh, yeah, recommending the Air Guard crew *had* been a mistake, he thought. But not for the reasons he'd been dreading.

He finally stood up and faced both men.

"Look, you meatballs," he said. "We're in the fucking military here. The service of the United States. You got a letter from the President, for Christ's sake. There's a mission to be flown and they asked for the best and I said you guys because you *are* the best at air-to-air. But I guess being an asshole doesn't make any difference when it comes to that.''

Ricco and Gillis were suddenly stumped. Was Norton really flag-waving, or was it just part of a bigger gag?

"I got no desire to fly anything involving you two," Gillis finally retorted. "Besides, I don't have the faintest idea how to fly a helicopter, nor do I want to."

Now it was Norton who was surprised.

"Helicopter?" he asked. "They want you guys to fly a copter too?"

"Don't play cute," Ricco told him. "Like you didn't know?"

Norton just shook his head. "How the fuck would I know? No one knows anything about what's happening here."

Gillis took one more step towards Norton. He really was a huge guy, and Norton was sure that if he wanted to, Gillis could squash him like a bug.

"Like I said, I don't want to be involved in anything that includes you two assholes," Gillis hissed.

"Ditto," Ricco chimed in.

Now Delaney was suddenly on his feet.

"So go ask to be relieved if you're going to cry about it," he told them angrily. He was about half Gillis's size in both height and weight. "Then you can go back to hanging out at the dump on weekends."

Gillis and Ricco started laughing at this.

"Hanging at the dump, eh?" Ricco said. "Well, it's sure beats being demoted from driving jet fighters to *choppers*!"

Norton's ears were stung by the comment.

"Think this is a come-down for us, do you?" he asked them.

"Who wouldn't?" Ricco replied. "Everyone knows that's where guys who can't cut it in fighters wind up. Either there or flying the President's hamster around the country."

This barb was aimed directly at Delaney; he looked

as though it had punctured his heart. His face reddened, his fists tightened. He was ready to fight both men. Of course, he was also fairly drunk.

At that moment, Smitz looked up and saw the growing confrontation. He seemed to be the only one in the room noticing something was amiss.

He tapped his pen on the podium and called the room to order.

"Gentlemen? Can we settle down, please?"

The four pilots continued glaring at each other.

"Gentlemen? Please? We have a lot of information to cover here. . . ."

The staring contest lasted a few more moments, but finally the pilots dispersed. Norton and Delaney sat back down. Gillis and Ricco walked to the opposite side of the room, down the aisle, and took the first two seats in the first row. Right in front of Smitz's podium.

"Candy-assers," Delaney said under his breath.

Only one person in the room laughed at Delaney's remark. It was the guy in the Angel cap. He was sitting three rows in front of them, yet somehow he had heard the whispered comment.

Smitz tapped the podium again, and now everyone else sat down. There were twenty-six individuals in the room, and all of them found seats as far away from the men with the needles as possible.

"Well, this is what you've all been waiting for," Smitz began nervously. "All of the human assets needed for this program have arrived. This being the case, we've finally been authorized to tell you a bit about where you'll be going and why."

A groan went through the room. Smitz nodded to one of his flunkies and the lights became dim.

Slowly the huge TV wall screen came to life. The room went absolutely silent. Smitz pushed a button and a video began rolling.

The title boasted that the video was prepared by the CIA's Foreign Intelligence Evaluation Section. Everyone in the room groaned again.

The tape began shaky and washed out. When it finally cleared, it showed an enormous hole in the ground shot by a camera from high above. The gash was about three hundred feet across, the length of a football field, and maybe a couple feet deep. It was blackened and stood out like a sore thumb in the relatively undisturbed field of long golden hay surrounding it. The hole itself was filled with burnt stuff. Tree limbs, brush, scarred pieces of metal, and what appeared to be hundreds of chalky sooty sticks.

In reality, they were human bones.

"This video was shot in Bosnia almost one year ago," Smitz said. "During a new flare-up in the fighting there, someone herded three hundred and fifty-two civilians into a field. This is what was left of them."

Those assembled stared at the video. This was not a bomb crater they were looking at. It was too shallow and the shape was all wrong. This thing looked like a perfect circle.

The tape continued. Now they were looking at a hill-top village somewhere in the Middle East. There was nothing left of the place either, except the foundations of some houses and the remains of a fountain, which was leaking rusty water out into the street, like a bleeding wound.

"This was once the village of El Quas-ri," Smitz went on. "It's in central Iraq. It was more than four thousand years old. We've determined it took about thirty seconds to wipe it off the map."

For the next ten minutes, the tape presented a ghoulish montage of burnt holes, charred bones, leveled villages, and other instances of selective destruction. The two-dozen perfectly square carbon smudges along a flat desert highway were the remains of twenty-four food-supply trucks heading for a Kurdish refugee camp, Smitz explained. The tiny seaport that no longer had a dock standing or a boat afloat had been a stopping-off point for people fleeing oppression in Iran, he went on. The small airfield flying a Red Cross flag that no longer

had any runways or buildings or airplanes had been a
UN-sponsored airmobile field hospital.

Everywhere, at every location, there were bodies.
Twisted, skeletal, all shapes and sizes, from adults to
children. Some still had skin clinging to their bones, others had been picked clean. They all looked as if they'd
been cooked alive, which was not far from the truth.
Most of the ghastly images were identified as being from
the Middle East; others had been shot in parts of Asia
and Africa.

But what had caused all this? Smitz wasn't telling—
not yet.

The tape finally ended, only to be replaced by another.
This began with a black screen emblazoned with three
red letters: NSA. Everyone in the room sat up again and
took notice.

"This is footage from an NSA airborne asset," Smitz
explained solemnly. "It was taken two months ago
somewhere over the Persian Gulf."

What appeared was a grainy, static-filled NightVision
video of two airplanes refueling in flight in the middle
of a very dark night.

The tanker was a Tu-16A, a converted Russian Air
Force bomber not seen much anymore. This one was in
bad shape; one of its engines was smoking heavily. The
plane carried no markings or country insignia.

The tanker was all over the sky, not at all staying
steady and true as mandated when gassing another airplane in the air.

"Amateurs," Norton heard Ricco stage-whisper all
the way from the front row.

The second aircraft was a bit harder to identify at first.
It had four propellers, a thick fuselage, and a nose that
was grotesquely elongated. As the footage get clearer,
though, it appeared this second aircraft was a C-130 Hercules cargo plane. But certainly not a typical one. This
one had been stretched considerably, and had a more
girthful fuselage to go with its weird nose.

It was taking on gas from the Tu-16A via a refueling

probe on its left wing. This meant some very tricky flying for the Herc's pilots, especially with Ivan bouncing all over the sky. Yet the odd C-130 was holding steady, and it appeared the refueling was going as smoothly as could be expected.

"Good drivers," Delaney whispered over to Norton. He knew a few things about C-130's.

They watched the refueling operation in silence for about two minutes. Finally, the Russian plane began smoking heavily and the fuel hose disengaged. Both planes gave a flick of the nav lights and then quickly fell away from each other.

The video went to automatic freeze after that.

The lights came up, and all eyes once again fell on Smitz. He had a laser pointer fired up and ready. He directed its red dot at the frozen image of the Hercules.

"This aircraft is an AC-130/SO-21D," he began as though he'd pronounced the mouthful of letters and numbers many times in the past few days. "It's attached to a classified joint program called ArcLight. Or, I should say, it *was*. . . ."

Norton's ears perked up. *ArcLight?* He'd heard that term somewhere before. So had Delaney.

"Weren't they an outfit that ran secret flights during the Gulf War?" Delaney whispered to him. "A kind of aerial special operations concept?"

Norton nodded slowly. He remembered now. During the Gulf War, he'd seen one of these weird airplanes returning from a mission one night over occupied Kuwait. The word around the bunkhouse later on was that the ArcLight guys were out looking for Scuds.

"Yeah, they were called the Air Rambos," Norton whispered back. "They flew snoop-type gunships. But I heard they were disbanded after the war."

Other murmurs were now going around. Smitz tapped his podium and the room went silent again.

He shut off the video and then looked over at the techs. One of them raised the lights a bit more.

"On the night of February 9, 1991," Smitz began,

"one of the ArcLight gunships went out on a Scud hunt. It left a secret air base in western Saudi Arabia at about 0230 hours, with a crew of thirteen. It was carrying three miniguns and a light howitzer, all fully armed. It was also hauling, among other things, various EW/ECM pods.

"After taking off, this particular airplane reached its first radio checkpoint, where it indicated everything was OK—and then it just disappeared."

Smitz paused for a moment. He was staring out at twenty-six people, all wearing very quizzical looks.

Now comes the hard part, he thought.

Smitz lowered his voice and began again. "Everyone at CIA and the Pentagon was certain this airplane had splashed that night and was at the bottom of the Gulf somewhere. They looked for it, but never very hard. Turns out it landed on solid ground—or it was shot down. We still don't know."

Another pause. A few people in the room began to stir.

"But whatever happened to it," Smitz went on, "it was refurbished by someone. And now . . . well . . ." He turned back to the frozen video again. "Here it is."

There was a long, disturbing silence now as Smitz let his words sink in.

"You mean *that* plane is responsible for tearing up all that real estate?" someone up front finally asked.

Smitz nodded soberly. "That appears to be the case," he said. "And obviously, it is no longer under our control."

Those gathered remained absolutely silent. Even Gillis and Ricco were transfixed.

"The ArcLight 4 gunship reappeared about sixteen months ago," Smitz went on. "It took out an Omani patrol boat that had been tailing some illegal arms shipments going up the Gulf. There were no survivors. Then it was reported over Somalia a few weeks later, firing at a rival faction of some warlord currently in power. Then it showed up again over the Gulf sinking a bunch of boats carrying ammo up to some Shiite rebels in Basra. But in the last two months it's been very active.''

''Who's pulling the strings?'' Delaney called out with a belch.

Smitz shrugged. ''Officially,'' he began, ''the Iraqi government is suspected of giving aid and comfort to this situation. The plane is now apparently based somewhere in Iraq. And the fact that it was used against some Iraqis nationals—well, that happens everyday over there. But . . .''

''But?''

''But it has also been reported taking out some Checs—and they are enemies of Iran. And as you saw, it was in Bosnia, at least once, doing someone's bidding. And in Somalia. And out over the Indian Ocean. And these are just the incidents we know about. There's a chance this thing is out there every night, shooting up something. It's only on the rare occasion that it leaves a lot of evidence behind.''

''Are you saying that someone is *renting* this thing out?'' Norton asked.

Smitz just shrugged again. ''It's a good question—and a hard one to answer,'' he replied. ''When we look at the targets it's hit, they have a few things in common. They are all low-priority stuff. Lightly defended, if at all. Many involve civilians. And they all seem to be, if you'll pardon the expression, 'small' enough not to cause a whole lot of attention.''

''Like flying hitmen,'' someone in front called out. ''Quiet. Efficient.''

Smitz paused; he was obviously choosing his words very carefully.

''To answer your question, no one knows for certain if this thing is flying around as a kind of airborne mercenary. That's why everyone here has been called in. That's why this unit has been thrown together.''

Another thirty seconds went by in absolute silence.

No one said a thing. No one moved. The briefing had suddenly taken a surreal turn. They'd all sat through thousands of mission pre-briefings, post-briefings, and backgrounds. They were always routine. But not this one. This seemed right out of a bad movie.

"Thrown together?" another voice finally asked. "As in thrown together to stop this thing?"

Smitz just nodded. "Those are our orders."

More silence, but now it was broken by some murmuring.

Delaney raised his hand as if he was in the fifth grade.

"Can I ask a question?" he said. "Who shot that last tape? The one of the refueling?"

Smitz checked his NoteBook. " 'One of the NSA's airborne assets,' is all it says here."

"Is that to mean a spy plane of sorts?"

Smitz just nodded again. The guy in the Angel cap shifted a little in his seat.

"Well," Delaney went on. "If you can get a spy plane in close enough to shoot that footage, and you really want to get rid of this thing, why not just go in with a couple F-15's loaded for bear and shoot the fucker down? Poof! End of problem."

It was another good question. If the rogue airplane is causing so much destruction and you know where it is, why not just go in and blow it out of the sky?

Smitz thought a long time before replying. Finally, he just said: "I believe the answer to that question is classified."

But Delaney was puzzled—they all were. "Classified? Well, let me rephrase it then," he said. "Why do you need *us* or anyone else to go in and take it out?"

Smitz just shook his head again.

"Because your mission is not to destroy that AC-130," Smitz replied. "Your mission is to *recover* it— and free the original crew. We believe they are being held captive at the same location the plane is operating from. If this is the case, then you will go in, rescue them, carry them out, and if possible, fly the plane out too."

Now a storm of gasps went through the room. No one could speak. Not even Delaney for a moment. But finally he managed to blurt out: "You mean you want us to fly over to Iraq, stop whoever is flying the airplane, recover it, *and* bring the original crew back?"

"Precisely," Smitz replied.

The briefing would last for two more hours.

Smitz wound up fielding the same angry questions over and over again. Why didn't the U.S. just send in some fighters to shoot down the rogue airplane while in flight? Why not destroy it with cruise missiles while it was on the ground—*then* go in and get the original crew? The people in the room came up with a hundred different ways how the gunship could be destroyed— and sending in a helicopter-borne force, manned mostly by inexperienced personnel, was not among them.

But Smitz stood his ground, answering truthfully that security concerns prevented all the remedies suggested— and mandated the one the CIA had put into motion. A helicopter force would transit to the Middle East, find the rogue airplane's base, raid it, rescue the original crew, and if possible fly the airplane back out. Those were the mission specs.

But *how* that was going to be accomplished would not be revealed to the unit just yet. There was still more training to do, Smitz explained. Live training. This meant the marathon sessions spent by the pilots in the simulators were coming to an end.

But there was little cheer in this. The lack of details about the operation itself upset those assembled to the point of revolt. If the most essential information on their mission wasn't going to be revealed to them now, one of them complained, then this wasn't "the mother of all briefings" as had been promised.

But Smitz held firm again. Later on they would learn the logistics of the raid. Those were the orders.

To that, Delaney declared with a loud burp: "Then you should call the next session the '*motherfucker* of all briefings.'"

Things deteriorated further after that. The comments

got more raucous, more acid-toned. But as it turned out, the one question Smitz had dreaded the most didn't get asked until just before the briefing ended. Oddly, it was one of the SEAL medics who brought it up.

"If the CIA believes the plane's original crew is being held prisoner," he asked, "then who is flying the gunship these days?"

Wisely, Smitz had prepared a response to this query ahead of time. Not an answer per se, just a response.

So when the question was asked, he just took a deep breath and with a straight face replied: "I'm sorry, that information is also classified."

It was dark by the time the briefing broke up.

Those assembled received two hypodermic injections each—booster shots to ward off any foreign germs they might run into overseas—as well as a cupful of pills that would supposedly do the same thing. They were told to report back to the billets and await individual mess call.

One of those attending the briefing would not be staying for evening chow, however. He was the man in the black flight suit and Keds sneakers and wearing the cap with the subtle-sexual phrase about angels on it.

The cap was actually an inside joke, a gift given to him by his wife. His name wasn't "Angel"—it was his code name. Even Smitz didn't know what this guy's real name was, or his rank, or even if he was in the military, or who he worked for if he wasn't. But the orders said he would attend all of the briefings on the program. Indeed his presence would be crucial to the success of the raid.

But at the moment, he had other places to be.

So he was glad that the sun had gone down before the briefing was called to an end. He waited, staying behind as the grumbling attendees got their shots, swallowed their pills, and filed out of the Big Room. Then, after a brief conversation with Smitz and Rooney, he slipped out the back of the restaurant and began climbing the sand dune located behind the building.

The dune was about fifty feet straight up and was by far the highest point on Seven Ghosts Key. He reached the top and took a good, long look around. The stars were bright already and the moon would be coming up very soon. If he squinted his eyes real hard, he could see a faint green light to the south. This was the ragged glow of Cuba. To the north, the night sky had a yellowish tinge to it. The color of Florida.

He could see no lights in between, though. No vessels in the nearby waters. No airplanes flying overhead. This was good. For what he was about to do, he could not have any witnesses.

Certain that the coast was clear—literally—he reached into his pocket and took out a device about the size of a TV remote control. He pressed three buttons in sequence and watched the tiny LCD screen light up. It began flashing the numeral .100 at two-second intervals.

Angel hit a few more buttons, and the numerals changed to .200 and began flashing every second. A few more buttons pushed, and now the screen read .300 and was not flashing at all.

"That was easy," Angel said to himself.

Now he held down a red button at the base of the device and then looked up. Off to the west, in the thick starry sky, a faint blue light appeared. It was moving very fast. So fast it was over the western tip of Seven Ghosts Key in less than ten seconds. That was when Angel let up on the red button. The deep blue light stopped directly above him, two miles up. He pushed the red button twice, and now the blue light began to descend.

Within fifteen seconds, it was no more than fifty feet above his head and still coming down. . . .

A minute later, Angel was one hundred miles away.

10

Off the west coast of India

The early morning sun was climbing over the East Arabian Sea.

The small fleet of fishing boats, trawlers, and motorized junks, having departed the west India port of Kordinar just after the midnight tide, was now making good headway as the winds shifted westward.

The vessels—twelve in all—were loaded with a variety of cargo: black-market computers, TVs, silk, American-made jeans and sneakers. A few political refugees. A few escaped criminals. Many families, some going on vacation to the Persian Gulf states. Many had children with them. Some were carrying infants.

They were heading for Oman, a full day's journey if the seas stayed calm. On arrival, those with merchandise to sell would become rich for a year's time. Those fleeing the authorities would be free. Those heading for a somewhat perilous shopping vacation would have the malls and sands of Oman, Bahrain, and the UAE awaiting them.

But because their cargo was considered precious in these waters, the small fleet of boats would have been prime pickings for the sea pirates known to ply this part of the ocean, preying on the defenseless. That was why there was a thirteenth vessel in the fleet—in fact, it was leading it.

It was an Osa-class gunboat. It had been hired by the voyagers to provide protection for their trip.

The Russian-exported gunboat was well equipped. It held a crew of sixteen, only four of which were responsible for the forty-four-foot vessel's operation. The rest were gunners, loaders, aimers, and computer guys. The gunship boasted twin OTO-Melara 76-mm guns both front and back, plus torpedoes with ultra-sound targeting capability. But the gunboat also carried the dangerous Starwind missile, essentially a knockoff of the terrifying Israeli-built Raphael antiship weapon.

The Starwinds were accurate, easy to use, and had an extremely high kill record. One could sink a midsize cruiser; two could devastate an even larger ship. The Osa gunboat had a dozen such missiles on board. As such, its firepower was equal to some of the capital ships of the world's biggest navies.

The travelers had paid the gunship's crew handsomely, and were cozy in the knowledge that the money had been well spent. Already during the voyage they had spotted pirate vessels sailing out on the horizon, like jackals shadowing a pack of wildebeests. But the pirates weren't foolish—they knew their smaller, lightly armed vessels could never take on the kind of firepower that the Osa gunboat carried.

That was why they had paid for a little firepower of their own.

They first heard the noise about ten in the morning.

There was a little wind and the sea was throwing some spray, and that combination made a distinctive sound. The noise caused by the thirteen vessels and their various power plants also made a distinctive noise—but it was rather high-pitched and mechanical.

This approaching sound was deeper, more ominous. As if the sea itself was groaning.

For most of the travelers, it was the last thing they would ever hear.

The airplane came out of the west.

It was flying low, its silhouette outlined by the heavy overcast, displaying its grayish, ghostly image.

The crew of the gunboat saw it first. One of their forward gunners doubled as a lookout, and he had picked up the thing on his binoculars about three miles out. It was little more than a growing speck at that point. Still, it didn't take long for the lookout to realize what it was.

He turned to sound the alarm, but before he knew it, a long stream of red and yellow fire went right over his head. It came so close to him that for an instant, he actually felt its heat, which was hot enough to short circuit his IF gear.

The next stream of bullets was more on the mark. It hit the lookout and the other three crew members at his gun station dead-on with a quick splash of fire and light. A mere three-second burst—four hundred projectiles in all—destroyed the gunboat's forward twin weapon, its turret, and one quarter of its crew.

The huge airplane roared over the stricken Osa several seconds later. The wash from its propellers kicked up the sea as no winds could ever do. Those still alive on board watched as the airplane did a long slow bank, passing over the rest of the ragtag fleet and back towards the gunboat again.

Bells rang. Whistles blared. A scramble siren went off. But none of this did any good. The gunboat's crew was already heading toward their battle stations, but there was nothing to scramble to. The sad truth was, for all the firepower packed in the gunboat, it was useless now. The travelers had indeed spent a lot for money and had spent wisely. No pirate vessel had come within fifteen miles of them.

But no one had expected anything to be coming from the air.

The AC-130 rose slightly in altitude as it approached the gunboat again. Its engines suddenly began screeching louder than before—this was the noise the four propellers made when their fuel was pulled back and they'd been ordered to reduce speed. Engines protesting, the pilots put the big aircraft into orbit about 1200 feet directly above the gunboat. The pilot dropped the left wing, and now all four doors on that side of the fuselage snapped open.

The stream of fire that came out of the gunship now lit up the sea for twenty-five miles around. It lasted no more than twenty seconds, just enough for the big airplane to make one circuit around the hapless gunboat. The violence it visited on the water was so quick, so intense, so heated, that steam enveloped the gunboat. A few of the vapors were blood red. When the smoke and the mist and the sea spray finally cleared, there was nothing left.

The gunboat and its crew were gone.

Its job done, the airplane departed in the same direction from whence it came. It would fly all the way to Bahrain. There it would land at a secret base and pick up a trunk full of dollars. This would be the second installment in its contract with sea pirates. The crew would split fifty percent of the take, and what remained would be sent to a special Swiss bank account controlled by others. The crew would then take off and refuel in the air, before returning to base. If all went well, they would be down and eating dinner by 1800 hours, another day's work behind them.

As for the travelers—they were now easy pickings. The pirates moved in and methodically attacked and boarded each vessel. Anything of value was taken; the captains and crews were immediately killed. All eligible females were snatched, along with all the guns and radio gear.

Once each boat had been visited by the pirates, the sea thieves would fire 22-mm cannon shells into its hull. A ten-second burst was usually all that was needed. Invariably something would catch on fire or the holes made would be big enough to cause water to pour in. No one remaining on any boat survived. All either drowned, or did not last long in what was some of the most shark-infested waters of the world. More than 160 men, elderly women, and children met their end this way.

The pirates, as always, made a clean getaway.

11

Seven Ghosts Key
Midnight

The storm came up so quickly, Smitz didn't have time
to close the window in his billet.

The rain and wind blew in, like a pair of unseen
hands, causing a small tornado to swirl madly around
his room. It scattered his previously orderly papers
everywhere, and soaked just about everything he considered valuable, including his fax machine, his change
of clothes, and his bunk. Then, just as quickly, it
stopped, even before he could get the window closed,
leaving him dripping wet and his room in a shambles.

His world turned upside down again. Just like that.

He'd been lying on his bunk, going over his Note-
Book entries for the day, when the sudden wind came
up. Located in base's tiny control tower, one floor down
from the control room itself, his ten-by-ten billet had
been a storage closet originally. When Smitz first landed
on Seven Ghosts Key, his rooming options were limited
to bunking in with the Marines in Motel Hell or staying

with the pilots in the basement of the building adjacent
to Hangar 2. Instinct told him that with this operation,
it was best that he didn't get to close to the personnel
involved. Especially the pilots.

So he'd tried sleeping in the Big Room the first few
nights. But between the laughing murals, the lizards
scurrying everywhere, and the tale of the seven CIA people who'd vanished from the island bouncing around his
head, the place had given him a major case of the yips.
Smitz valued his sleep, and wanted to lay his head somewhere that was not overrun with reptiles or ghosts. When
Rooney suggested that the empty supply room in the
tower might be more comfortable, Smitz jumped at the
chance.

He lay back down on his bunk now, disgusted that in
just a few seconds his place had become a small disaster
area. But this was nothing new. This assignment had
been a struggle from the start, and nothing he'd seen
lately indicated that it was going to change anytime soon.
A small twister in his room was just more of the same.

The screwiness had not ended that night in Bethesda.
If anything, it had grown worse. Not only was he almost
as much in the dark about this operation's goals as the
personnel called in to do the job, but since arriving on
Seven Ghosts Key, Smitz had been fighting a silent, but
nonstop battle with his office back in Washington for
both the information and equipment he needed to see the
thing through. Getting the intelligence assets. Getting the
humans. Getting the Tin Can software. Getting bunks
for the Marines. All of it a battle. For some reason, he'd
had to fight for every last nut and bolt of the essentials,
and with his nemesis Larry Stone back in D.C. control-
ling the spigot, it was even harder than expected.

Smitz was getting so weary of it, he'd wished more
than once that some ghost would swoop down and spirit
him away. But then they'd have to change the name of
the island.

The strange thing was, only stuff relating to the upcoming operation seemed to have a hard time squeezing

itself through the supply pipeline. Espresso for the restaurant, fresh steaks for chow, tapes for everyone's VCRs—all these things he could get, via the twice-weekly visits by CIA-contracted cargo planes. But trying to secure the correct-size computer disk for the Tin Can's hard drive had taken three weeks. Getting the two tapes he'd shown at the recently completed briefing had taken nearly as long. These selective delays were stupid and weird, like just about everything associated with the project. Yet every time he cabled Stone to ask why it seemed some things were being held up intentionally, he never received an adequate reply.

It was like fighting a losing battle from the start.

Smitz put his last dry towel under his head now, took off his glasses, and tried to rest his tired eyes. This operation was the biggest and most complex he'd ever been assigned. He was, after all, still a junior officer in the CIA's Special Foreign Operations Section. His job for the past two years had been essentially carrying spears for the section's bigger operatives. Cleaning up their dirty work, getting funds to them if they were offshore, writing their reports if they were not. The solo projects he'd handled had been appropriately unimportant. Meeting with Cuban dissidents, interviewing fake Russian nuclear scientists, telling half-truths to disaffected mullahs. Kid stuff . . .

Why then had Jacobs given him this assignment literally from his deathbed? Had it been a vote of confidence from the old dog to a young wolf making his way up the ranks? Or had it been just the opposite—a chance for him to fail and get weeded out to some real crappy CIA desk job, like the Agricultural Intelligence Section. Was that the reason Stone was squeezing his balls so hard on this one? Smitz didn't know. He was the first to admit that the project was a little over his head. The question was, could he still rise above the waves and see it through?

He rolled over on his bunk and stared at the dripping-wet wall. He suddenly wished that he smoked cigarettes or drank liquor. He suddenly wished he had *a vice*. He wasn't sure why. It was a strange thought. But it seemed if he did have some nasty habit to fall back on, it might make what he had to do go a little easier.

But alas, he had none of these things.

He wasn't that lucky.

He somehow drifted off to sleep in his messy wet little room. His dream began again. He's playing first base in the sixth game of the 1986 World Series. Two outs in the tenth. The crowd is roaring. He's tapping his mitt. Voices are whispering in his ear. But this time, before the ball is even hit to him—the one that would go through his legs and cost him the world championship— the rain pelting his window started up again. He awoke with a start and saw a red light flashing in his face. It was his scramble-fax's remote beeper. There was a message coming in for him from the Office.

He reached over and activated the remote-control device, then plugged it into his laptop, praying that his stuff would work after getting seriously drenched. He was heartened to see the laptop's little green light pop on. He hit the enter button, and the message began scrolling across his laptop screen.

"Situation fluid. Further matériel arriving your location within the half hour," was all it said.

Half hour? Smitz sat straight up on his bed.

He couldn't possibly clean up his room in that short a time!

The wind was howling and the rain coming down even harder when Smitz reached Hangar 2.

It was now almost 0100 hours and he was awaiting the "further matériel" as the scrambled message had told him to do.

But what was he waiting for exactly?

He didn't know. But he had a good idea.

Rooney drove up in one of the pink jeeps. He had had the sense to wear a rain slicker. The storm was getting worse now, and the wind was positively screaming.

Rooney climbed out of the jeep, soggy cigar still stuck between his teeth. He was a powerful if paunchy individual, with an Ernest Hemingway look to him. A team of air techs was waiting a little further inside the hangar, wondering why they'd been called out to duty so late and in such weather.

Rooney walked over to Smitz, huddled just inside the door of the aircraft barn.

"You got to get yourself some foul-weather gear, Smitty," he told him. "Things can get mighty strange out here in the straits."

"You're telling me," Smitz replied.

No sooner were the words out of his mouth when his cell phone rang. It was the tower. Four planes were on their way in.

"I suppose they didn't tell you exactly what we're getting," Rooney asked as he tried to relight his cigar in the pouring rain.

Smitz resisted the temptation to ask him for a puff.

"They weren't specific," Smitz replied. "But I've got a pretty good guess."

"Yeah," Rooney said. "Me too."

Their words were drowned out by the sound of the first airplane approaching. The high-pitched whine meant only one thing. This was a huge C-5 Galaxy cargo jet coming in.

The monstrous plane appeared out of the mist a moment later. It slammed down with a great screech of tires and smoke, and roared by them with oceans of spray flying in every direction.

"Damn!" Smitz exclaimed.

"Not the kind of plane you'd expect to land in a hurricane," Rooney said.

Right on its tail came a second Galaxy. Behind it, a third, then a fourth. The four airplanes touched down as if they'd been choreographed. By the time the last plane had landed, the first C-5 had reached the end of the long runway and had taxied back around towards the hangar.

It pulled to a stop in front of Smitz and Rooney, its nose opening like a gigantic set of jaws.

The insides were packed so tightly, it was hard to see exactly what the flying beast was carrying. But the aircrew hopped to it, and soon two dark canvas-covered forms were being pushed out of the gaping maw and into the hangar.

"Damn, look at that," Rooney said, somehow puffing his water-soaked cigar. "It's like a whale giving birth through its mouth!"

"But what the hell are these things?" Smitz asked.

Rooney finally threw the cigar away and lit up another.

"Let's find out," he said.

As soon as the first bundle was inside the hangar, Smitz had a word with the first C-5's loadmaster. Smitz signed a slew of documents, and then asked that the C-5's crew remove the canvas covering one of the objects. This took a few minutes, but when they were done, Smitz just stared at what had been revealed.

That was when his boss's last words came back to him.

Try to stay out of the helicopters, Jacobs had said.

Finally Smitz knew what the old man had meant.

12

Jazz Norton didn't dream very much.

He didn't know why exactly. A flight surgeon once told him that as someone who dodged flak and SAMs for a living, and who, when not in combat, flew dangerously at air shows, Norton lived a much too exciting a life to dream. After going twice the speed of sound miles above the earth on a daily basis, his subconscious needed a rest too. Besides, the doctor had asked him, what would a person like him dream about?

But this night, Norton was sure he was dreaming when he saw a ghost looking down at him from the foot of his bed.

The figure was dressed all in white. It's skin was wet and runny. With a bright light coming from behind, it looked almost transparent. A crash of thunder and a flash of lightning only added credibility to the apparition.

Norton sat up with a start, his fists clenched, ready to punch the ghost.

That was when Smitz pulled back the hood of his rain slicker to reveal his soaking-wet head.

"Sorry to bother you like this, Major," the young CIA man was saying. "But we need you over in Hangar 2 right away."

The storm was growing worse. Lightning flashes were tearing holes in the dark sky; thunder rumbled, shaking the tarmac right down to its foundation. And the rain was coming down in torrents. Norton and Smitz ran through the deluge, heading for Hangar 2.

"If you guys were so smart, you would have picked a better place to hide yourselves!" Norton yelled over at Smitz. "The weather here sucks!"

"Who said we were smart?" Smitz yelled back without missing a beat.

They finally reached the huge hangar and Smitz banged heavily on the front door. They could hear several techs struggling to open the big sliding piece of metal on the other side. Finally, the door was pulled back and the two men jumped inside.

Norton yanked back his hood and wiped the rainwater from his eyes. When his vision cleared, he saw before him a very strange aircraft.

Something ran through Norton at that moment; a jolt went from his head to his toes and back again. Was it adrenaline? A bit of lightning? Fear? He didn't know. But he staggered a bit, causing Smitz to reach out and catch him.

"That's how I felt when I saw it too," Smitz said.

Norton took a closer look. For a tiny instant, he thought he was looking at a jet aircraft here—an elderly A-6 Intruder, to be exact. Bathed in the weird greenish hue of the hangar's sodium lights, the snout of this odd aircraft, when viewed head-on, resembled the Intruder in a perverse way.

But in the next blink Norton knew this was no A-6. He should be so lucky. No, this thing was a helicopter. The massive rotors were proof enough. But it was a copter that had wings as well. And the cockpit was actually a double-seat tandem setup—a place for a pilot in back and a gunner up front, with bug-eyed bubble glass all round. And the wheels, though looking like a fighter jet's, were squat, their attending gear very heavy. And hanging off those stunted wings were multi-barreled guns and rocket dispensers. And hundreds of different attachments—antennas, speed vanes, gun muzzles, God knows what else—seemed to be poking out all over the fuselage.

Norton blinked again. This thing was a beast—and it was staring right at him. And his first urge was to run, very fast and very far away.

"Do you know what it is?" Smitz asked him.

Yes, Norton replied. He knew exactly what it was.

It was an Mi-24 Hind. A massive Russian-built helicopter gunship.

"Where *the fuck* did you get this thing?" he asked Smitz incredulously.

"I can't tell you that," Smitz replied. "The Russians built a couple thousand of these monsters. Let's just say we were able to *procure* a few."

They walked further into the hangar. The techs who had spent all night putting the gunship together gave way with a nod from Smitz.

"Grab some coffee, guys," he told them.

Norton was simply awestruck by the size of the helicopter. It was huge. Much bigger than an Apache or a Cobra or any attack chopper of American design.

"The Russians came up with this concept after studying our experience in Viet Nam," Smitz explained, "They saw the pickle we were in, landing troops into hot zones with only a few machine guns sticking out of our Hueys for cover. So they set out to build a combination gunship and troop carrier. That's why it's so big."

They began walking around the machine.

"It weighs 21,000 pounds empty," Smitz continued. "Got to be the weight of at least a couple Apaches."

"At least," Norton said with a whistle.

"Half inch of plating around the cockpit," Smitz

went on, sounding not unlike a car salesman. "Protection for both gunner and pilot. The Russians were so afraid of getting their asses shot off in Afghanistan, they put the flight crew in steel bathtubs. Same thing for the engines and the guts. Supposedly you can take a 62-mm round in the power plants and keep flying."

"Not bad," Norton mumbled.

"Thick glass all round," Smitz continued. "Those windshields have more strength than the steel tub the crew sits in. They can stop a high-caliber bullet, maybe even a cannon round or two."

"But this thing has wings," Norton said, stopping to study one of the not-so-stubby appendages.

Smitz turned on his NoteBook. "Says here they are nearly the size of the wings on an F-104 Starfighter."

"But why?" Norton wanted to know. He patted one of the huge weapon-dispensers attached to the long downward-slanting wings. "Just to carry these things?"

Smitz consulted his computer again.

"Says here the wings provide approximately one fourth the lift required to get the aircraft up and flying. I guess that means the damn thing is one-quarter jet fighter, three-quarters helicopter."

Norton just shook his head. "Only the Russians could think of that."

"They *are* known for their helicopters," Smitz said, a bit sly.

And that was when Norton stopped in his tracks. He felt like an anvil had just landed smack on the head. All those hours in the Tin Can. The screwy cockpit setup. The ass-backwards flight regimes.

He looked Smitz straight in the eye. "Damn, you're going to ask me to *fly* this thing, aren't you?"

The young CIA officer could only shrug. "That's the plan," he admitted. "We can't go into Iraq in American-built choppers. Our cover would be blown in a minute. So we have to use the kind of copters the Iraqis fly. And they fly Russian-built jobs. All those hours in UIT were intended to get you up to speed on this baby. The simulator software was reverse-engineered from this thing to give you a feel for flying a Hind. End of mystery.''

Norton just shook his head, not able to take his eyes off the sinister Hind. "Man, what am I *doing* here?" he mumbled.

Smitz let the moment pass, then said to him: "Look, why not just get up there and try it on for size?"

Reluctantly, Norton climbed the ladder and eased himself into the rear seat of the cockpit. And of course there was a problem right away. There were switches and buttons and dials and levers and lights and handles going from his left elbow to his right. Indeed they seemed to surround him, and there seemed to be twice as many as needed. The interior did resemble what he'd been "flying" in the Tin Can, but with double the number of doodads. For someone so used to driving clean aircraft like F-15's and the F-17 Cobra, the Hind cockpit looked like a madhouse.

"Christ, what is all this extra crap for?" he cried out.

Smitz climbed the ladder and peered into the electronics-laden tub himself. It did look like it had been built back in the fifties.

"I've been assured all the crucial flight systems match your simulator training," Smitz said. "The unimportant stuff is just redundant backup readouts they felt compelled to jam in there, I guess."

But the cruel joke continued. Norton took a closer look at the control panel and discovered that in the multitude of lights, switches, and buttons, not one of them was labeled in English. Instead they all had nameplates with Cyrillic lettering on them.

"Jesus, even a Russian would have a hard time reading all this," Norton said. "How am I supposed to?"

"Well, that's a temporary problem," Smitz replied. "When we get a chance, we'll label all the crucial stuff for you. But a lot of it should be somewhat familiar to you already."

Norton tried to make some sense of the alphabet soup

of Russian words swimming before his eyes. He felt as
if all the air was leaking out of him.

"How long do I have to figure this out?" he asked
Smitz. "A year or so?"

Smitz took a deep breath.

"The specs say the maximum flight-training time is
thirty days," he said. "That's to be considered combat-
ready in this thing."

Norton just stared back at him.

"*Thirty days?* To be combat-ready? Better check your
little computer there. You must be reading it wrong."

But Smitz didn't move a muscle. "Nope," he said.
"Thirty days. That's the spec."

Norton reached up and pulled the CIA man closer to
him.

"Are you crazy?" he hissed. "It probably took a Russian five times that long to get combat-ready in this shit-
box—and they *built* the goddamn thing."

Smitz tactfully disengaged his collar from Norton's
fist.

"Look, Major, our timetable is already behind schedule. *Way* behind. So, we've really got no choice in this
matter. Thirty days worth of flight orientation is all that
can be allotted. That includes group-flying exercises.
Then—"

"Wait a moment," Norton interrupted him. "Did you
say 'group flying'?"

Smitz just put his thumb over his shoulder. For the
first time Norton realized there was another Hind, just
as big, just as fierce, parked at the rear of the hangar.

"And there are three more, even bigger Russian copters, in the other two hangars," Smitz told him.

Norton just shook his head as it all fell into place.

"You're sending us *all* into Iraq, riding in Iraqi choppers?" he blurted out. "The Marines? Me? Delaney?
The whole crew?"

Smitz nodded. "More accurately, in aircraft that *look*
Iraqi. From the little I know, the plan requires being on
the ground for a long period of time. Remaining mobile

and remaining secure will be essential. Flying back and forth to an aircraft carrier or a friendly base is not an option. So the unit has to become autonomous and stay in-country, until the mission is done. To do that, a cover is needed. These helicopters will provide that cover— and the mobility.''

Norton just couldn't believe what he was hearing.

''Man, you guys have been watching too many bad movies,'' he said, starting to get out of the cockpit. ''But you can do this one without me.''

Smitz decided it was time to get tough. He reached over and firmly sat Norton back down into the cockpit.

''Major Norton, you're a military pilot, correct?'' he began sternly.

Norton felt his jawbone tighten. ''Yeah, that's right.''

''And you've seen combat? And you are on the short list for shuttle flight training. And you wanted to fly black missions out of Dreamland? Right?''

Norton could only shrug. ''Yeah, so?''

''So then flying is not the concern here, is it?''

Norton shook his head. ''No, it isn't the flying,'' he mumbled. ''I can *fly* anything. But—''

Smitz cut him off. ''And to tell you the truth, Major, I'm not even sure why you were selected for this mission. But one reason, I believe, was your high rating on the adaptability section of the PS2. So—we know you can fly anything and we know you can adapt to just about any situation. What is the problem here then?''

''The problem is that there are about a million things that can go wrong with this plan,'' Norton shot back. ''Whatever the plan is!''

''But if you don't know what the mission spec is,'' Smitz argued, ''how could you possibly know what could go wrong?''

Norton took a moment and tried to compose himself. He was losing this debate and he knew it.

''Look, you're putting us in Iraqi copters, in Iraqi uniforms, I assume,'' he said slowly, rolling each syllable off his tongue with contempt. ''If just the slightest thing gets fucked up, and we get caught, they can shoot us all as spies. That's just one reason.''

Smitz just shook his head. He was the exact opposite of Norton. He preferred to hash things out, compromise, with level heads and calm voices. It was the Harvard way of doing things.

"Then, Major, I suggest you and the others should do everything in your power *not* to get caught,'' he said calmly. "I'm sure everyone from the President on down would prefer it that way.''

Norton could feel his face go red. His hands went into fists again. He was stuck and he knew it.

He took another survey of the Hind's byzantine control panel. "Does anyone even know how to start this goddamn thing?''

Smitz looked to the small cluster of aircraft techs who had gathered nearby, drawn back from their coffee break by the raised voices. They'd heard Norton's question, but their only reply was a chorus of shrugs. One man held up a manual that looked about a foot thick.

Smitz turned back to Norton.

"Let's just say we're working on that,'' Smitz told him.

Norton groaned and put his head in his hands. "Man, I should have stayed in show business.''

Smitz gave him a friendly pat on the back. "Look on the bright side, Major,'' he said.

Norton looked up at him. "There's a bright side?''

Smitz nodded. "You could have been assigned to the aircraft that your friends Gillis and Ricco have to fly.''

This was true enough. In the next hangar over, Gillis and Ricco were going through their own trauma.

They were sitting side by side in a helicopter even larger than a Hind. Also of Russian design, it was known as the Mi-6 Hook.

This copter was not a gunship. It was a dedicated troop carrier/cargo hauler of immense proportions. When it first entered service in the mid-fifties, the Hook was the largest military helicopter ever to fly—so big, in fact, it had to be shipped to Seven Ghosts Key in pieces, and still it barely fit inside the second C-5 that had landed earlier in the night.

Put together, it was an astounding 136 feet long— more than a third of a football field. Its rotors were a gigantic 133 feet in diameter. Its power plant was a brutally strong pair of engines capable of nearly six thousand horsepower per engine. As a result, the Hook was the first helicopter to ever surpass three hundred kilometers an hour. This was extremely fast for any chopper.

Its vast cargo hold could carry seventy-five fully equipped soldiers or even a tank or two inside. It could lug a total of twelve tons in its belly and another nine with a pull line underneath. The copter also had wings sticking from its midsection. Again, their function was to provide lift for the enormous machine.

None of this was making a positive impression on Ricco or Gillis, though. They were sitting in the vast cockpit—it too was adorned with a multitude of lights, bells, buzzers, switches, and levers. All of it with Russian nameplates. All of it looking like it was made in the fifties, which it was.

The only things the pilots recognized were the steering columns, the throttles, and the refueling suite—all of them were similar to the instruments on their KC-10 Pegasus tanker. But this provided them with little comfort.

Rooney, the CIA base chief, had drawn the short straw and was giving them their first look at the Russian-built behemoth.

"You *really* don't expect us to fly this thing, do you?" Ricco was asking him for about the hundredth time.

"Those are the orders," Rooney told him for about the hundredth time.

But Gillis persisted—he was by far the most infuriated of the two.

"You have to be nuts," he lashed out at Rooney.

"We fly jets. Big jets. Big fucking American jets! This is a helicopter. A *Russian*-built helicopter. We can't drive this thing."

"You'll have to learn," Rooney said matter-of-factly. "It's as simple as that. Look—they went through the trouble to modify it to your experience. With the steering columns and all. I've been assured that once you get the feel of this thing, it will handle just like your big tanker. That's why you guys didn't have to suffer inside those simulators."

But Gillis and Ricco couldn't be had that easily. Sticks and throttles did not a flying machine make. As it was, the cockpit looked like the dashboard of a tractor-trailer jammed into that of a compact car.

But it was the modifications to the back cargo bay that *really* had them worried. The vast insides had been stripped out and two enormous fuel bladders had been installed. Per the mission specs, they were presently full of aviation fuel, the stink of which was permeating the vast flight cabin.

"And is someone expecting us to fly all that gas somewhere?" Ricco demanded of Rooney. "If so, I can suggest to you about a hundred better ways to do it. Like, in a fuel ship. You know, the kind that floats on the water? I'm sure the Navy's got more than a few of them."

Rooney just shook his head. He wished now that he'd volunteered to orient Norton to his craft instead of these two.

"The idea is not to carry the fuel from one place to the other," he explained calmly and slowly, like a professor to a couple dumbos held after class. "The idea is to carry it upstairs—so you can refuel others in flight. That's what you two boys are good at, am I right?"

The pair of pilots looked back at him. This was the first they'd heard of this.

"Yes, we are fucking great at refueling—in a big go-damn jet!" Ricco half-shouted at him. "Why doesn't anyone listen to us here? We're not chopper pilots. No one here is.''

Rooney just stared at the ceiling of the copter's cockpit. He was astounded by the number of tubes and wires running along its length. What the hell was inside them all? he wondered.

''And you really expect us to learn how to refuel other aircraft in flight with this thing?'' Gillis asked him.

Rooney nodded.

''What kind of aircraft?''

''Other helicopters, of course,'' Rooney replied.

At this, Ricco and Gillis both slumped into their seats. Like Norton, they couldn't believe what they had gotten themselves into.

There was a long silence as both men looked over the huge cockpit and its dozens of instruments and controls.

''And how long are you going to give us to learn all this crap?'' Ricco asked.

Rooney was uncharacteristically lost for an answer. He ran his hand over his balding dome. Outside, it sounded like the storm was at last letting up.

''I'll get back to you on that,'' he said finally.

13

0830 hours

Delaney woke up to a cloud of steam hovering above his head.

He rubbed his eyes, took a sniff, and said: "There had better be sugar in that. . . ."

Norton and Smitz were standing over him, cups of steaming coffee in their hands. Delaney just stared up at them.

"Unless you're going to pour it on me . . ."

"We should," Norton replied. "It took us five minutes just to make sure you were still alive. How can anyone sleep so fucking soundly?"

Delaney yawned and managed to sit up. He stretched and yawned again. Then he snatched the cup of coffee out of Norton's hand.

"I take my sleep very seriously," Delaney said after a few noisy slurps. "It's one of the reasons I got divorced. I'd give her the happy stick, roll over, and be out for the next ten hours. I slept through a tornado once."

Norton and Smitz looked at each other and did a simultaneous eye roll.

"Good," Norton said, throwing him his clothes.
"You'll need that experience for where we're going."

Delaney had half-drained the cup of scalding hot coffee by now.

"Why? Where are we going?" he asked, pulling on
his flight suit and boots.

"For a little ride," Norton replied.

Two minutes later the trio walked into Hangar 2. Delaney took one look at the Hind gunship, turned on his
heel, and began to walk away.

Norton caught him by the collar and spun him back
towards the gunship.

Norton said grimly, "You know what that is, don't
you?"

"Yeah, of course, it's a fucking Hind," Delaney said,
his eyes now glued on the frightening machine. "Is it
real?"

"Too real," Norton said, nudging him a little further
towards the Russian-built gunship. "But it's a beauty,
isn't it?"

"It's a piece of shit," Delaney replied. "And if you
got me up to go for a ride in this thing, you wasted your
time and mine."

He began to walk away again. Smitz blocked his retreat.

"You're the one wasting time, Major," the CIA officer told him. "This bird has to go up on a shakeout
flight. And we need someone to fly front seat. And that
someone is you."

Delaney turned back to Norton.

"Don't tell me you know how to fly this thing," he
said.

Norton just shrugged. "They seem to think I can. And
if I can't, then they're going to put you behind the
wheel. Because there's one in the back of the building
for you too."

Delaney squinted his eyes to see that, indeed, there was a crew of air techs praying over a second Hind gunship.

Delaney put his hands to his face and just shook his head. "Gawd . . . I'd give anything to be flying poodles around again. Anything . . ."

Smitz stepped forward, his NoteBook out, its screen blinking in the muggy post-storm breeze.

"We've got a satellite window of three hours coming up," he said. "We've got to get this thing started, taxied out, and airborne. Like right now . . ."

Delaney looked as if he could have punched the CIA man. But then his face brightened a bit. His mind had switched to another mode.

"Let me ask you something, Smitty," he said. "If we're in such a secret place that no enemy of this country knows we are here, then whose satellites are you so worried about passing over and seeing us?"

Smitz just shrugged. "Our own, of course," he replied simply.

Norton wiped his brow at that one. It was getting very hot, very quickly. The bad dream was continuing.

He turned Delaney back toward the Hind.

"Let's just get this over with, OK?" he said.

Norton and Delaney pulled on a pair of helmets, strapped themselves into parachutes, and climbed up the access ladder to the Hind's tandem cockpit. A squad of air techs was buzzing around the gunship now. They seemed to know what they were doing, Norton thought. Or they were giving a good impression that they did.

Delaney eased himself into the forward compartment through a hinged thick-glass door that looked not unlike something found in a gull-wing sports car. He settled into the seat, which was comfortably plush, leather-covered, and sturdy. The number of dials and buttons and buzzers in this compartment rivaled those in the pilot's hold in back. There was a spare set of flight controls in the gunner's seat, but Delaney was cautious not to put his feet anywhere near the rudder pedals or his hands anywhere near the stick.

An air tech appeared beside him and plugged a wire from his helmet into one of dozens of inputs on the multi-layered control panel. This done, he slapped Delaney twice on the head—and a second later, Delaney could hear Norton's voice through his headphones.

"Ever see leather seats on an American bird?" Norton asked him.

"Yeah, they're real comfy," Delaney replied. "This thing have a CD player?"

"More likely an eight-track," Norton told him. "You see a primary switchboard up there?"

Delaney scanned the control panel—that was when he first noticed just about everything was labeled in Russian. But a few primary systems had masking tape covering up their Cyrillic nameplates with hastily scrawled English printed over them. Most said the word: "Override." Delaney started switching them all with wild abandon.

"Tell me when to stop," he called back to Norton.

Meanwhile, Norton was switching on all of his own masking-tape-labeled switches, going systematically from left to right. He could hear things begin to whir, and the sounds were vaguely familiar to him. Where had he heard all this before? Then it hit him—in the simulator; these were the sounds they had piped into his headphones during his crash course inside the accursed Tin Can.

A tech started hand-signaling him.

"Want to move it out now?" he was asking Norton. Norton just shrugged. "Sure, why not."

With that the squad of techs began pushing the huge gunship out of the hangar, with Smitz and a few guards lending a hand.

Out in the bright sunshine the cockpit began warming up quickly. By the time they were on the tarmac, Norton had completed all of his switching. Everything seemed to be set—green lights indicated each system was on-line and ready to go.

Now it was time to start the engines. Smitz had given him a photocopied, heavily edited version of the Hind's translated flight manual. Norton now had it in his lap, opened to the page entitled: "How to Start the Engines."

"Hang on, partner," he called ahead to Delaney after reading the instructions. "This could be interesting."

He saw Delaney tighten his helmet and assume a crash position. Norton did one last check of the bizarre control panel, and then activated the switch marked APU. This stood for Auxiliary Power Unit, a kind of outside battery pack that would jump-start the gunship's two powerful engines. Or at least that was the plan.

But when Norton hit the APU panel, he heard an explosion that sounded like it was ripping the big gunship apart. There was a bright flash of red from behind him, the reflection lighting up the cockpit. He turned and saw a six-foot flame shooting out of the APU vent.

Shit . . .

This did not look good. Norton was convinced that he'd blown off the rear end of the copter somehow. He looked down at the air techs and saw panic wash across their faces. In front of him Delaney was already struggling with the clasp on his cockpit door, in the first stages of abandoning of the aircraft.

But before full-blown hysteria could set in, Norton saw Smitz run into his field of vision, simultaneously waving and flashing the thumbs-up sign—while still looking worriedly towards the rear of the copter.

"It always starts up like that!" he was yelling up at them.

"Damn!" Norton heard Delaney curse in his head-phones. "I thought we'd blown the fucking thing up and gotten out of this."

And a moment later, sure enough, the huge rotor be-gan turning over their heads. Now the gunship was rocking back and forth with a mighty vibration, lifting Norton an inch or so off his seat.

"Jeesuz, are you sure we're not on fire!" Delaney yelled into his microphone.

Norton *wasn't* sure. He did a scan of the control panel and found the warning light that he believed would indicate an engine fire. It was safely on green.

"Just hang on," he called ahead to Delaney. "We aren't even having fun yet."

The crew chief was hand-signaling him again. Norton got the message right away. He and Delaney were to seal their cockpits.

Norton told Delaney to button up, then did the same. And that was when everything seemed to change. When the door clamped down and was sealed, it became very quiet within the gunship. The only sound Norton could hear besides the *whupp-whupp-whupp* of the increasingly spinning rotors was the soft rush of air. The Hind's cockpits were pressurized, a luxury Norton didn't believe was afforded to many American chopper pilots.

"Hey, cool, I can hear my heart beating again," Delaney called out from in front. "Or, at least I think it's my heart."

Norton got another signal from his crew chief. The rotors were turning at full throttle now. He waved the man off, and the small army of techs began moving away from the gunship.

He consulted the crude instruction book, turning to the page detailing a quick course on how the Hind should get into the air. He began reading as fast as he could.

The Hind wasn't like any other copter. That much was certain now. It didn't take off vertically because it was so damn big. It had to be rolled down a runway, just like an airplane.

"Hang on, partner," Norton called ahead to Delaney. "Let's see just how good the Russians build helicopters."

"I have just one question first," Delaney asked. "Why are we wearing parachutes?"

Norton consulted the crude manual again. "If this thing goes unstable, we open up and step out."

"With that eggbeater still turning above us?" Delaney cried. "Are they nuts?"

Norton couldn't argue with him. It seemed like a choice between two deaths. Go down with the ship or step out and be sliced and diced by the rotor.

"We won't need them," Norton said back to him. "Don't worry."

"Yeah, that's what my first wife said about using rubbers," Delaney replied, his voice trailing off and leaving Norton wanting some kind of punch line.

Did Delaney have kids? Norton wondered. He didn't even know.

But his mind was soon back on other things. He booted power and adjusted to 60-percent torque, just as the photocopy instructions told him to. Then he popped the brakes, and the huge gunship began moving.

"Oh, Christ," he heard Delaney gasp. "This ain't going to be good. I just know it. . . ."

"Relax, Slick," Norton reassured him. "Think nice thoughts."

The ride was bumpy, and Norton's steering very herky-jerky, but in good time they had reached the main runway. Turning left and creeping up about fifty feet, Norton finally touched the brakes and the gunship came to a stop.

He did one last check of the control panel, and then tried to think back to all those hours in the Tin Can. It seemed odd, but this was not that much different from flight-testing an airplane for the first time. But had he really learned enough about the Hind to actually fly it?

There would be only one way to find out.

"You still breathing?" he called ahead to Delaney.

"I assure you I'm going through several bodily functions at the moment," was Delaney's reply.

"OK, then," Norton said. "Get ready to do one more."

With that, he took a deep breath of the artificially cool air, hit the gas, and off they went.

About a quarter mile away, Ricco and Gillis were rolling out in their new aircraft too.

The two refuelers were less sullen than when they'd first stepped into the cabin of the gigantic Mi-6 Hook. The interior control work done on the huge copter's controls *had* been extensive. Through the use of microprocessors and a hundred miles of rewiring, nearly sixty percent of the controls had been converted to look and act like those on their KC-10 Pegasus. Even the steering yokes and throttle bars were the same.

So the tanker pilots were more comfortable with their new set of wheels. But they had not left the ground— yet.

It was a tribute to his professionalism and toughness that Rooney, just months away from retirement after thirty-five years in the CIA, had agreed to go along with them on this initial flight. He was now sitting in the flight engineer's hole, parked directly behind Ricco, who was sitting in the left-hand pilot's seat.

The huge Russian helicopter was moving slowly towards the southern end of the runway. Rooney had to admit that the tanker pilots—for all their complaints— were handling the big bird pretty well so far. Taxiing out to the airstrip was no more or less comfortable than the bouncing and jostling one experienced in a commercial airliner. The only difference was the constant roar of the copter's huge rotor blades and the never-ending sloshing of the fuel bladders in the rear of the cavernous cargo hold.

The pilots expertly brought the big helicopter out to the end of the airstrip, then did a quick check of their vitals. Ricco was handling the controls; Gillis was reading their own photocopied flight manual. The Hook also had to take off like an airplane.

"OK, what next? We roll out for five hundred feet or so?" Ricco was saying as he ran a quick systems check.

"Or was it six hundred?" Gillis murmured, checking the manual.

"It's six hundred and fifty," Rooney reminded them, looking at his copy of the flying manual.

They bumped to a stop at the end of the runway and did another system check.

Ricco turned back to Rooney. "Are you sure that we can take this thing up and fly it like a KC-10?"

Rooney nodded. "This bird has been rewired so you will feel like you're flying a tanker. Up is up, down is down, fast is fast, and slow is slow. It will respond to your touch, convert the energy to what you want the copter to do. The only difference is your takeoff speed and distance."

"That sounds great, but are you *really* sure?" Gillis asked him.

"I wouldn't be here if I didn't believe that," the CIA man replied calmly.

Secretly, though, he wanted very much to light up a cigar and calm down a bit. But the load of fuel in the back prevented that.

One last check of the systems and everything seemed set. They made a brief report to the control tower and received their takeoff clearance. Ricco and Gillis shook hands—a preflight ritual of theirs. Then Ricco gave her the gas. They began rumbling along the runway at a very slow speed, the rotor blades screaming in protest as more fuel was laid on the gigantic engines.

"Let's have a count-off up to the sixty-fifty and our rotation speed," Ricco said, already battling the shaky controls.

"OK, we're at one hundred feet," Gillis called out, reading the distance indicator. "Speed at thirteen knots already."

Ricco had a firm grip on the controls, his eyes glued to the bumpy potholed runway. The ride was getting rougher with each passing instant, however. He added more power.

"Why not spend a few hundred bucks and get yourself a new runway?" he complained back to Rooney.

"Two hundred feet, speed at twenty-two knots," Gillis said. "You got the right power levels? We should be going much faster quicker."

Ricco checked his board and was certain that the power settings were OK.

"It's all green," he said, his grip on the controls now giving him white knuckles.

"Three-fifty on the roll, speed at twenty-five knots," Gillis said, his voice sounding more concerned with each word. "Maybe those recommendations were for high-altitude stuff."

"You're all right," Rooney said, not knowing if in fact he was speaking the truth. "Just stay with it."

"Four hundred feet on the roll, speed only thirty-two—make that thirty-one knots," Gillis reported anxiously.

Ricco added a bit more power—but as a result everything in the chopper began shaking even more violently.

Five hundred on the roll . . ." Gillis intoned. "Speed holding at forty-one . . ."

"Shit, we're not going make this," Ricco said.

"Stay with it," Rooney said again—but even he could tell they seemed to be standing still while the engines were screaming and every nut and bolt in the aircraft seemed to be coming apart.

"Six hundred on the roll—speed is not yet forty-five knots," Gillis warned.

They were supposed to be at least fifty-five knots, or more like sixty, but it was no time to wonder why.

"What's it say in that book about aborting takeoffs?" Ricco yelled back to Rooney, who was already madly flipping through the pages.

"Nothing!" he called ahead, his voice losing a bit of wind.

They continued rumbling along, engines screaming, fuel sloshing. The aircraft seemed ready to break apart at any second. But they were beyond the point of stopping. The rotors were so torqued up, to kill power now would most likely flip the copter on its side, blowing the fuel and no doubt killing them all in the process.

That was when Ricco, usually the more cautious of the two, had to think quick. Finally he just declared, "Fuck it!" goosed the throttles, and yanked back on the controls.

A second later, they were airborne.

It was amazing how well the aircraft smoothed out! Once its wheels had left the ground, the engines took on an almost symphonic hum. The fuel in the back stopped sloshing. The bolts stopped rattling.

All three men breathed a sigh of relief.

"Piece of cake," Ricco declared, adding power and lifting the huge copter higher into the early morning sky. "A big piece of *fucking* cake . . ."

It had been a long night for Joe Cool's Marines.

It started the previous afternoon, when they bivouacked on the northern end of the island, setting up tents among the rocks on the craggy beach and establishing a defense perimeter just as if they were in a combat situation.

They had spent the worst of the night's rainstorm here, huddled in their ponchos, more concerned about their gear getting blown away than keeping themselves dry.

When the storm began dissipating slightly around 0330 hours, some of the Marines were finally able to go horizontal. But at exactly 0345, they were roused out of their tents by their sergeants, and told to muster up with full packs and be inside Hangar 3 in fifteen minutes.

Much rushing around ensued as men grabbed their gear and suited up. The entire contingent was lined up and ready in under four minutes, though. What faced

them now was the mile-long hump from their present
position down to Hangar 3.

There were eighty-two of them in all and as one, they
began running. Across the beach, over the dunes,
through the isolated maintenance area, past the "motels," and over the main runway. The first of them were
at the front door of Hangar 3 by 0358 hours.

There, waiting for them, was their CO, Captain Chou
Koo.

The last man staggered in at 0402 hours, but Chou
did not mind. Not many soldiers could endure near-
hurricane conditions and be in full pack a mile away on
strictly leg power on fifteen minutes notice. And Chou
knew it.

He had trained them well.

Their official unit title was actually a secret. They
were known instead by various nicknames, depending
on the operation. Organized in 1991 to take care of some
post-Gulf War messes around the Persian Gulf, the classified Marine unit had first been tagged Zebra Company.
When the scene shifted to Bosnia, they were coded
Company 801. In Somalia, they were known as Task
Force 22. Since then they had bounced around Africa,
Asia, and the subcontinent, putting out fires too small
for the big units like Delta Force or taking on things the
SEALs simply weren't interested in, or were too busy
to do. These days they were known as Team 66.

This was a good name because Chou likened the unit
to a team of utility infielders. Indeed, most of them had
just missed making the big leagues. Many were jarheads
who couldn't quite pass the training for the SEALs or
Delta Force, or any number of other deep programs run
by the U.S. military. Some had missed making it into
these higher-echelon units simply because of things as
minor as a 5-percent hearing loss in one ear or a rare
allergy. One guy was missing the tip of his left hand's
index finger. Several others were color-blind. Many of
the men wore glasses or contacts. Some had flat feet.
This made them no less strong, no less capable, no less

loyal or effective. They took on the jobs no one else
wanted with gusto. As a result, their mission record,
though little known, was full of success stories.

Chou had been in charge of them since 1996 and since
becoming CO, he had emphasized their versatility. That
was now their real forte. They could do wet operations
with the best of them; they could do para-drops. They
were as adept in the jungle as in the snow. They were
excellent at hand-to-hand and silent combat; they could
work the latest and biggest infantry weapons. They ex-
celled at rescuing hostages, tracking terrorists, handling
nuclear or biological threats.

They were a very special group and their handlers at
the Pentagon knew it. That was why they never hesitated
to loan them out to the CIA or the NSA or any other
Spook outfit needing some quick firepower somewhere
around the world.

But for all their successes and experience, there *was*
one thing Team 66 had never done: They had never
worked from helicopters.

And this worried Chou.

For many reasons.

Thus the need for this unusual drill.

He had them form up again, and then ushered them
wordlessly into the huge hangar.

There they found two helicopters, the contents of the
third and fourth C-5 deliveries earlier this stormy night.
About the same size as the Hook, and also designed by
the Russian military, they were Mi-26 Halos. They were
pure, dedicated troop carriers with cargo holds nearly as
big as that of a C-130 Hercules. The Marines just stared
at the huge copters. Just about all of them could fit inside
one. That was how big these choppers were.

"We will be conducting ingress and egress exercises
with these helos for the next few hours, gentlemen,"
Chou told them. "I suggest that in between, you famil-
iarize yourself with these rather unusual aircraft. You

will be seeing a lot of them in the future."

Chou then split his company into two, and with the aid of a whistle and a stopwatch, loaded them onto the two helicopters. Then, with the blow of the whistle, the doors were opened again and his men piled out and deployed in protective rings around each chopper.

On the first try, it took the eighty-two Marines forty-eight seconds to completely deploy out of the choppers and set up their defensive perimeters.

Not bad, Chou thought. But he knew they would have to cut that time at least in half. So he had them do it again. And again.

And again.

By 0630 hours, the Marines had done the drill no less than fifty-eight times and had cut the time to thirty seconds. Again, not bad at all for so many fully equipped troops to stand up, straighten their gear, pile out of each copter, and go into a full combat mode by surrounding each aircraft in its own protective ring.

But Chou knew more drilling would be needed to shave another ten seconds off that time.

Still, he was pleased with their performance and told them so. Like their endless mock assaults on the Motel Six building, they never stopped trying to get better. But the most difficult part of this early morning was still ahead. It was heralded by the arrival of Smitz at Hangar 3 around 0645 hours. His ever-present IBM NoteBook out and turned on, he told Chou simply: "It's time to get going."

Moments later, a Humvee arrived and four men piled out. They were wearing the distinctive green flight uniforms of U.S. Army Aviation.

These men were introduced to Chou's company as being part of the Army's OPFOR unit based at Fort Polk in the Louisiana swamplands. It was from there, Smitz revealed to Chou, that the Russian-built choppers had come originally. In this upcoming mission, the Army guys would be flying the huge Halo copters.

Chou shook hands with them, then turned back to his men.

"OK, troops," he said. "Pile back in. We're all going for a ride."

By this time, both the Hind gunship and the fuel-laden Hook had been airborne for about thirty minutes.

Norton was putting the Hind through its paces over a section of the Florida Straits known as Military Reservation Box 31.

He was falling in love with the massive copter—strange as that seemed. Once in the air, it flew as easily and smoothly as a small airplane. The controls were ultra-responsive, and somehow its size and bulk were offset by its powerful engines and the two stubby wings helping out with the lift. The presence of the stubby wings also allowed for the gunship's huge rotor to dedicate most of its work to pushing the copter forward.

And this made the beast fast.

Damned fast!

He was carving through the warm morning air at speeds he thought impossible for such a huge rotor aircraft. And the odd thing was, it seemed as if he'd been flying the Hind for weeks—and he couldn't get rid of this feeling. He was actually beginning to think that all the simulator work had been worthwhile.

As for Delaney, he was having the time of his life.

The front seat of the Hind offered its passenger a view and an experience different from any other aircraft. Because of its ultra-forward position and its bubble-like enclosure, it gave the rider the sensation that he was flying *without* the aircraft.

To this end, Delaney had his nose pressed up against the glass, looking out over the sea, his arms spread as far as the cockpit allowed, as if he was a bird.

Several times Delaney's enthusiasm rose to such a level, Norton was forced to remind him not to use curse words over the radio. But typically Delaney was letting a slew of them slip.

"Jeesuz Christ!" he kept yelling. "God damn! What a fucking view!"

The fact that Delaney was a fighter jock—and one who had seen combat—meant that his excitement level was, like Norton's, ice-cold most times. But this was different. The Hind was a monster on the ground, but an eagle in the air.

"Maybe this *has* been all worth it," Norton caught himself thinking.

Twenty miles to the northeast, Ricco and Gillis were plowing through the early morning air in a slightly less robust fashion.

The big Hook fuel ship was very fast, but there were several factors working against it at top speed. First of all, there were many tons of gas in the cargo hold. Secondly, Gillis and Ricco were not jet jocks—they flew the big planes. As such, they were not ones to go gallivanting around the sky. To them, smooth and level was the norm.

But this did not mean they weren't enjoying themselves.

"This is remarkable," Ricco said several time times over. "How can something so awkward-looking sail like this thing?"

"The Russians can build a great chopper, we have to give them that," Rooney told them.

He too was enjoying the smooth ride. If it weren't for the constant sloshing of the jet fuel and the smell from it, it would have been a totally pleasant experience.

"I suppose we can't ask exactly *why* we're flying this bird, can we?" Gillis asked Rooney.

"You can ask," the CIA man replied, "but I can't answer."

"I have the feeling we are supposed to fly it long-range. Am I wrong?" Ricco asked.

"You may be underestimating your upcoming mission," Rooney replied in a rare bit of candor.

Ricco was about to reply when their radio started crackling.

"This is SGK Base . . . come in?"

"That's for us," Rooney said. "We are call sign Beta Two-Six."

Gillis grabbed his radio chin mike and turned it on.

"Go ahead base."

They next heard the unmistakable nasal voice of Gene Smitz. He was in the base control tower.

"Proceed to coordinate five-nine-five at east-northeast . . ."

Gillis wrote down the instructions, and Ricco began to turn the big chopper northward. His maneuver was met with a great splashing sound from the fuel bladders in back.

"If this is just a training mission." Ricco asked, "why can't those things be filled with water—instead of fuel?"

"I really don't know," Rooney replied truthfully. "But my guess is, someone figures this training mission could go real at any hour."

Ricco and Gillis eyed each other. Rooney's tone was a tad unsettling.

"And you didn't hear that from me," the CIA man quickly added.

But at that moment Ricco wasn't listening. He was looking out his side window. In the low clouds he thought he saw two aircraft heading in their general direction.

"Damn, are we supposed to have any other traffic up here with us?" he asked Rooney.

Rooney leaned forward in his seat and saw what Ricco had spotted. There were two large helicopters flying about a mile below and two miles off their left side. They seemed almost as large as the Hook. Larger even.

"Don't worry," the CIA man said nonchalantly. "They're ours. That's who we're being vectored to meet."

Gillis looked down at the choppers and back at Rooney.

"Really?"

Rooney settled back into his seat. "Yep. Those, my friends, should be the Marines."

It *was* the Marines.

Their two huge Halo copters had taken off from Seven Ghosts Key ten minutes before, and had been vectored to the same spot that the huge Hook was now heading for.

Inside both choppers, the Marines were packed in tight. Full loads, weapons ready.

The Army pilots were driving the big Russian cargo copters with ease. Of all the pilots at the Seven Ghosts base, they were the most experienced in flying Russian aircraft—and it showed. Now, looking out the windows of the transports, the Marines could see the huge Hook being flown by Gillis and Ricco.

The Army pilots slowed a bit and allowed Gillis and Ricco to take up a position just ahead and slightly above the two troopships.

Now there was only one piece missing. . . .

Norton took the call from Smitz just seconds after Ricco and Gillis did.

He increased throttles and poured on the coals, and was soon approaching the three other choppers as they entered Box 31.

Once in sight, he radioed back to Smitz, reporting that he had spotted the trio of aircraft. Smitz quickly briefed him and Delaney on the fuel-filled Hook and two Marine-carrying Halos. Then he told Norton to take a position about a quarter mile in front of the big Hook.

Norton did so, and this was how they flew for the next thirty minutes.

So for the first time since the operation began and all the principals had reported to Seven Ghosts Key, the still-unnamed unit was one. They were aligned in a ragged, uneven formation. Heading into the unknown.

But they were flying together at last.

For the next seven days, Norton and Delaney did little more than eat, sleep, and drive the Hinds.

Most of this flying was done at night; most of it in Hind #1. The second Hind, while being nearly identical to the first, was actually a few years older and had more air miles on it. To preserve its operational status, it was decided that the majority of the initial orientation flights would be done in the younger model.

The two former fighter pilots had quickly settled into a routine. As soon as the sun set around 8:30 P.M., Hind #1 would be dragged out of the hangar after being prepped. By 8:45, Norton and Delaney would be suited up and ready for their preflight inspection. Going over the Russian-built chopper with flashlights, checking for leaks, making sure every bolt was still tight and every flying surface was still clean would take about fifteen minutes. Only then would they be ready for launch.

As each flight mandated that both pilots have equal time behind the controls, they would usually fly for three hours, land back at the base, switch positions, and go out again. To see who would serve as pilot first, though, they would flip a coin. In the first few days, Norton won every one of these coin tosses, much to Delaney's consternation. Flying the first half of the night flight was much more exciting than the second half, and Delaney always seemed stuck with the second shift. At one point, he even accused Norton of having a double-sided coin. From then on, he insisted on flipping his own coin and doing it the full view of witnesses.

It was no surprise that the two fighter jocks were anxious to get behind the wheel and drive the Hind first. The massive chopper was butt-ugly, but it was a real gas to fly. It could do things an F-15 couldn't. It could fly lower, turn sharper, slow down, speed up, all at a touch of the controls, which both of them knew by heart now.

Its powerful engines and its substantial wing area really did make it part jet fighter.

(One strange thing about the helicopter, though, was that it could not hover—or at least not for long. Putting the Hind into a hover for more than a minute would likely burn out its engines. Like the aircraft itself, the power plants were designed to be moving forward all the time. This was not an aircraft that wanted to stay still for very long.)

Most nights they were airborne by 2130 hours. From that point they usually had a six-hour satellite window during which they could fly just about anywhere within Box 31. Much of this time they spent flying below five hundred feet. Occasionally they were forced to change course to avoid getting too near to an off-course private plane or fishing boat. To be spotted might put the whole operation in jeopardy. But their proximity to Cuba actually helped in this regard. The Cubans were known to have Hinds. If one were spotted over these waters, there could be a fairly plausible explanation: The Cubans were simply doing night maneuvers. Over the ocean. In unmarked copters.

Riding up front in the Hind was not such a bad thing. You could shoot the guns from the front seat and the Hind was loaded for bear. Its wings supported two gun pods and two missile launchers, not of Russian design, but made to look that way. Hind #1 also had an outrageously long cannon attached to its nose. This monster was able to fire gigantic 76-mm shells at a very fast rate. Get caught in the sight of this big gun, and it would be the last thing you did.

After some flying and shooting, at fish mostly, they would usually land and switch places. That was when the boring part of the night began, for the next few hours would usually be concentrated on formation flying. The Halos and the Hook would launch around midnight. Together they would proceed to a predesignated spot where the Hind would be waiting. Then they would form up and fly around in circles until 2 A.M. or so. Flying in

formation was not nearly as much fun as driving the
Hind solo. Doing endless orbits over the fluorescent Caribbean waters tended to drag a bit. But the mission spec
said flying together and learning how to stay close in
the air at night was very important, so the formation
flying was done, usually with Delaney grumbling behind
the wheel of the Hind throughout.

During all this, Gillis and Ricco were getting the hang
of their huge copter as well. The crazy sleeping hours
being what they were, Norton and Delaney rarely saw
the tanker pilots on the ground—which was good for
both sides. But in the air, the refuelers never missed a
rendezvous point, were always on time, at the right altitude, in the right spot. Always. The CIA had asked for
the best in the aerial refueling business—and they had
gotten their wish.

All of the copters were rigged with in-flight refueling
probes, and usually at least one hour of a night flight
was devoted to hooking and unhooking with Gillis and
Ricco's fuel ship. Taking on gas in the air between two
choppers was not that much different from a fighter
hooking up to a KC-10 tanker, except the speeds were
slower and it was all done through hoses and not static
booms. Still, it didn't take much time at all for Norton
and Delaney as well as the Army Aviation pilots flying
the Marine-laden Halos to learn the art of connecting
with the Hook and drinking in a bunch of gas.

But in addition to all this, Gillis and Ricco had another exercise to drill for—this the most dangerous one
of all. For not only were they charged with keeping all
of the unit's choppers fueled up, they also had to learn
how to take on fuel themselves. From a higher source.

According to Smitz, this aspect of the mission was
extremely important. So every night that first week, a
C-130 Marine Corps tanker was called down from Eglin
Air Force Base. With Norton and Delaney riding shot-
gun and spotting for the fuelers, Gillis and Ricco would
maneuver their giant copter up and under a fuel hose
being let out from the C-130's right wing. On connec-

tion, the fuel would flow from the C-130 to the depleted bladders in the cargo hold of the Hook. It took the refuelers some doing to get it right the first few times, but experience and intuitive flying skills eventually won out. By the third night, the two tanker jockeys had the difficult hookup down pat.

Each time Norton saw this, he felt a little bit better about recommending the National Guard pilots for this program.

But there was still one last sticking point: The operational details of the mission were still unknown to them. They knew pretty much where they were going. And why. But they didn't know exactly what they were supposed to do once they got there. And more important, *when* they were going.

But because of events on the other side of the globe, these questions were going to be answered very soon.

14

The name of the oil platform was Qarah al Khalif #6.

It was a three-tiered, six-shaft exploration and pump-ing assembly located equidistant from the eastern shore of Iraq and the western shore of Iran, in the northern-most region of the Persian Gulf.

The platform got its name from a nearby island, and it was indeed one of a half-dozen sea pumping facilities in the area. It was owned by a consortium of oil whole-salers whose main office was located in Bahrain. Also known as Qak-Six, the platform and its five cousins held the distinction of being the only offshore pumping fa-cilities in the region to continue operations during the Gulf War. In fact, the six Qak platforms had been pro-tected throughout the conflict by U.S. Navy aircraft and ships, this even though both Iran and Iraq held a sub-stantial stake in their ownership and operation. Such was the quality of crude pumped from their wells.

This was a special day on Qak-Six. It was the last day

of the month. This meant not only payday for the 313
workers on the huge platform, but also the beginning of
a ten-day vacation granted most of the workers once
every five months.

Three ferries had been engaged by the platform's
owners to carry the workers down to Bahrain for their
furloughs. Bahrain was the destination of choice for the
majority of the workers—Filipinos mostly—as it was
considered the most westernized of the Gulf States.
Translation: There was a night life there, and if one
looked hard enough alcohol could be found, and even
female companionship.

It was just before ten in the morning when the first
ferry, fully loaded, pulled away from the platform's
docking area. It was a cloudy raw day, not unusual for
this time of year in this part of the Gulf, and the water
was choppy. But this did not dampen the spirits of the
workers, their pockets full of money, their bellies filled
with the anticipation of stepping on dry land again.

The first ferry had just cleared the platform and the
second one was maneuvering into place when a long,
loud, guttural groan shook the rig. The noise was so
sudden and so distinct that those few workers still left
on the top tier thought it was one of the rig's automatic
stabilizers suddenly losing its footing. But the platform
itself was not moving, and the catastrophic shift to one
side indicating a leg was failing did not occur. Thank-
fully, the problem was not with the rig itself.

That was when many people saw an airplane appear
on the murky horizon and relaxed. In a freak of atmos-
pherics, the growl of the plane's engines had proceeded
it, carried, no doubt, by the twenty-five-knot westerly
wind. This had caused the sudden thunderclap.

With much relief, the loading of the second ferry re-
sumed.

It was not unusual to see aircraft flying by the oil rig.
Both Iraqi and Iranian patrol planes passed by every few
days, and occasionally a British, American, or even Saudi aircraft could be seen plying the skies this north in

the Gulf too. Most gave the oil rig a wag of the wings and they would be off.

The second ferry was about halfway full when the plane finally went by the oil platform. It was flying very low and its engines seemed extremely loud. The plane was painted all black with a charcoal-like quality to the tone. Traces of a camouflage scheme could be seen on the wings and tail.

Many aboard the platform knew what kind of airplane this was: a C-130 Hercules, the ubiquitous American-built cargo hauler and general all-round workhorse of many nations' air forces. What did mildly surprise some people was that the airplane carried no markings, no tail numbers, no insignia to identify what country it belonged to—this, and the fact that its nose was so long and its fuselage so thick.

The plane passed about one thousand yards to the south of the oil rig and kept on going, disappearing into the mist to the east, possibly heading towards Iran, just forty miles away. The loading of the second ferry was nearly completed, and the third boat was being signaled to come in. That was when the people on the platform heard another thunderclap. All eyes turned east and to everyone's surprise, they saw the airplane had turned and was coming back.

The workers on the first ferry would have the best view of what happened next.

The plane passed so close to the oil platform this time that the whole structure shook from top to bottom. The water below was suddenly foaming, kicked up by the plane's engine exhaust. Suddenly three long streaks of flame erupted from the side of the airplane. This fire came so quickly and was so vivid, many on the ferry thought the plane was in trouble and had doubled back, perhaps to attempt an emergency landing near the oil platform.

But a moment later, a geyser of flame erupted from the top of the platform itself. Had the plane flown so close to the rig that it had hit something? No—the plane was still flying. It roared right over the first ferry. Then came a tremendous explosion. It sent shock waves through the ferry and the water around it. All eyes looked up to see the oil platform's mast disintegrate in a puff of smoke. Now a second explosion went off, louder than the first. An instant later, the entire upper tier of the rig was engulfed in flames. Only then did the people on the ferry realize the airplane had fired on the oil platform.

And now it was coming back again. . . .

The airplane swept by the platform a third time, a continuous stream of fire pouring out of its left side. The oil rig began to shudder, and hundreds of small explosions peppered it up and down. Flame was suddenly everywhere. Many workers began leaping into the water, some on fire themselves. Others were trapped and quickly engulfed in flames.

The plane roared by again. Now a huge gun muzzle could be seen protruding from its left side. It was firing large-caliber projectiles at a frightening rate. The workers on the ferry saw the control house go up first in this fusillade. The main pump hut went next. Then the living quarters, then the turbine station. Oil was gushing wildly out of some pipes now and being ignited in many places.

Inside of ninety seconds, the oil rig was a burning wreck. Bodies were in the water; many more workers were badly burned on the platform itself. The plane went by twice more, delivering high-powered shells in such a methodical fashion, it seemed unreal to the people on the first ferry. Was this really happening? Why would anyone want to destroy Qak-Six?

Stunned, the ferry captain finally started pounding on his vessel's radio, intent on sending out an SOS. But as soon as he switched his comm set on, it made a loud crack and went dead, a victim of the gunship's high-powered electronic-jamming suite. The plane went by the oil rig one last time, but there was no shooting this time. This pass was just to survey its deadly work. The sixty-six workers on the first ferry stood on the rail, astounded by what they had just seen. The few people still left on the platform could not have survived the brutal assault—and those injured and in the water would not live for more than a few minutes in the choppy cold sea.

Still, the ferry captain had to make an attempt to rescue any survivors. So he ordered his vessel to turn about and head back toward the burning oil rig.

That was when those aboard the ferry saw the big plane turn once again—and point its nose right at them.

The USS *LaSallette* was not an ordinary ship.

It was one of the oldest operational vessels in the U.S. Navy, its keel having been laid in the winter of 1955. It boasted very few weapons. Twin .50-caliber machine guns on the stern and bow were its only outward defenses. Its helicopter, a small OH-51, carried only rudimentary antiship missiles and a single .30-caliber machine gun on its nose mount. There were but a dozen M-16's on board, with a total of three hundred rounds of ammunition available. The only other potential weaponry consisted of some smoke grenades and flares.

The *LaSallette* was not a warship per se. Its superstructure was a forest of antennae, satellite receivers, radar dishes, and microwave arrays. More than half its crew of 214 worked on monitoring data pulled in by these various devices. Officially, the *LaSallette* was a C3 platform, for command, control, and communications. In reality, it was a spy ship. It cruised the upper reaches of the Persian Gulf periodically, snooping on Iraqi radio and TV transmissions, gathering intelligence, watching for any military movements. It had been compared to a floating AWACS plane, and this was not entirely inaccurate.

This day it was on a typical SigInt mission. A number of Republican Guard units had been on the move in the upper part of Iraq recently, some heading south, others moving east. Routine maneuvers perhaps. But the *La-*

Sallette had been sent into the northern gulf to troll the airwaves for any indications as to what these elite Iraqi units might be up to.

It was by fate then that its course brought it steaming over the horizon just as the AC-130 gunship had finished off the last survivors of Qak-Six's number-one ferry. With its long-range snooping radar and TV equipment, the *LaSallette* was suddenly flooded with data emanating from the burning oil platform and the mysterious airplane orbiting above it. There was no doubt among those interpreting this information that the gunship had attacked the oil rig and had killed just about all of its occupants. The proof of this was pouring into the hard drives of the ship's main computers.

And for the first time in a year and a half of rampage and destruction, the people flying the gunship suddenly had a very big problem on their hands.

They had witnesses.

By the time the *LaSallette*'s crew were called to their battle stations, the AC-130 was heading for the ship at full speed.

The captain immediately ordered his helicopter to launch. Gunners assigned to the .50-caliber deck guns scrambled to their positions. Everyone above the rank of CPO was issued an M-16 and a clip of ammunition. The communications shack was sending out messages to any and every Allied ship in the immediate vicinity— but the airplane's jamming suite prevented all but the first few seconds of any message to escape. It made little difference. The captain had already done a sweep of his immediate area. The nearest U.S. ship was sixty miles away.

The *LaSallette* was trapped and very much alone.

The secure photo-fax machine in Smitz's billet started beeping at exactly 3 A.M.

The CIA man rolled over, sleepily checked his alarm clock, and then clicked the fax machine's Receive button.

A red sheet was the first to emerge. It was covered with black dots and a thick black band running diagonally down its side. This indicated the message he was about to receive was of the highest security—Eyes Only—and should be destroyed as soon as he was through reading it.

Smitz finally got out of bed and stumbled into his pants and shirt. He was used to these late-night interruptions by now. They had a certain rhythm to them. The fax would take sixty seconds to print out, long enough for him to reheat a half-filled cup of coffee from earlier that night. He slipped it into his microwave, and then visited the head. The fax machine and the micro beeped at exactly the same time. "Message received," he typed into its keyboard. The machine clicked twice and then went silent.

He took his coffee from the micro, burning his fingers in the process. Finally he sat down to read the missive.

The cover sheet was protecting a photograph Smitz recognized as being shot from an aerial recon camera called an ICQ-23. It was a secret type used on U-2's and some versions of the new RF-18 Navy recon fighter.

The photo showed a smoldering hunk of metal in the midst of an oil-slicked sea. Smitz didn't know whether he was looking at the remains of a ship or an airplane or something else. It took the explanation on page three to tell him this was all that was left of an oil platform in the upper Persian Gulf known as Qak-Six.

The summary was brief. There were 322 people dead. No known survivors. The rig was perforated with holes, big and small. They were almost symmetrical in their placement. Smitz bit his lip. There was no doubt in his mind what horror had been visited on the oil platform. The AC-130 had struck again.

No sooner had he finished reading the grim report when his fax began beeping again. He hit the Receive button and started another blurry photo printing out.

This one he watched from the first moment of its inception, and as it scrolled out, he felt his eyes go wider and his jaw drop lower. There was no mystery about this image. It was a high-altitude photo of a ship, one that was in the process of sinking. It was obviously taken from a passing satellite just seconds before the vessel slipped beneath the waves. In the very northwest corner of the photo was a very small indication that looked like the rear end of an airplane in retreat.

Below the picture was a simple caption. "USS *La-Sallette* C3 vessel sinking this day 705 hours GMT. With loss of all life."

"Damn," Smitz breathed.

He was still staring at the photo when his phone rang. The noise startled him so much he whacked his head on the ceiling of his tiny billet. He leapt for the phone, snagged the receiver, pulled on the cord, and finally brought it up to his ear. His eyes passed over the hands of his luminescent watch. It was 3:15 in the morning.

Who the fuck could this be?

The man's voice at the other end sounded very far away.

"Hold for the President," he said.

15

This night had started out pretty much like any other for Norton and Delaney.

They'd lifted off about 2300 hours with Norton in the pilot's seat of the Hind and Delaney riding up front.

Their first order of business was to transit fifty-five miles out in the Caribbean and do a routine navigation exercise around a spit of land called Whiskey Rocks. After this, they linked up with the other choppers and practiced formation night flying and refueling exercises. This completed, they all returned to base. While the other choppers were done for the night, Norton and Delaney took on more fuel, switched positions, and then took off again. They had two more hours of flying time available, and Delaney wanted to get more time behind the wheel. Yet no sooner were they airborne when they got a call from the base telling them to return immediately.

This had never happened before. They turned around, both thinking that the satellite window was closing sooner than anticipated. But as soon as they were down again, they saw the ground crew meander out of Hangar

2 to take care of the chopper. They didn't seem to be in any hurry, indicating a satellite pass-over was not the problem. It had to be something else.

With Delaney agreeing to watch over the care and handling of the Hind, Norton hurried over to the Big Room to find out what was up.

He burst in, like a kid late for class, to find most of the usual suspects were there. Smitz, Rooney, Ricco, and Gillis, of course. The SEALs. The Army pilots. The CIA security people. As Norton was walking in, they were all starting on their way out. Everyone looked grim. No one said a word to him as they passed by.

"Jeesuz, what's happened?" Norton asked Smitz, who was trying to hurry out of the room himself.

"The people running the gunship just fucked up," he said breathlessly. "They sank a Navy C-3 ship. In the Gulf. Two hundred guys went down with it. They also nailed an oil platform, killed everyone on board that too."

Norton just stared back at him, letting the news sink in.

"A Navy spy ship? Damn, that's not good," he mumbled.

"As a result, we just got our orders, right from the top," Smitz told him, each word landing like a hammer blow to Norton's stomach. "We're moving out. Now."

"*Now?*" Norton asked incredulously. "You mean like today?"

"No, I mean as in 'now,'" Smitz replied. "*Right* now. The transport planes will be here in ten minutes. We take off in one hour."

Norton shook his head as if to clear it.

"Wait a minute," he began to protest. "We're not ready to go anywhere. We've been barely flying those choppers for a week. No way are we ready for combat. I thought the plan was for thirty days of practice."

"Well, the plan just changed," Smitz said, turning to leave. "Don't ask me why, but when the gunship was shooting up refugees and villages, it just wasn't this high a priority. But now it is. So we're moving out.''

He started for the door again, but Norton grabbed him.

"Wait a minute! We haven't even been briefed on the fucking mission yet," he protested. "Not on the operational stuff anyway. How are we supposed to know what the hell to do?''

Smitz pushed his hand away.

"We'll get our final briefing once we're on-site,'' Smitz said. "Now, I want you to find Delaney, get suited up, and both of you get down to the flight line, ASAP! I've got to go wake the Marines.''

With that, Smitz ran out the door.

Norton was suddenly alone in the big empty room with the garish murals. The one by the front door looked particularly eerie at this moment. Norton stared at it, then felt a shudder run through him.

The three jumbo black women with pots on their heads were really laughing at him now.

Ten minutes later, he stumbled into the preflight ready room.

He'd looked all over for Delaney. In Hangar 2, back at their billet, out on the flight line. But his partner had disappeared. No one seemed to know where he was. Nor was Norton in any mood to search any further for him. Let someone else deliver the bad news. At the moment, he needed time to absorb it himself.

He always had nerves before any combat mission— any pilot who denied this was lying. But in every mission Norton had ever flown, he'd made a point of checking, double-checking, and triple-checking every last detail before his feet ever left the ground. This was the reason he'd been to war many times and had come back without so much as a scratch.

But now, he and the others were being rushed into a very dangerous situation, probably the worst thing anyone could do when it came to combat. Despite how well they had all taken to their foreign-built choppers, they were still not fully prepared for this. Far from it. No operational briefing? No idea where they were going exactly? No more than a few live-firing exercises? It was a recipe for disaster.

Yet there was nothing he could do about it. This was the price he had to pay for agreeing to join up with the Spooks. He could only buck it up, do the mission—whatever the hell it was!—and hope for the best. Or die trying.

He opened his locker to find a new combat suit waiting for him. Unlike the threads he'd been wearing since arriving on Seven Ghosts Key, this outfit was part fighter-pilot g-suit, part survival pack. It was desert-camouflaged and festooned with pockets—on the arms, the legs, the chest, Velcro pockets everywhere. The built-in utility belt carried small packets of survival stuff, including food pills, a tiny water-purification kit, morphine candy, bandages, an electronic compass, a mini-phone, a GPS transponder, and so on.

The helmet was also a combination of a pilot's regular bone dome and a standard GI-issue Fritz battle hat. It was covered with camouflage netting similar to that used in Marine Aviation. The boots were waterproof, fire-proof, and lined with pyrofoam, which would heat up at the crack of an inside seal. By experience Norton knew how cold and miserable the desert could be. There was a chance these heat-lined doggies might come in the handiest of all. The suit also came with a gun, a standard-issue Colt .45 automatic, with two clips of ammo.

So this would be his wardrobe for the mission. He could only pray that the length of time he'd be wearing it would be measured in hours and not days.

Norton climbed into his suit as quickly as he could. He would search for Delaney once he was suited up, he decided. But just as he was adjusting his helmet's strap, Delaney blew in to the room.

Through the open door behind him, Norton could see the quartet of C-5 transport planes had landed and were already backed up to the flight line, their engines still turning. The unit's Russian-built helicopters were being pushed up the loading ramps and into the cavernous cargo holds. The Marines were moving single file to take their places on the C-5's as well. From all indications, they were less than thirty minutes from departure.

Delaney was already suited up in his futuristic combat suit; somehow he'd beaten Norton to the suit-up room. He was also carrying a small duffel bag with him. He came up to Norton and whacked him on his helmet.

"Ready for the big show, Jazzman?" he asked sarcastically.

"Unless they stop shooting people for desertion," Norton replied.

Delaney laughed at the grim joke.

"We ain't that lucky," he told Norton, adding, "What kind of gun you bringing?"

Norton just shrugged. "The one they just gave me," he replied, taking out the .45 and showing it to Delaney.

Delaney looked at it and just shook his head. "What are you? A girl?" he asked, exasperated.

Delaney tore the gun out of Norton's hand and casually flipped it into the wastebasket.

Then he unzipped the duffel bag, reached in, and came out with an enormous pistol.

"Here, man," he said, handing the massive handgun to Norton. "I got a *real* gun for you."

Norton's wrist almost buckled under the weight of the hand cannon. It was at least twice the size of the .45, with a long thick clip sticking out of the handle. The bullets in this clip looked like tiny artillery shells. The pistol itself was big and black and shiny. A true monster.

"What the hell kind of gun is this?"

"Beats me," Delaney said, taking out his own huge pistol and examining it. "I got them from the same guy who's been giving us the beer. He's also the armorer here. He gave one to Smitz too."

"Smitz? What's he need one for?"

Delaney checked his weapon's ammo clip. "He's going with us, I guess," he said simply.

This was news to Norton.

"Now if we get into a situation where we have to use pistols," Delaney was saying, holding the huge gun out in front of him, "what would you rather have? A GI peashooter. Or this baby?"

Norton just looked at his gun, then at Delaney, and then back at his gun. His partner was making sense.

"This one, for sure," Norton replied.

"Atta boy!" Delaney said, slapping him on the back. "Believe me, these things will come in handy. You'll see."

With that, Norton put the massive weapon in his bag, and together they walked out to the waiting C-5's.

In a large, smoky, windowless room two thousand miles west of the Florida Straits, seven men were sitting around a table, smoking cigarettes and drinking coffee.

They were all in their late sixties. Those not bald had gray or white hair—overgrown, to the shoulders in a few cases. They were all wearing Western-style shirts, jeans, and cowboy boots. And even though the room was dimly lit, they were all wearing sunglasses.

"This is a very big gamble," one man said. "There are so many things that could go wrong now."

"It has to be done," a second man said. "We knew we'd have to deal with this situation eventually. No one else was doing anything about it."

"It *was* left up to us to take some action," a third man said. "It shouldn't have come to this, but it did."

More cigarettes were lit and more coffee poured. The room became even smokier.

"But we're walking such a thin line here," the first man said. "Our people at Langley agree; what few we have left. Our lines of communications could be discovered. Just what the hell we've been doing here all these years could be revealed. That would be a disaster."

"Doing nothing about this situation would be a disaster too,'' a fourth voice said. ''Our reason for being is not just to sit here and do nothing. Our reason for being is to act as a last resort. That's what we've done in this case. That's what we had to do.''

''Personally, I think we should have acted long before they sank the *LaSallette*,'' a fifth man added.

This opinion was seconded by the sixth and seventh men present. The first man just shook his head and finally shrugged.

''OK, I just hope these guys can pull it off—it's such a high-wire act,'' he said. ''They're professional military men and I just hate pulling their strings like they are puppets. They haven't got the faintest idea what is really happening and that's just not right.''

''It's better that they don't know,'' the second man said. ''We agreed on that long ago. Just let them fly the mission. We'll give them what we can along the way. We'll have our friend look in on them from time to time. Who knows? They might just get lucky and things will work out our way.''

There was almost a laugh around the table.

''And in thirty-five years, just how many times have we got lucky?'' someone asked.

''Just about every time,'' the second man said. ''I think.''

PART TWO

THE MAN IN ROOM 6

16

The palace was called Qom-el-Zarz.

It was located in a very unusual part of the world. Just fifty miles northeast of Baghdad, it straddled the border of Iraq and Iran, tucked away in the very rugged foothills of the Suhr-bal. This area was so barren and desolate, at one time NASA had considered using it as a training ground for U.S. astronauts heading for the moon. In many ways, it did look otherworldly.

The palace was built into the side of a 3500-foot mountain. It looked like a cross between a modern-day fortress and something from the pages of *Arabian Nights*. Though it had been seen by very few eyes, its architecture was among the most beautiful in the Middle East. It featured four minarets, each one housing a Rapier surface-to-air-missile platform. Its main building was a pale-blue domed affair, looking not unlike a mosque, ringed with satellite dishes and Bofors antiaircraft guns. It was surrounded on all sides by high, thick walls. Their parapets were patrolled day and night by heavily armed mercenaries.

A dozen smaller buildings were scattered around the

palace compound itself, which in turn was surrounded by another heavily guarded wall. One building housed a vast collection of rare automobiles. Deusenbergs, Bugattis, Mercers, a half-dozen Lamborghinis, several special-order Jaguars—there were thirty-five of them in all, this despite the fact that only one road led in and out of the palace and it was poorly paved at best.

Another building contained an immense art collection. Rembrandts, Reubens, Titians, Monets, Renoirs. Some sculptures. Some modern pieces. All of the artwork was priceless. Most of it was stolen.

The second-largest structure in the compound was a six-story, twenty-two-room affair located near the outer southern wall. It resembled a five-star hotel, which in some respects it was. It featured great views of the snow-capped Rabat Mountains to the east or the equally pleasing Divila River to the west. Some of the most notorious figures of the last half of the 20th century had come to this place to drop out of sight. Carlos the Jackal had stayed here. So had Idi Amin, Abou Abbas, Carl Letiner of the Cali Cartel, and various members of Hamas, the IRA, and the Red Brigades. Lesser-known art forgers, jewel thieves, wealthy billionaires who'd faked their deaths, and high-up government officials who'd felt the need to disappear—many of them had also spent time as guests in the "Hotel."

It was said that exactly one half of the Qom-el-Zarz palace sat in Iraq, and the other half in Iran. There was no real proof of this; the border here was hazy at best. But if true, neither Iran or Iraq ever tried to lay claim to the place. This was out of respect for—and fear of—the person who lived here.

His name was Azu-mulla el-Zim, more simply known as "Zim." He was an odd, mysterious figure, weighing nearly four hundred pounds, with a scraggly beard and Coke-bottle-thick eyeglasses. He was a modern-day sultan of sorts, rich beyond dreams. He had no friends, but no enemies either, as they said in the Middle East. And he was a true paradox. He was a sadist, ruthless in many ways, but also a connoisseur of great art. He was responsible for the deaths of countless innocents over the years, yet tears never failed to come to his eyes when listening to a Wagner opera. His stolen art collection was among the largest in the world, yet he'd made many substantial if secret contributions to the Louvre Fund over the years.

Zim began life as a smuggler at the age of ten, swallowing packets of opium for Syrian drug dealers and then walking across the border into Lebanon to sell them on the other side. As he grew older, he went into dealing arms, heroin, and much later, black-market computer chips. He'd amassed a great fortune simply by eliminating anyone he saw as a competitor. He'd murdered dozens of people himself, and had paid to have hundreds more killed. He read *The Wall Street Journal*, the *Financial Times of London*, and at least a dozen other financial sheets cover-to-cover every day, and held huge interests in every large world market. Yet very few people in the West knew he even existed.

His wealth was estimated at several billion. But with Zim, it was not really about money. It was about control, power, and the love of playing two sides against one another. He was ruthless, a misogynist, a charming liar. He lived a fabulous life. He owned many things. He owned many people.

He also owned the AC-130 ArcLight gunship.

Just how Zim had come to possess the special operations plane was a deep mystery to those who knew him.

Some believed Zim had "willed" the airplane to land near his compound the night it disappeared. Others claimed he had somehow interfered with the plane's navigational system and forced it down that way. Still others said he'd managed to get into the dreams of the pilots flying the plane and had introduced a hypnotic suggestion forcing them to land that night. Another tale said he'd secretly paid off the crew weeks before, and that they came willingly.

But however he'd come to own it, he considered it more than just another weapon or another piece of art.

In many ways, it was his most prized possession.

On this day, Zim was sitting in his main chamber, perched upon exactly one hundred large silk pillows, reading the latest edition of *Le Monde*.

He was of indeterminate age; though he looked to be in his mid-fifties, it was thought he was at least twenty years older. His usual attire was a simple silk gown, sandals, and a kufi. His beard was somewhat gray, his skin tanned on his face and hands, but nowhere else. When he spoke English, he did so with a pronounced lisp.

He was surrounded, as always, by a dozen girls, most of them from Japan, most of them barely in their teens. A pot of calming tea was steaming on a table nearby. The remains of some small biscuits littered the tea tray. The room was filled with the stench of plum incense. A bank of computer screens glowed at one end of the room. They were filled with the latest financial information from Zurich, Paris, London, New York.

Zim clapped his hands, and one of the young Japanese girls crawled up the hill of pillows and knelt before him. He raised his right eyebrow a bit—the girl knew what this meant right away. She reached up, took off his thick-rimmed glasses, wiped a speck of dust from the right lens, and returned them to Zim's nose. Then she slipped back down to the floor.

Zim was reading a piece on the fluctuating uranium market, and was thinking about organizing a coup in the Ivory Coast that would bring him closer to the uranium fields at Daloa, when the door at the far end of his chamber opened.

Two heavily armed men stepped in. Dressed all in black, they bowed and made way for a third person. This man came in on his knees, inching forward a little bit at a time. He was one of Zim's legion of flunkies, glorified servants who ran errands and carried messages for him from the various parts of his palace. They were all required to enter into his presence this way.

The man had made it about fifteen feet inside the room when Zim finally shouted at him: "OK, get up, you ass!"

The man immediately obeyed and began tiptoeing across the room toward the mountain of pillows. The Japanese girls made way for him as, with trembling hand, he proffered a note on a silver tray up to Zim.

On a signal from Zim, one girl took the note, climbed up the pillows, and presented it to him with a long deep bow.

Zim put his magazine aside, adjusted his thick glasses, and opened the note.

A hush came over the room. This was not considered pleasant news, and the man who had delivered it was in desperate fear of his life at the moment. It was not unknown for Zim to kill the messenger when the news was bad.

Zim read the note silently. He seemed confused at first—again not a good sign.

"Who sent this?" he asked.

The man at the base of the pillows quavered a bit.

"Your guest in Room Six," he replied with a shaky voice. "He's been on the phone all night."

Zim considered this, then reread the note.

"Is he being intentionally vague?" he asked the messenger.

"I have no idea, sir," the man replied, his voice equal parts terror and confusion. "Shall I go back and ask him?"

Zim shook his head. "No, I think I know what he means."

He crumpled the note and threw it down on the mountain of pillows. Then he put his hand to his chin in thought.

"Tell Major Qank to activate the Third Ring," he told the messenger. "He is to report to me anything unusual that those in the Ring might see. Understand?"

"I do," the man replied, backing up slowly. If he

could just get out of the door alive, it would be a major victory.

"And one more thing," Zim called after him. "Thank my guest in Room 6."

"I will, sir," the man said, disappearing back out the door.

Once he was gone, Zim yawned, stretched his enormous body, and then put his head on a pillow and went to sleep. This was a normal ritual for him at about 9 A.M. every day.

Only when they heard him snoring did one of the Japanese girls retrieve the crumpled-up note and carry it over to the others who were waiting in the corner.

Quietly, they opened it and read it.

It contained only two words: *They're coming*.

Major Ali Bus Qank was not really a major. Nor was he a military officer of any kind.

He was, however, the man in charge of Zim's intelligence operation, and for this Zim had conferred the rank of "major" upon him arbitrarily. For all the work Qank wound up doing, he secretly believed he deserved to be given at least the *faux* rank of colonel—yet he would never tell Zim this.

Qank was a Syrian. He worked out of an office located beneath the west wall of Zim's inner sanctum. From there Qank and a team of four collected intelligence from a variety of sources—newspapers, TV broadcasts, the Internet—as well as from the network of informants Zim had in place around the world.

This network was broken down into sectors known as Rings. Zim had organized the network himself many years before, and it was brilliant in its simplicity. The Third Ring was made up of freelance spies who had access to all airports, both commercial and military, as well as all major shipping ports stretching across southern Europe to the Middle East. Through simple observation, intercepted radio traffic, and purloined passage logs, the Third Ring knew just about every airplane and surface vessel, military or not, that moved from America through Europe to the Middle East.

Of the entire network, the Third Ring was the most reliable at revealing the American military's objectives. Like Zim, Qank knew some things about the Americans. First, they always entered military action reluctantly. Yet when they made their minds up to act, they usually acted quickly. *Too* quickly, most times, especially when it came to secret operations.

That was what Qank knew Zim was now anticipating. The sinking of the USS *LaSallette* had been a big mistake. But mistakes happen. The destruction of the Qak-Six oil rig had been a job, paid for by a rival oil consortium, just one of dozens Zim had contracted for the gunship in the past year and a half. That the star-crossed American ship had happened upon the scene was something that could not have been prevented. And actually, there had been some luck in this. Because the *LaSallette* was a spy ship, there had been nothing heard about its sinking—not in the media, not in the back channels. Not yet anyway. Qank knew the Americans would want to keep quiet for now about the ship's sinking, rather than admit what it was up to at the time of its demise.

But Qank also knew the Americans could not let the sinking go unpunished. Refugee camps, food convoys, Bosnian innocents—their liquidation had registered little on America's moral radar. But the sinking of the *La-Sallette* had changed that. Some of their own had been killed—by a weapon they had lost control of many years before. And now the Americans were coming to get that weapon back. Finally.

Qank and Zim had discussed this eventuality before, of course. In their scenario, they expected at least a thousand American troops, probably special forces of some kind, to transit to the Persian Gulf area, probably offloading in Bahrain or in the United Arab Emigrates, but definitely not in Saudi Arabia or Kuwait. The prepositioning of this force would likely be accompanied

by the appearance of an aircraft carrier or two moving
into the upper Gulf area. Then all U.S. forces in the area
would be put on alert—and then the Americans would
strike.

The only question was, when?

That was where the Third Ring came in. If anyone
could identify the means of transport and the timetable
of the oncoming American force, the freelance spies in
the Third Ring could.

So Qank worked his secure phones for the rest of this
day and far into the night. Giving orders to his informants and getting back their reports, he spoke to more
than 150 individuals in eighteen hours. If a thousand
special troops were moving to the Persian Gulf area by
air, Zim's spies would have detected a small parade of
C-5 or C-17 cargo planes making their way across the
Atlantic. These planes might land at Rota, Spain, or on
Sardinia. (Nonstop transits were not common, if only to
preserve the crews and prevent suspicion.) If such a
force was moving by ship, the spies would likely see a
fast-assault vessel or even a nuclear-powered aircraft
carrier suddenly make an appearance in their region.

The Middle East was like a sieve. Very few things
happened that weren't spoken about somewhere by
someone. Qank was sure that the American troops coming to get the gunship would show up somewhere. But
after a long day on the phone, he was left with an odd
fact: None of the Third Ring spies had seen anything. It
was business as usual at all their locations. No extraordinary activity at American air bases, no aerial tankers
taking off in unusual sequences, no areas cordoned off
for classified flights. Nothing.

The ring reported no unusual shipping activity either.
No assault ships had been spotted, no vessel at all that
might be carrying the size of the force Qank and Zim
were expecting. In fact, there was little U.S. military
shipping happening anywhere at all. This was very
strange.

A bit desperate, Qank commenced scouring the Internet, searching the web pages of all the major U.S. newspapers on the East Coast. He was looking for any stories that would have indicated a small specialized military unit moving out, farewell celebrations at a military port or at an air base—that sort of thing. But this turned up nothing as well. He had one of his men do the same thing for all newspapers in the U.K., Italy, and Germany—perhaps the Americans were moving troops down from Europe to do the job. But this proved a dead end too.

Finally, he had his men check their informants in place in the handful of American bases in the Persian Gulf itself. Maybe some specialized troops already in the region would be called on to retrieve the gunship. But again, there was nothing to indicate that was taking place.

After thirty-six straight hours of this, Qank was stumped. If something was happening, the Third Ring would have sniffed it out simply because when it came to covert military operations, the Americans were not very good at sneaking in the back door.

Yet the man in Room 6 said they were coming.

So, where were they?

17

Delaney was sick. Very sick.

Possibly sicker than he'd ever been.

He'd been riding the rail of the freighter for days, watching as waves that appeared to be the size of skyscrapers rose and fell before him. He'd lost all track of time, didn't know what day it was, or even what body of water he was on. All he knew was that he'd thrown up so many times he couldn't believe his stomach could hold any more.

It was embarrassing. Of the entire unit, he was the only one who was still expelling bits of food he'd eaten weeks ago. He'd tried all sorts of things to stop. Holding his breath. Drinking warm water. He had even tried prayer. Nothing worked. He felt as if he'd been throwing up his entire life.

And that was a shame, because this trip had started off so differently.

Upon leaving Seven Ghosts Key, the unit, contained in three C-5's—men, choppers, and all—had flown to an even more exotic location: a place called Xetu on the outer Canary Islands. The C-5's set down at a large privately run airport on the island's secluded northern end. Because the unit had not been briefed about the details of their transit, everyone just assumed that the C-5's were simply refueling there, and would leave as soon as the gas-up was complete.

But as Delaney and the others learned that day—and would learn many times in the next week—they had assumed wrong.

The C-5's sat on the runway for hours, not moving, their insides getting hotter with each passing minute. Finally the unit was unloaded, aircraft and all. It was dark by this time. A half mile away was a small port facility. At its dock was the lowliest, crappiest-looking cargo freighter Delaney could have ever imagined.

Under instructions from Smitz, the unit pushed the choppers over to the dock, which, despite much grunting and groaning, took under an hour. Once they were at the dock, an ancient crane lifted the choppers onto the freighter, putting the Hinds into the hold first, and then settling the big Hook and the even bigger Halos onto the deck. Once they were in place, the crew covered the helicopters with black tarpaulin and then arranged empty metal containers on top of them, hiding them completely. Then the unit itself was loaded aboard.

Then they sailed.

Delaney had gotten sick soon after chow the next morning. At first he thought it was the food. The freighter was so dirty and grimy and rusty, Delaney was convinced the CIA had dressed it up to look that way, and the food was absolutely horrible. When Delaney found himself bent over the railing an hour later, he would have bet his lunch the greasy eggs had made him sick.

But then he noticed the ship was rolling. Up and down, up and down. And then he noticed that there was a nauseous rhythm to this motion. And once that thought was firmly entrenched in his mind, there was no turning back. He became sick and had remained sick ever since.

He'd spent so much time on the rail, he actually had

a favorite spot to throw up from: about midships, port side. Crew members—when he saw them—totally ignored him. Members of the unit did too. The Marines had done their morning calisthenics no more than fifty feet away from him and no one had given him a sideways glance. He was insulted and relieved at the same time.

Only Norton showed him any sympathy, bringing him pints of water so he wouldn't get totally dehydrated. But vomiting was a solitary practice, so Delaney just took the water and waved off any of Norton's attempts to converse or distract him.

After more than one hundred hours of this, Delaney was convinced that Hell actually floated on an ocean.

It was now the fifth day and though Delaney didn't know it, his nightmare was about to end.

It was Norton who brought him the news. The pilot arrived on deck with a pint of water and, for the first time, a cup of coffee.

"You don't expect me to drink that, do you?" Delaney asked, looking at the steaming mug.

"Yeah, I do," Norton replied.

Norton looked different. It took Delaney a moment to realize why. Finally it hit him. Norton was unshaven, in need of a haircut, and his clothes weren't exactly spiffy. For the first time ever, his friend actually looked unkempt.

"Look in a mirror yourself," Norton told Delaney, reading his thoughts. Then he passed the coffee cup into Delaney's shaking hands.

"What makes you think I can actually keep this down?" Delaney asked him.

"Because I have good news for you," Norton replied.

Delaney stood up straight for what seemed like the first time in years. "And that is?"

Norton pointed to something just off their bow. They were in a thick fog, and Delaney tried hard to focus his bleary eyes. After a few moments, he could just barely make out the outlines of something floating in the middle of the bluish-green water. It looked like an extremely large sludge barge.

"What the hell is that thing?" he managed to blurt out.

"It's our destination," Norton told him. "We're finally here."

Their destination was named *Heaven 2*. It was presently anchored near the island of Halul, about fifty miles off the coast of Qatar in the lower Persian Gulf.

It was an old sludge barge, 250 feet long and sixty feet wide, and originally built to move all kinds of unsavory cargo up and down the Red Sea. It was rusty, what paint that remained was peeling, and the vessel had a distinct 15-degree list to the port side. There was a small control house at its bow, and a steering hut/chart room on its stern. Belowdecks there was room enough for a crew of six, a mess, a head, and little else.

The CIA had purchased the barge in 1987, and brought it into the Persian Gulf in order to run small amphibious operations against Iran. But it hadn't seen active duty since 1993. And it hadn't been cleaned since 1991.

A thick wooden platform covered the top of its hull; this created an area large enough to carry all five of the unit's helicopters with little room to spare. The barge moved about by means of two tugboats, and from the air or to the uneducated eye, it could have passed for a scow. A crew of six part-time CIA-paid seamen kept the barge afloat.

The freighter docked with the vessel and painstakingly unloaded the five helicopters. It was about one hour before sunrise when this operation began, and the fog drifting up from the mouth of the Gulf was getting thicker. Together, the mist and the dim light gave the unloading operation some much-needed natural cover.

The entire unit pitched in getting the choppers onto the platform and back under wraps. They were under orders to handle the aircraft "as if they were handling eggs." One of many sticking points of the operation was the maintenance of the choppers. The Army Aviation guys knew a little bit about fixing the Russian machines. Plus a dozen air techs from Seven Ghosts Key had come along for the mission. But between them, they could fix only small problems such as frayed wires, bum generators, blown fuses, and the like.

If anything major went wrong with one of the choppers—if a critical part failed or broke—the mission would be doomed.

One hour after getting the choppers stowed away, Smitz called a meeting in the barge's tiny chart room.

All of the principals drifted in. They were tired, dirty, anxious. Delaney, still pale, asked why the barge didn't have a swimming pool. No one laughed, least of all Smitz. Always earnest, the young CIA officer especially didn't appear to be in the mood for any jokes now. In fact, he'd seemed to have aged ten years during the five-day voyage. His beard was erupting, his hair was tousled. He was wearing a tattered pair of Army fatigues. He certainly wasn't sporting the schoolboy look any longer. He was now one of them.

"You're all finally going to get your wish," he began soberly once everyone had arrived. "Though it's not how I imagined it, this is what you've been waiting for: 'the motherfucker of all briefings.' "

There was a round of tired, mock applause as Smitz laid out a long piece of paper that had scrolled out of his NoteBook's printer. It was about three feet long, six pages in all. It was crowded with text, maps, photos, crude illustrations, and code-word lists. It looked very unimpressive.

"These are our operational orders," Smitz said, examining the document. "They were just sent by my office. Why it took so freaking long, I'll never know. But here they are. Here's what they want us to do."

He flattened out the length of paper and held it in

place with help from some empty soda bottles found in a nine-year-old bag of trash. He indicated the first photograph on the document. It was a satellite image of a very deep valley surrounded by some very high mountains. There were a half-dozen buildings lining one side of what looked to be a perfectly straight two-lane asphalt highway. One of these buildings looked like a Western-style ranch.

"We're attacking Arizona?" Delaney quipped.

Again, no one laughed.

"This is a site located somewhere in the Suhr-bal in northeast Iraq," Smitz began, using a chewed-on pencil as a pointer. "It has no known name. However, it is about two hundred klicks from where we are now. Six buildings in all. One appears to be a barracks. One is a very smoky factory."

"A hole in the wall," Ricco said. "So what?"

"Well, it's an ingenious hole in the wall," Smitz said. "Look at this building. It's large enough to be a hangar. And notice this roadway. It appears to begin and end nowhere. But it's just long enough to handle both heavy cargo planes and jet fighters."

"An airport in disguise?" one of the Army pilots asked.

"That's the thinking," Smitz replied.

He pointed to the high mountains.

"Look at the topography of this place. Everything around it is at least 2500 feet high. The angles of these peaks are so sharp this place is likely be covered in shadow for most of the daylight hours."

He pointed to the factory-like building.

"And no one has any idea what this place does, what it makes, if anything. But those three stacks seem to be belching out some kind of black smoke on a continuous basis."

Smitz paused for effect.

"Bottom line: Some people in my office believe the ArcLight gunship operates from here."

Those gathered pulled in a little closer. They were

now studying the satellite photo with renewed interest.

"So the highway is a runway, the mountains provide the shadows to hide in, and the factory smoke obscures the airplane when the shadows don't," Norton said. "Someone kept his thinking cap on for this one."

"That's the guess," Smitz confirmed. "This place looks innocent and unimpressive. But whoever built it went a long way to make it nearly impossible to get a good satellite read on it. Or even a U-2 flyover."

He indicated the long ranch-style building. It looked a bit like Motel Six, back on Seven Ghosts Key.

"Note this structure," Smitz said. "Some people in my office believe the plane's original crew is being held here. Going in and getting them out is what Team 66 has been training for."

He pointed to an even larger building further down the "highway."

"This might or might not be a hangar," he said. "It's big enough to house—or hide—a C-130. Whether that's its function or not, my office isn't sure. And note what could be AA gun emplacements."

He pointed to several dark spots in the lower hills surrounding the base. If they were AA gun or missile sites, they were in the correct position to provide the valley with maximum air defense coverage—unless something was coming in real low.

Smitz took a moment to collect his thoughts. There was no talk among the men gathered. Just a grim silence and the gentle rocking of the barge.

"OK then," Smitz began again. "That's the target. Now here's the plan. . . ."

The men gathered even closer around the chart table.

"After the place has been reconnoitered," Smitz said, "we will determine the most opportune time for the raid. We'll go in as one. The Hinds arrive first, ride in low, and take out the AA threat. Then they will sweep the area of ground opposition. The Halos will land and half the guys from Team 66 will crash the prison building, eliminate any opposition, and free the original crew.

"The rest of the Marines will go to the hangar, hopefully find the gunship inside, and secure it. By that time"—he turned to Norton and Delaney—"you two will have landed and—"

Delaney quickly began waving his hands.

"Whoa!" he said. "You want *us* to land? Shouldn't we be providing the air cover?"

"Under usual circumstances, yes," Smitz replied. "But there are two things you have to do on the ground. First, as senior officers for the mission, it's up to you two to appraise the situation inside the prison building, whether it's good or bad. But more important, you have to get on board the ArcLight and determine its flight capability."

"Well, how long will we have to do that?" Delaney asked innocently.

"About ten seconds," Smitz replied without even looking up. "You'll have to very quickly determine whether you can fly the thing out of there or not. If you can, then you will load everyone aboard, abandon the choppers, and get the hell out of there."

"What if we can't fly it out?" Norton asked.

Smitz took a breath. "Well, then we put everyone on the choppers, wherever they will fit, and take off. We leave explosives inside the ArcLight, blow it up before leaving. Should that not work, you guys use your choppers' weapons on it. Fuck it up to the point of never flying again."

They could all see Gillis and Ricco getting fidgety.

"Where the hell do we come in?" Ricco finally asked. "Why are we even here?"

Smitz turned to the tanker pilots.

"You're here because you will perform the most crucial aspect of the raid," he told them.

Both men brightened immediately—a small coup of diplomacy for Smitz.

"Now, depending on how it goes, you two will have either one of two missions," he went on, turning everyone's attention back to the satellite photo of the raid site.

"If the ArcLight is not airworthy, you will have to refuel the air assets once everyone has lifted off for the flight back to the ingress site. If the ArcLight is flyable, but is low on fuel, or if its tanks have been drained, then you will land and the fuel in your chopper will be pumped into the airplane. I've been assured it will be compatible. Now there's a list of other contingencies, but there's no question that fuel is the key to this whole operation. And you guys will have all the fuel."

Gillis and Ricco were smiling so widely, it was as if they'd won the Medal of Honor already. Delaney glanced at Norton, who did a mile-high eye roll. After all their bitching, *now* the tanker pilots were happy?

Smitz moved the pencil pointer further down the piece of scrolled paper.

"Now for the ingress site," he began again, pointing to another hazy photograph. This one was accompanied by several crude drawings. The photo showed a lone mountain at a location very different from the disguised air base. This mountain was a giant, so high there was even a wisp of snow at its peak. Yet it was a solitary place, surrounded by vast open desert. And it had an odd geological quirk to it. About halfway up on its southern side was a long, flat overhanging cliff. Looking from the south then, the mountain actually appeared to be half mountain, half mesa.

"This place is called Ka-el," Smitz said, rolling the Arabic name off his tongue with some aplomb. "It was last used as an advance base by British SAS prior to the Gulf War."

He pointed to the cliff. "You can see this area is flat as hell and long. We believe it's long enough to accommodate a moving chopper takeoff."

"You 'believe' or you're sure?" Delaney asked.

Smitz looked up at him. "We *believe* we'll find out soon enough," he replied, leaving Delaney to scratch his head.

Smitz went on: "We ingress to this site, set down, and wait for the Hinds to recon the gunship's base. Once we've determined the most opportune time to go in—that is, when the gunship is actually on the ground—then we saddle up and do the raid.''

Norton studied the photo of the oddly shaped mountain.

"Won't we be very exposed up there?" he asked. "Anyone flying overhead will see us for sure. They'll have to think it's a bit strange that five choppers are sitting in the same place halfway up a mountain, even if we are painted like Iraqis."

Smitz just shook his head. "That's the beauty of this place," he said. "We don't have to be exposed at all."

He pointed to the crude drawings under the mountain photo. One showed a cascade of vegetation coming down the side of the mountain and ending at the flattened-out area.

"All this vegetation is fake," he said.

He pointed to the next drawing. "Behind it is this place."

The drawing showed what appeared to be an enormous cave. If the dimensions penciled in were correct, this cavernous maw was larger inside than Hangar 2 back at Seven Ghosts Key.

"Damn, who lives there? Batman?" Delaney asked.

"Close," Smitz replied. "Like I said, the SAS used this place as a forward chopper base during Desert Storm. Apparently it's been around since the First World War. The Brits had enough room inside for a chopper squadron and a company of men. Just about what we're packing. The Gomers never caught on.

"This is where we will go to first. We wait here until the right time arrives to strike, then we do the job. If everything goes according to plan, we'll be in-country for less than seventy-two hours. . . ."

A gasp went through the room. "You mean *seven* hours, I hope?" Delaney said.

"No," was Smitz's reply.

"Here's the reason why," he explained. "The cave is about a hundred klicks away from where everyone thinks the disguised air base is located. But that hidden base is in a part of Iraq that is so remote and the terrain around it so rugged and yet similar to everything else in the area, it might take a few recon flights just to find it and pinpoint its exact location. Then we have to wait until we know the gunship is there. Between the two, I believe we will have to reconnoiter the target at least a few times before we go on. This means we have to be prepared to spend some time in that cave. Maybe a few nights. Maybe a week. Maybe even longer.''

A groan went through the chart room. But Smitz ignored it. He was used to that reaction by now.

''So here are the setups,'' he began. ''Step one, we leave here. Step two, we reach the cave. Step three, we await word from my office that the gunship might be at the base while step four, the Hinds go out and recon its location. Step five, the Hinds return. Step six, the whole unit goes out, we hit the base, recover the crew, and, we hope, the airplane itself. Step seven, we egress out, fly the AC-130 to Al-Khadi, in western Saudi.''

''The place from whence it came?'' Norton asked. ''Nice touch.''

Smitz looked up from the document for a moment.

''I must emphasize one thing,'' he said. ''Once we leave, we will be totally autonomous. We have to operate on our own, without expecting or getting any help from outside assets. That's how secret this mission is. After we lift off from here, it will be like we never existed.''

This statement was met with nothing but grim stares and the shuffling of some feet.

Smitz returned to his missive. The scrolled paper was now totally flattened out and getting smeared from much use.

''Next item: code words,'' Smitz announced. ''As usual, complicated. Let's see, the office wants the first Hind to be Delta Tango One. The second Hind will be Foxtrot Tango One. The Hook will be Alpha Tango Six. The first Halo will be Delta Tango Larry. The second

Halo will be Delta Tango Curley . . . Jeesuz, who makes up this stuff?''

He read further down.

''The cave will be known as Target Point Zero. The objective will be known as Target Minus One Alpha. The—''

That was when Delaney interrupted him. ''May I make a suggestion?''

Smitz looked up at him. ''Sure, I guess . . .''

Delaney took the paper from Smitz's hands and to the astonishment of all, tore off the paragraph listing the code words, crumpled it up, and threw it out an open porthole into the sea beyond.

''We're going to have enough to worry about without trying to keep all that crap straight,'' he declared.

Then he turned to Gillis and Ricco and said: ''You guys will be Pumper.''

He pointed at the Army Aviation pilots. ''You guys: Truck One. Truck Two.''

He pointed at Norton. ''Hound Dog One . . .''

He pointed to himself. ''Hound Dog Two.''

He pointed to the photo of the flattened mountain. ''That will be the Bat Cave.'' He pointed to the hidden air base. ''That's the Ranch.''

Then he looked up at everybody. ''Any objections?''

They all just stared back at him. Delaney really was a nutty guy, Norton thought. But there was no one better at cutting through the bullshit.

''Fine by me,'' Smitz finally replied.

A chorus from the others echoed that sentiment.

Smitz rolled up what was left of the scroll and stored it in his briefcase. He then passed out two-page sheets that he'd previously printed out of his NoteBook.

''Here's a bit of information on some of the Arc-Light's original crew,'' he explained. ''It's very sketchy, but I thought it might be best to see who we are going in to rescue.''

Once everyone had their info sheet in hand, Smitz stood up straight and stretched his back.

"We'll be taking off at 2100 hours tonight," he announced. "You should all get some sleep if possible. Any questions? Comments?"

Only about a million, Norton thought to himself.

But before he could say anything, there came a voice from the back of the small room.

"Yes, sir. I would like to go on record as saying this plan is total bullshit."

Everyone turned.

It was Chou Koo—Joe Cool.

The room was suddenly very tense. Chou was the kind of guy who had never questioned an order in his life.

And now he was speaking up.

"Something to say, Captain?" Smitz asked him calmly.

"I think what you are proposing is impossible," Chou replied. "With all due respect, sir."

"Why is that, Marine?" Smitz asked sternly. "Share with us."

Chou stepped forward.

"Simple really," he said. "What if one of the Halos develops a mechanical problem? There are no backups. With everyone who is going on this ride, the air techs and so on, there probably won't be enough room on the other aircraft to bring everyone back home. What do we do then?"

It was a tough question, but Smitz had to answer.

"If that happens, the others continue on," he said. His words were absolutely ice cold.

Chou's jaw clenched.

"Well, what if we lose the fuel chopper?" he asked. "How will the entire unit proceed then? Or even get back to friendly lines? Or if we get stuck on that mountain and the Gomers get wise at some point, how will we get out?"

Smitz just stared back at him.

"We probably won't," he replied.

Chou stood frozen for a moment, then finally turned away.

Smitz looked at the rest of them. His eyes were narrow and absolutely dark. Yeah, he'd changed—*a lot*.

"Any more questions?" he asked.

There were none.

Below the steering house on *Heaven 2* was a room just big enough to fit a dozen bunks stacked three on top of each other. This was where the pilots were sent to sleep before the mission jump-off.

Norton climbed up onto his assigned bunk and collapsed. The cubicle was small and stuffy, but at least he didn't have to sleep inside his chopper as the Marines and the air techs were doing.

No sooner had he laid his head down when he heard Delaney in the next bunk over let out a burp and then a moment later, start to snore. Norton was simply amazed. Apparently Delaney could fall asleep almost anytime, anywhere, no matter what the circumstances. Norton envied him. Considering what lay ahead for him and the rest of the unit, sleep was the furthermost thing from Norton's mind.

He pulled out the two-page information sheet Smitz had given them on the gunship's original crew. The questions began flooding in. What had happened to them that night the plane went missing? What had they been going through ever since? Were they really still alive, as some in the CIA believed? Or had the Iraqis cooked and eaten them a long time ago?

He began reading the info sheet. It contained the names and rank of all on board the ArcLight plane that night, but only photos and detailed information on the pilot and copilot.

Both men looked just like hundreds of flyboys Norton had run into during his military career. Clean-cut, clear-eyed, rock-jawed, kinda dopey, but actually very smart, just in a very different way. Pilots were always easy to pick out of a crowd. That all had that same look.

Both men also looked like candidates for the pulpit. That was another thing about flyboys. They were always so Christian, so religious, so goddamn holy.

But what shape were these two in now?

The pilot of the plane the day it took off was a guy named Jeff Woods. He was a colonel in what the info sheet called "a U.S. Air Force Special Section." He was buzz-cut blond, late forties, a slight resemblance to astronaut John Glenn. Married, two kids, pretty wife, at least in 1991. Little League coach. Community volunteer. Deacon at his church. Whiter than Wonder Bread.

The second in command was an Air Force major named Pete Jones—could you get a more American-sounding name than that? He too was rock-jawed, poster-boy handsome, jet-black hair, worn a bit more stylish than Wood's. A rake. But a Christian one, according to his file.

He had no kids.

Very cute wife.

Something to come back for . . .

Where the hell was she *now? What was* she *doing at this very moment?*

The next thing Norton knew, Delaney was shaking him awake.

Norton sat up with a start, drool rolling down his chin. Somehow nine hours had passed by. Delaney was dressed in his futuristic flight suit, helmet and all.

"C'mon, Jazz," he was saying. "Nappies are over. Time to go to work."

18

It was dinner time at Zim's palace.

As usual, Zim was eating alone, perched high above his chamber on his mountain of pillows. There were no young Japanese girls around to watch him eat or to wipe his mouth clean after an exceptionally messy bite. There were some things the little nubile ones just would not do.

Even his personal guards preferred to wait outside the chamber while Zim was dining. He wasn't sure why. His fare was always so appetizing, if a bit regional and esoteric.

Zim had a huge bowl before him with two forks as his only utensils. In the bowl was a combination of raw lamb's brains, horse's eyes, and salmon guts, all mixed together in plain yogurt.

Truth was, Zim loved to eat alone and in peace, as he was loath to share his meal with anyone. That was why he was surprised when just into his second bite, the doors to his chamber opened.

Two guards came in, followed by a man on his knees. Zim looked up and immediately frowned.

It was Major Qank.

"I am eating," Zim said with a wave of his hand, dismissing his intelligence officer.

Qank bowed deeply and took a deep breath.

"A thousand pardons, sire, but . . . this is very important."

"What could be more important than my meal?" Zim asked Qank as if he was actually awaiting an answer.

Qank was stumped for an adequate reply.

"Well, this is *equally* important, my sire," he finally replied.

This answer gave Zim pause.

Finally he said: "OK, get up. And what is so urgent?"

"A note, sir, from the man in Room 6 . . ."

Qank tiptoed to the bottom of the pillow pile. He was just tall enough to hand the note up to Zim.

Zim finished chewing an elongated fish intestine, slurping the last few inches as one would a spaghetti strand, and finally opened the note.

Again the message within was simple. It read: "They are here."

Zim read the note several times, then wiped his mouth with his sleeve and stared down at Qank.

"Is he being intentionally vague here, do you think?"

Qank just shook his head. "No, sir. I think he's being quite clear. The Americans have somehow managed to sneak by the Third Ring and they are now in the area."

Zim put his hand to his chin and pretended to be in deep thought.

"Hmmm, what shall we do then?"

Qank had anticipated this question. They actually had a contingency if the Americans ever got this close. He just hoped Zim's memory was as good as his.

"We *do* have a plan, sir," Qank started. "It involves a purchase. In South Yemen, I believe . . ."

Zim thought about this for a moment.

"Ah, yes!" he finally exploded with a laugh. "The Three-Card Monty plan . . ."

Qank rolled his eyes involuntarily. "Exactly, sir," he said. "Shall we proceed?"

Zim took another mouthful of his disgusting food. "Do we have the time, though?" he asked with a burp.

"I believe we do," Qank replied.

"Then make it so!" Zim called out with a laugh. The guards laughed too.

Qank looked around at them and wondered for a moment what was so funny. Then he began backing up.

"As you wish, sir," he said, heading for the door in reverse. "As you wish . . ."

South Yemen
2200 hours

It was very hot in Sayhut-ru.

The sun had baked the city all day; the temperature at noon was 122 degrees. Now that night had fallen, it had cooled off—to 103. And more hot weather was expected for at least the next two weeks.

The small city was actually a military air base with a few hundred houses around it. The base housed one unit of the Yemeni People's Air Defense Force and functioned as a civilian port of entry as well. But civilian or military, there was no activity at the base on this sweltering evening. No flights were scheduled to fly into this little piece of Hell. No flights were scheduled to leave either.

That was why Captain Rez Bata was so surprised when he saw a Learjet land unannounced on the main runway. He checked the time. It was 10 P.M.; he was just getting ready to go home for a bath. Who was this coming to disrupt his plan?

Bata was the air base night manager, one of only twenty captains in the tiny YPADF. In addition to his duties watching over the civilian part of the airport, Bata also ran the base's air defense squadron, which consisted of exactly one rather broken-down airplane.

Oddly, it was that airplane that the man in the Learjet had come to see him about.

He heard the footsteps coming up the stairs and finally into his office. Bata took one look at the man and instinctively knew who he was right away. Though he had never seen the man before, his gut instinctively told him he was a representative of Azu-mulla el-Zim. He had that *look* about him. Bata straightened up; his heart began pounding. This was the Middle East equivalent of getting a visit from a lieutenant of a Mafia Godfather. Bata knew it would be important for him to say the right things, and do whatever this man wanted.

"My employer sends his greetings," the man said as Bata offered him a seat. There were no introductions; there was no need.

"And mine to him," Bata managed to croak.

The man put a briefcase onto Bata's desk and snapped it open. Inside the case were twenty packets of money held together with rubber bands.

"This is two million American cash," the man said. "We believe it is sufficient payment."

Bata was totally confused. "Two million? What for?"

The man pulled back the drawn curtain. In the fading light they could just barely see the base's one and only military plane. It looked very old, standing out on the tarmac, rusty, with pools of oil and other fluids dripping from it. It was obvious it hadn't been flown in a very long time.

"For that," the man said simply. "My employer wants your airplane."

Bata looked at the man, then at the airplane, and then at the briefcase full of money.

"But I can't sell that airplane," he stuttered. "Certainly not for two million."

The man just smiled and said, "But you see, you have no choice in the matter. My employer wants the plane. Now. Tonight. And he *always* gets what he wants."

Bata was sweating now. His superiors would never go for this. No matter who was making the offer.

He told the man as much.

"But you misunderstand," the man replied. "This is not a payment from my employer to your government for the airplane. This is a *personal* payment. To you. To do with what you wish."

The man looked at the case full of thousand-dollar bills. "And with money like this, I think my first instinct would be to resign my commission."

With that, the man stood up, made a courteous, heel-clicking bow, and went out the door.

Bata sat for a long time looking at the money. Then finally, he took out a pen and paper and wrote out a very hasty letter of resignation. There would be no time to collect his family, of course. They would have to stay behind. But if he could get a car service tonight to carry him to Alwar, he could be anywhere—the Bahamas, South America, Monaco—by morning.

He took a handful of valuables from his desk, threw them in the briefcase, and then closed it and grabbed his hat. He looked out the window again to see that the airplane he'd essentially just been bribed for had a team of mechanics already swarming over it. He took a closer look. What were they doing?

It seemed like they were attaching some kind of elongated snout to the airplane, hastily riveting it in place. They were also painting it in an odd charcoal-gray color. One man was busy painting numbers on the underside of the fuselage. Another was standing up on the tail wing, doing the same thing.

What was this about? Bata wondered. Maybe Zim's people were preparing the plane for an arms shipment, or for a drug run. Or maybe for a pickup of young girls for the white slavery market.

But in the next instant, Bata knew that it didn't make a whit of difference to him what they were doing to the airplane. He took one last look around his office, sighed, shut off the lights, and left, the briefcase full of money tucked safely under his arm.

Yes, they could fly the airplane to the North Pole for all he cared.

Though he had heard that C-130's were good for that sort of thing too.

19

Considering everything involved, the takeoff from *Heaven 2* went well.

The platform was just long enough to fulfill the need for a running start for all five helicopters. The Halos went up first, followed by the Hinds, and then finally, the gas-laden Hook. Once airborne, they formed up at one thousand feet and headed west.

During the day, *Heaven 2* had inched its way up the Persian Gulf so that by launch time, it had positioned itself just off of Bubiyan Island, a lonely spit of land near the coast of northeast Kuwait. From there, it was only a matter of thirty-five miles to Iraq. The flight plan called for them to pass over land north of Basra, in a sector known as Khorra-sul-el. It was rugged, mountainous country, with few radar sites and known to be a slice of airspace rarely traveled by Iraqi aircraft because of its proximity to the very hostile border of Iran.

Once over this region, the five choppers turned north. They stayed in the same formation they'd practiced endlessly back over the Florida Straits. The two Hinds out front, the Halos next in line, with the Hook bringing up the rear. If all went well, they would reach the mountain hiding place just before midnight.

Both Hinds were equipped with a medium-range air-threat-warning radar. They were crude setups, but enough to tell Norton and Delaney if there were any other aircraft up there with them. There wasn't—and that was not unexpected. First of all, the Iraqi Air Force didn't fly very much, mostly because they had so very few airplanes to fly. Secondly, nearly two thirds of the country was covered by two U.S. patrolled No-Fly zones. Only helicopters could fly in these zones, so if they were to meet anyone up here, it would most likely be another chopper. But thirdly, the Iraqis rarely flew anything—choppers or warplanes—at night. Too super-stitious, was how this was once explained to Norton.

Either way, the combination of these three factors gave the small helicopter force an open sky through which to infiltrate.

Norton just couldn't help wondering during the flight, though, if the Iraqis knew something about flying at night that he didn't.

The unit flew for exactly ninety-three minutes, over flooded marshes, rugged hillsides, vast desert.

At 2340 hours, Norton's GPS scope began beeping. They were nearing their landing zone. He flipped down his NightScope eyepiece and sure enough, he could see the huge mountain of Ka-el looming in the distance.

But there was a problem.

A big problem.

On the other side of the mountain was a cloud of sand so large, it looked like a tidal wave rolling in on a beach.

Norton began blinking his navigation lights madly—and soon saw Delaney flying right beside him start blinking his in return. Now the other three choppers were signaling as well. They all saw the gigantic sand-storm. The question was, what to do now?

But this really wasn't a question at all. There were no other options. They didn't have enough gas to turn around and go back—not without a risky nighttime air-to-air refueling.

So they had no choice.

They had to keep going.

Norton was the first one to descend through the sand-storm.

His heart was beating right out of his chest. The love affair with the Hind was on hold for the moment. High winds were buffeting the Russian chopper all the way down. It sounded like he was being hit with a million rocks, especially around the canopy. He hoped the much-ballyhooed protection for the Hind's power plants would prove true. Just one gust of sand sucked up into the copter's engines, and it would be lights out forever.

Four hundred feet from landing and he was fighting the controls mightily. The Hind was great at going forward, but hovering was not one of its fortes. He was doing his best to keep the chopper level, but his biggest problem now was not the fiercely blowing sands, but something more devious: disorientation.

Keeping an airplane steady in relation to the ground was a hard enough job. Holding a chopper level in zero visibility was a real chore. It was really a mind-over-matter thing. The eyes won't believe what the instruments are telling them, and the pilot puts the aircraft in a position he *thinks* is level. Trouble is, the instruments are almost always right—and the pilot's instincts almost always wrong. There were recorded instances of chopper pilots running into sandstorms or heavy rain and actually turning themselves upside down—until they tried to land or went into a mountain. Disorientation was like breathing. If you thought too much about it, you got all fucked up.

At that moment Norton was trying his best not to think about either.

The chatter from his radio was not helping. All attention to security gone, the Army Aviation pilots were calling out numbers and positions to one another in breathlessly clipped fashion, a sure sign the pilots were getting stressed. Even Delaney was sounding a little nervous, yelling out his altitude readings as if the very sound of his voice was enough to will his chopper to the ground in one piece.

But finally, just like that, Norton broke through the bottom of the storm. He caught a quick, glimpse of the cliff face, and knew that he was much lower than he'd thought and going way too fast. He immediately gave the stick a yank and increased power. The front of the chopper bucked upwards, slamming his helmet against the top of canopy.

A second later, there was a mighty bump, a bounce, and a large crashing sound. And then nothing.

He was down.

Norton began frantically shutting down all the crucial systems aboard the Hind, lowering his electrical exposure as quickly as he could. His headphones were filled with the stern relief of the other pilots as they too broke free of the sandstorm and came down on the deck— hard, but at least in one piece.

"Truck One down!"

"Truck Two down . . . copy."

"Pumper down . . . and breathing . . ."

"Damn! Ouch . . . Hound Dog Two here . . ."

Norton smiled a moment. The last report was from Delaney. His chopper bounced in not a hundred feet from Norton's own. His partner was just barely visible through the continuing swirl of sand.

Then the radios went silent again.

The wind got louder; the sandstorm was descending on top of them now. All sight of Delaney and the other choppers was quickly gone. Norton rechecked his control panel; everything that had to be shut down was off. Only the bare minimum of instruments were still lit.

He did a quick GPS check and confirmed that they had come down in the middle of the grid they had planned for. They were on the vast cliff halfway down the high mountain. The satellite systems never lied.

He killed the GPS screen, and found himself suddenly surrounded by complete darkness. The sand swirling, the wind screaming the aircraft rocking back and forth. Darkness . . .

He hated it.

But then an idea hit him. He turned on his NightScope and sure enough, he could see the Marines, pouring out of the choppers, some of them going into their defensive ring despite the howling winds. Others he could see running up to the waterfall of vines and pulling them aside. Thank goodness, there *was* a cave behind them.

"Hot damn!" Norton heard himself say for the first time in his life.

The next thing he knew, he was moving. He pressed his face against the cockpit window and saw two ghostly faces staring back in at him. They were air techs, two of the dozen who were part of the mission. All twelve were all around his chopper now. They were pushing it toward the cave opening. Just as they were supposed to.

Once inside the cavern, Norton could finally see again. He just stared out at the place. It was enormous, as big as if not bigger than Hangar 2 back at Seven Ghosts Key. The Marines already had a generator hooked up, and now some very dim bulbs were burning within. It gave everything, and everyone, a very ghostly appearance. And true enough, he could see bats fluttering around on the ceiling of the place.

Norton could hear voices and lots of banging. Finally he reached over and undid the clasp on his cockpit window. Someone on the other side flipped the glass door upwards. It was Delaney.

"Welcome to Bat Cave," he said.

20

The sun rose hot and burning over the hard desert.

The night had passed without incident in the cave. The Marines had dispensed a battery of motion detectors all over the flattened cliff as well as hanging many over the side of the mountain itself. Two squads of Marines had spent the night out on the ledge. Well hidden in their unmarked, Iraqi-style camouflage uniforms, they had set up powerful NightScopes, one pointing in just about every direction possible from the cliff's location. The combination of the motion detectors and the Night-Scopes gave them eyes and ears that extended out for miles.

About a half mile from the base of the mountain, there was a highway that ran east to west. It was known to be little traveled, and true to form, not a single vehicle was seen on the roadway all night. In fact the unit's electronic picket line had detected no movements—other than nocturnal animals—anywhere near the hiding spot.

By 0500, Norton and Delaney were ready to go.

The air techs had worked all night getting the Hinds in shape to do the first recon flight. Most of the long hours were spent extracting sand from critical systems. Norton and Delaney did their own extensive preflight inspection as well. Their weapons check went well, as did a communications test. Everything seemed to be in order aboard the tough Russian gunships.

They could only pray it would stay that way.

The Hinds were finally pushed out of the cave and into the dim sunlight at 0530 hours.

There was still an hour before sunrise. A sweep of the area proved their position had still not been compromised. The picket line of Marines on the cliff's edge reported no activity in evidence, no traffic on the road to their south. Nothing flying anywhere overhead.

Norton and Delaney started their engines. The Russian choppers responded with the usual bang and storm of fire and smoke. But within seconds, the big rotors began turning, and soon were whirring with unbridled Russian efficiency.

They took off cleanly. Using extra power and the hard sand in front of the cave as their runway, they were up and away in less than 250 feet. The pair of Hinds immediately climbed up to five hundred feet and turned northwest. The first of what would probably be many recon flights was under way at last.

The desert now spread before them like a vast, golden vista. Norton had seen it before, of course. Nearly ten years ago, during Desert Storm, he'd flown over some of this same landscape. It was flat hard terrain in this region mostly, interspersed with rugged low hills. Moonlike. Desolate. Beautiful in the oddest way.

They flew northeast, following a course suggested to them by Smitz's CIA bosses. They passed over a few scattered villages, some goat herds, some wheat fields, the occasional roadway. It was still very early in the morning, and very few people could be seen about. Those that did see the choppers had no noticeable reaction, even though flying as low as they were, the racket they were making must have been unbearable.

Maybe this was what the people had come to expect
from the Iraqi military. Waking up early to the sound of
helicopter gunships was the least of their problems.

The open spaces and the sparseness of the land aided
Norton and Delaney greatly in preserving their cover.
And again, their disguise was simple. The sight of two
Hinds roaring through the sky at sunrise was nothing
new to anyone who spotted them from the ground.

Just as long as they acted like they were Iraqis, they
would stay out of trouble.

They flew for forty minutes. Hugging the contours of
the earth, following the flight plan, Delaney was leading
the way, Norton off his wing.

Over the lowest of the Bala Ruz Mountains, between
the Tariq-sum Hills, up and along the Al Vzayn River,
skirting the edge of Baghdad's suburbs, and then moving
northeast towards the Divala River basin.

It was odd, because it would have seemed that in a
combat-imminent situation, one's mind would be focused to the max. But this morning, for whatever reason,
Nortons thoughts began to wander.

What would happen if he and Delaney returned to the
cave after this recon to find their position had been compromised and everyone butchered? A grisly thought,
Norton told himself. Almost too grisly to enter his mind.
Besides, if they had been compromised, wouldn't they
have been intercepted by now? Or would they find Fulcrums waiting for them when they returned to the hiding
spot?

How about the gunship's original crew? What were
the chances that they'd all survived ten years of captivity? Would they be like Buchenwald prisoners when
they were finally freed? Would they be insane? Brain-
washed? Would their families still be waiting for them?
Would they be heroes once they got home? Would they
be hounded by the press? Asked to write books? Do the
talk show circuit? Make movie deals?

Norton blinked, and suddenly he was inside the accursed Tin Can simulator again. In all those hours of training he never did figure out a way to nail the T-72 tank before the Fulcrums—or the SAMs or the AAA guns—nailed him. Maybe that was the reasoning behind the simulator training after all. Maybe that was a problem that just *couldn't* be solved. Maybe he was actually on a suicide mission here, just another piece of fodder given up so the U.S. military could get back something it should never have lost in the first place.

Maybe, he was just a damn . . .

"*Jazz!* Jazz? You awake, man?"

Norton's headphones were suddenly filled with the sound of Delaney's very excited voice. He hit his silent-scramble-mode key and responded.

"I'm here . . . what's up?"

"What's up?" Delaney came back. "Open your eyes, man. Dead ahead."

Norton shook the last of his morbid thoughts away and took Delaney's advice. His jaw dropped.

"Damn. Will you look at that. . . ."

About five miles straight ahead was exactly what they were looking for. The shadow-filled valley. The prison building. The smoke-belching factory. The high, sharp-peaked mountains. Everything. It was the Ranch, just as it had been presented to them.

And sitting out on the highway that doubled as the runway was the ArcLight gunship. It was partially covered in tarpaulin, but Norton could see its elongated nose and its extra-wide fuselage poking out of the covering. Figures could be seen moving around the airplane and at various points on the base itself. The suspected AA guns and SAM sites were in evidence. There was even a T-72 battle tank sitting alongside the asphalt roadway.

"We just hit a home run," Delaney was telling him through his headphones. "On our first at bat!"

Norton was so surprised by their sudden luck, he yanked back the throttles and slowed down a bit to take a better look. It had been almost too easy, but there was no denying that the CIA's directions had brought them precisely to where they wanted to be. All the pieces fit. The buildings. The runway. The mountains. The billows of black from the factory smokestacks. And best of all, there was the gunship, sitting so fat and pretty, Norton felt he could reach out and touch it.

"Damn," he said again. "This *must* be the place."

Smitz was checking his NoteBook when he got word that the Hinds were returning.

He alerted Chou, and quickly a dozen Marines began clearing the opening to the cave. It was now 0830 hours, and the sun was up and visibility extremely clear. Getting the Hinds out of sight would be their number-one priority.

The two gunships came in for bumpy landings. No sooner had they stopped rolling when the air techs flooded out of the cave and began pushing them towards the opening.

Because of the Hinds' long, low still-turning rotors, many of the techs had to lie down and push the choppers' big wheels by hand. But finally the rotors stopped turning and both aircraft were pushed completely inside. The cave opening's covering was put back in place. A check with the perimeter men confirmed that the landing and recovery had gone unnoticed.

Norton was out of his Hind even before the cave opening was sealed off. Smitz and Chou were waiting for him.

"We found the place," he exclaimed to them. "First time. Just like that."

Delaney was right beside him. "It was just where they said it would be. Right on the fucking money."

"Damn, really?" Smitz breathed.

"Your office got the number of blades of grass right. And the ArcLight is there. Ripe for the picking."

Smitz was having trouble absorbing the news. No way did he expect the timetable to be moving this fast.

"Either my office is getting real good, real quick,"

he muttered, "or we're just the luckiest bastards on God's Earth."

"Either way," Delaney said, "we *know* where the place is. And the gunship is on the ground. I say we get our asses in gear and do this thing right now—so we can get the fuck out of here."

Smitz bit his lip. There was nothing in the plan that said they couldn't move fast once the target was established. But *this* fast? After everyone assumed that finding the hidden base would take more than just one recon flight?

He had to think for a moment. His stomach was getting tight—a sign sometimes that all was not right. What should he do? Should he send a scramble-burst message back to his bosses and tell them what had happened? Ask for further orders? Or would this just waste time? The forte of the unit was they were supposed to be autonomous. They were supposed to be able to think on their feet, take advantage of any situation.

But he was also under orders to report extraordinary events back to the office, both good or bad. Did an incredible stroke of good luck qualify as "extraordinary"?

"Fuck it, Smitty," Delaney cursed, reading his thoughts. "Don't call those assholes back in Washington. They'll just fuck it up. Let's just do it. Before we think too much about it. Besides, I got some shit to do back home."

Smitz looked up at Norton. His rock of good judgment. Surprisingly, Norton was smiling.

"You heard the man," Norton said, indicating Delaney. "He's got 'some shit to do.' "

Gillis and Ricco were now standing nearby as well. They were nodding in agreement. So were Chou and the Army pilots.

Smitz slammed his NoteBook shut and turned off the power.

"OK, screw it," he said finally. "Let's go."

21

They came out of the sun, like a thunderstorm of fire and burning metal.

Red tracers. Streaks of flame. Blinding yellow explosions. Palls of smoke rising in seconds. The noise, the screech of engines. Deafening enough to puncture eardrums, enough to make them bleed. Every sound of combat could be heard now—except the screams.

Norton had gone in first. His Hind's gigantic nose cannon was pumping out its enormous shells as soon as he came over the top of the mountain. His first target, of course, was the T-72 battle tank sitting astride the fake highway. There was no simulated nightmare here. He threw more than thirty high-explosive shells into the mammoth tank, and it blew apart like a kid's toy.

Next, he looped up and took out the first suspected AA gun emplacement, the one on the ledge about two thirds of the way up the south mountain wall. This took fifteen of the big shells before exploding in a ball of fire and dust. What Norton believed was a SAM site located on the west mountain wall appeared in his targeting circle next. He let his wing guns take care of this potential threat, shredding it with a five-second twin burst.

Another quick turn and he was firing at the second suspected AA site. Three seconds from his side guns and it was vaporized. Another 90-degree turn, another pair of five-second bursts, another suspected SAM site reduced to twisted metal and flaming embers.

Just like that, his first strafing run was over. He'd taken out the tank, two AA gun sites, and a pair of SAMs in less than thirty seconds. Without getting so much as a ding on his aircraft.

And not a Fulcrum in sight.

Delaney was now on his tail. They turned as one and like two World War One Spads, they swept over the hidden base, back and forth, firing their massive guns and hitting everything but the building where the prisoners were thought to be kept.

Norton was screaming at the top of his lungs now— an involuntary quirk of combat he'd picked up in Desert Storm. He was shooting at anything and everything he thought looked target-worthy. The gaggle of metal and wires on a perch overlooking the factory. Was it another AA gun or some kind of weather station? No matter. It was gone in a three-second burst. That glint of white plastic sitting on a trailer with four wheels near the roadside. Was it a mobile SAM launcher or a satellite dish in disguise? It made no difference. A barrage of missiles from his wing pylons and the thing was gone.

That garage, at one end of a narrow street. Could there be another T-72 hiding inside? Again, it didn't really matter. A ten-second burst from the monster nose cannon and the place was left a pile of smoking debris.

Delaney was making it his job to decimate the smoking factory. His chopper was buzzing around the substantial three-stack structure, pouring cannon fire and missiles into every part of it. Secondary explosions were going off all over the building, indicating flammable materials were inside. Soon there was more smoke smothering the area as a result of Delaney's handiwork than there was originally from the factory's smoke screen.

The combined Hind attack lasted no more than three minutes. It was so sudden and so determined and extensive, not a single shot was fired back at them. And so far the two targets they wanted untouched—the Ranch house and the covered aircraft—hadn't received so much as a scratch.

With much excitement then, Norton sent a message to the other three choppers loitering just over the mountains.

"Come on in," he told them. "The water's fine."

The trio of big choppers arrived over the scene not a minute later.

They found themselves looking down on the swath of destruction Norton and Delaney had caused with their huge Russian choppers. There was smoke and fire everywhere, as if the place had been carpet-bombed. Confusion itself seemed to be rising up into the winds.

Norton and Delaney went sweeping up and down the hidden valley again, firing their guns almost randomly as the first of the two Marine-laden Halos came in and touched down in a perfect three-point landing.

The huge chopper landed about 150 feet away from the Ranch house. As soon as it was down, the Marines began pouring out—just as they had practiced.

"Truck One down and clear," came the message in Norton's headphone. "Join the party, Hound Dogs!"

That was all Norton had to hear. He put the big Hind on its tail, did an almost impossible 180-degree loop, and with some twisting and turning, brought the chopper in for a bumpy, neck-wrenching landing. Delaney bounced in right on his tail, nearly colliding with him in the process. Only a last-second swerve by Norton prevented a catastrophic collision.

Predictably, Delaney was up and out of his cockpit even before the Hind stopped rolling. He nearly decapitated himself with his hasty exit, but jacked up as he was on adrenaline, not even the still-spinning razor-sharp rotor could interfere with what he wanted to do next.

Norton exited his own aircraft quickly as well. Delaney was positively on fire when he ran up to him. Somehow he'd gotten a hold of two M-16's.

"C'mon, Jazz!" he yelled, throwing one rifle to Norton. "Show time! Let's do it!"

Delaney began running towards the Ranch house. The Marines were still pouring out of the nearby Truck One. There was much shouting in the air. The sound of gunfire crackled all around them.

Norton started running too. He and Delaney were about one hundred yards from the prison building. Between them and their goal stood the T-72 tank, smoking heavily. They ran past it—but then Norton suddenly skidded to a stop.

"Wait a second, Slick!" he yelled to Delaney.

Delaney put on the brakes so fast he nearly fell on his ass.

"What?" he yelled back to Norton.

But Norton was already climbing up onto the burning tank.

"Jeesuz, Jazz!" Delaney screamed at him. "What the fuck are you doing? That thing could blow at any second and . . ."

But Norton was not listening to him. He was burning the tips of his fingers trying to pry open the tank's turret hatch. It took a few massive pulls but finally the thing sprang free. Norton had the presence of mind to stick the snout of his M-16 into the hatchway and fire off half a clip. He didn't want to meet anyone on the inside coming out. But all he could hear was his bullet rounds clanging off the sides of the crew compartment.

Finally he stopped firing. Then he leaned down and looked inside the tank.

It was empty.

It was as if time stood still for an instant.

Empty? The word rolled around in his mind a few million times inside one heartbeat.

Why would it be empty?

The big Hook roared over, very low, Ricco gunning his engines as he passed above the little scene on the tank. The tanker pilots carried a small but workable radarscope in their cockpit. If any enemy aircraft were coming their way, the plan called for them to send out a flare barrage as a warning. Jazz could see no flares now, thank God. No—Ricco's loud revving of the big chopper's engines was meant to be another kind of message: The tanker pilots were telling Norton to get his ass in gear, don't waste time fucking with a burning tank. *Get on with it!*

Delaney was down below him now, trying to scream the same thing up at Norton through the din.

"Jeesu! Jazz, get the fuck off there! C'mon!"

Norton finally did jump down, but he was still in a slight daze.

"Empty," he said aloud. "That tank was empty."

Delaney stopped for a moment too; he also had to think about it.

"Well, maybe the crew got out, you know, before you nailed it," was his only explanation.

"Yeah, maybe," Norton said.

The roar of an explosion going off behind them knocked both pilots back into reality. It sounded like an atom bomb being detonated.

"Gawd! What the fuck was that?" Delaney yelled as they both hit the ground.

They looked towards the Ranch House building to see indeed a small mushroom cloud rising above the front gate. The Marines had just blown the huge metal door leading to the place off its hinges. Now they were surging inside—again, just the way they'd rehearsed. Guns up and firing, flash grenades going off everywhere.

"Damn, these guys don't fuck around!" Delaney yelled, getting back to his feet. "It's time to rock and roll!"

Next thing he knew, Norton was running again. Rifle up, helmet clanging against his head, he was running

faster than he'd run since he was a kid. Delaney was
right in front of him, firing his M-16 into the air, adding
to the cacophony of gunfire all around them. Another
huge explosion went off, this one on the far side of the
prison building. More flash grenades exploded. They
were so bright and Norton was getting so close to the
objective, they were partially blinding him.

But he was running even faster now. Spit coming
from his mouth, a strange guttural laugh coming from
his throat.

Damn, this *was* rock and roll. . . .

He was suddenly aware of two people running right
beside him. It was one of the SEAL doctors and Team
66's videographer. The doctor was carrying his medical
bag the way a running back would carry a football. The
video guy was hauling his camera as if it was a weapon
of some kind.

"Stick close to me, Doc!" Norton yelled out for no
reason other than the excitement of the moment.

"Yeah, sure!" the SEAL yelled back.

They all reached the front of the building at the same
time. The door was still hot and searing where the Marines had blown it off. The inside of the building was
thick with smoke. Marines were swarming all over the
place, like an army of ants. Through the haze, Norton
could see one huge open room. Many bunks were lined
against one wall—just like back at Seven Ghosts Key.
A string of flash grenades went off, blinding him again.
There seemed to be a lot of trash on the floor, but he
could not make out exactly what it all was. One thing
looked like a smashed TV—but he was probably mistaken. All this trash had to be something else. He
stepped over the debris and kept moving deeper into the
building.

More smoke. More fire. A flash grenade still burning
in one corner. Gun shots from the far end of the building. Shouting over the din. More flash grenades. More
blinding explosions . . .

And then, suddenly, everything just stopped. All the

shooting. All the shouting. The sound of angry footsteps, boots hitting the concrete floor.

Everything stopped. . . .

"Company, hold fast!" Norton heard Chou yell from somewhere inside the cloud of smoke. "Secure positions. Cease firing!"

The calm that settled on the building came so quickly, it was almost frightening. In seconds, all that could be heard was the crackling of flames and the whistle of the wind outside.

Then came the voices. Not yelling. Not the cries of excitement of men in battle.

No—these were gasps, curse words of disbelief. The voices of men in the process of grisly discovery.

"Doc! Up here!" they heard someone shout. The SEAL doctor began moving through the haze, Norton on his tail, Delaney close behind. They reached a small open area about halfway down the length of the barracks. There they saw a very disturbing sight.

Lined up side by side on the barracks' floor were nine bodies. Facedown, hands at their sides. They were arranged in such an orderly fashion, it was obvious someone took a bit of time to do it properly.

They were Americans. They were all wearing plain gray flight suits that were about ten years out of date. All still had their names sewn on them. One of Chou's men was doing a quick check, but there was no doubt who these people were. They were the DIA and Special Forces guys assigned to the ArcLight gunship.

Each one had a bullet in the back of his head.

Smitz was hanging out of the side window of Truck Two, out of breath, sweaty, and getting dizzy.

Something was wrong here, he just knew it.

There were circling the ArcLight gunship. The smoke from the battle going on inside the prison compound was obscuring his vision, even though they were just a few hundred feet above the airplane.

The Marines inside the giant Halo were chomping at

the bit to land and get on with the mission, but the Army chopper pilots were playing it by the book: They would not land unless they were sure the area was secured. But with the swirling sand and smoke, it was impossible to see if any opposition was waiting for them on the ground. The Hinds would have taken out any AA and the SAMs, but what about the regular grunts that might be guarding this place?

Try as he might, Smitz could not see any potential enemy soldiers anywhere near the runway or the airplane. Of course there were only a few thousand places they could be hiding.

Finally Smitz had to make a decision. He crawled up to the copter's cockpit and tapped the pilot on the shoulder.

"Bring her down!" he yelled. "We've got to go in now."

"The LZ is not secure," the pilot said back. "The orders were for us not to . . ."

Smitz had no time for it. He wasn't questioning the Army pilot's courage—the guy was just doing what he was supposed to in these cases. But Smitz was throwing away the book, or at least ripping a few pages out of it.

"Bring her down," he said again. "I'll take the heat if anything goes wrong."

The two Army pilots just looked at each other. It did seem stupid just to keep circling. And they were as anxious to get the show on the road as anyone. So they nodded and told Smitz to tell the Marines to get ready. Then they leaned on the controls and the big chopper began falling out of the sky.

Smitz scrambled to the back and gave the high sign to the Marines, but they already knew they were going in. They were crouched in their ready positions, weapons up, helmet visors down, tension and excitement very thick in the air.

Smitz checked his own weapon; it was a standard-issue rather boring-looking M-16 that he had never fired.

His plan for the next half minute was very simple: wait for the chopper to land and then get the hell out of the way as the Marines exited the aircraft and did their thing.

And that was just what happened. The big chopper landed with a tremendous thud. The downwash from its huge rotors caused the interior of the cabin to fill with smoke and exhaust, but this did nothing to dampen the Marines' verve. No sooner had the chopper stopped rolling when the big rear doors opened up and the Marines went running out. The copter's engines were still screaming, and Smitz was sure he heard gunfire as soon as the Marines hit the ground. He checked the clip in his own gun a second time, noted the time, took a deep smoky breath, then ran out of the copter's tail. This would be first time he'd ever been in combat.

He tripped coming down the ramp, of course, landing ass over teacup and sending his Fritz helmet flying off his head. Now came a bizarre piece of business as the Halo's rotor wash started blowing his helmet down the runway, away from the airplane, which was sitting about fifty yards away in the opposite direction.

It was weird because Smitz's first instinct was to chase his helmet—and that was what he did. But the damn thing was traveling faster than he could run. Still, he pursued it, not wanting to be without it when the bullets were flying, and not thinking that he was presenting himself as a very easy target to the hundreds of gunmen who could be hiding anywhere.

So he ran and tripped and got up and scrambled in a crouch some more, until he finally caught up with the helmet. Snatching the damn thing by its strap, he slammed it back down on his head. Then he turned around and focused his attention back to the matter at hand.

But something very odd was happening here. He was sure he would see the Marines storming the ArcLight airplane, and maybe hear the sounds of a fierce gunfight in progress. But when he turned back to the action he was surprised to see that the Marines were more or less . . . standing around.

This wasn't right.

Smitz got back to his feet and began running towards the airplane. He met one of the platoon leaders running for him in the opposite direction.

"What the fuck is happening?" Smitz yelled at him over the roar of the waiting chopper.

"It's the wrong airplane!" the Marine yelled back.

Smitz stopped dead in his tracks. He grabbed the Marine by his collar.

"It's *what*!?"

"It's the wrong airplane," the Marine yelled again. "It's not the gunship."

Smitz let the Marine go and together they ran up to the aircraft. The other team members had stripped off the tarpaulin covering, and Smitz could see the plane was definitely a C-130. And it was painted just like the ArcLight aircraft, or at least the same as the pictures he'd seen of the rogue gunship. But the numbers on the side of the fuselage and the tail appeared to be very crudely painted on. And many of the cockpit windows were either smashed or gone completely.

Smitz's heart sank to his feet. He climbed inside the airplane and saw it was completely empty. No guns. No computers. No nothing. Just an empty cargo bay.

"Jessuz, did you check the numbers up front?" he asked the Marine.

The soldier nodded. "They don't match," he replied. "Nothing does. This plane doesn't even have portholes for any guns. See?"

Smitz felt the air just go right out of him. He couldn't believe it.

They had come all this way . . . for the *wrong* airplane?

There were tears in the eyes of the Marines when Smitz arrived at the prison building.

When he scrambled through the blasted-away front

door, the first thing he saw was a bunch of Team 66 men hunched over, turned away from each other, silently crying.

Smitz passed by them slowly—his first thought was that many of their comrades had been killed in the attack. But when he reached the area where everyone else was gathered, he took one look at the nine bodies and knew this was a different horror they had to face. It was unreal for a second or two. No one was talking. No one acknowledged his presence. Everyone was just milling about. And the nine dead Americans didn't look dead at all. They looked like they were asleep. All lined up in a perfect row. With small parts of their skulls blown off. And tiny trickles of blood flowing out. Some with eyes open. Some with smiles frozen on their faces. It was almost as if they had been expecting what had killed them—yet did not resist.

How strange a thought was *that*?

Smitz staggered back for a moment, catching himself just as he was about to fall over. It was starting to sink in now. All those long days. All the stress. All the training. All the bullshit. And for what? To come after the *wrong* airplane? To be fooled by a dupe set up to foil them? And to get nine countrymen they were supposed to rescue killed in the process?

No wonder the Marines were crying.

Smitz felt a lump growing in his throat as well. His eyes were glued on the nine corpses as a very distinct fear gurgled up from his stomach. How could he ever sleep again after this? And what dreams would come to him if he did?

He finally sucked it up and cleared his throat to speak.

"Have . . . have you checked this place for booby traps?" he asked Chou.

The stoic Marine officer just nodded once. "It's clean as far as we can tell. Plus, I dispatched three antiambush teams to watch the outside. But I believe we are the only fools at this place. Live fools, that is."

Smitz then told the others about the decoy airplane.

No one was surprised to hear it. It had been just too easy from the beginning, they were mumbling now. Getting into Iraq undetected. Finding this place on the first try. Happening upon it while the AC-130 was supposedly on the ground. Things just didn't go that smoothly in combat. Usually, if there was any luck floating around, it was bad luck.

And now the unit had a ton of it.

"Yeah," Smitz heard Norton whisper to no one in particular. "Someone *definitely* knew we were coming. . . ."

Smitz and Norton stayed with the video man.

They wanted to make sure every inch of the prison was caught on tape. Delaney stayed with the doctor. He supervised getting the dead airmen loaded into body bags. As the grim process began, the vibes inside the prison building began to change. Shock and sadness were turning into anger and fury. Team 66 had been in tight spots before, but never had they been compromised. And never had they had such a failure. But to be fooled so completely—the whole unit had to share the blame. What really twisted the gut was that the culprits had gotten away unscathed. That was why there were no enemy bodies anywhere. There *had* been no enemy. The Marines and the Hinds had done all the shooting. Whoever was responsible for the grand deception had left the hidden base before chopper unit arrived.

That was probably the worst of it. It was obvious the nine Americans had been dead for only a short while. After enduring ten long years of captivity, they had been killed when help was just minutes away.

Tragic heroes in all senses of the term.

Or so it seemed . . .

They loaded the nine bodies onto Truck One. Then Team 66 dynamited the prison building, the dupe C-130, and anything else they could find of value. Norton and Delaney climbed back into their choppers and were soon airborne. The Marine choppers took off and met Ricco

and Gillis at 1500 feet. Per the alternate plan, each aircraft quickly took on fuel, then turned as one for the
long ride back to the Bat Cave.

For the entire flight, in Norton's eyes, everything had
turned a shade of red.

22

Maybe the oddest thing that happened to Norton that day occurred shortly after they returned to the Bat Cave.

Landing went as smoothly as could be expected. His Hind was the last to be pushed into the cavern before the fake vegetation was put back in place, sealing them in once again. All the important gear was promptly stowed away and the Marine pickets were quickly dispatched outside.

To say the mood inside the cave was somber wasn't close to capturing the right word. Everyone in the unit was walking around red-faced, with fists clenched, agitated. Restless. *Angry*. They had failed, miserably, and now living with that truth had begun.

Returning to the cavern itself was a source of contention, though not verbally. Shortly after leaving the hidden air base, Smitz told them they were now operating under orders contained in something called Contingency #2. Which said, if the first attempt at the raid proved unsuccessful, they were to return to the ingress site and evaluate the situation before pulling out completely.

Had it been put to a vote, it would have been unanimous that the unit just go home. But Smitz was following orders—and the orders said return to the Bat Cave, even if it meant using up the fuel they would need to get out of hostile territory. So that was what they did.

But even this prospect wasn't foremost on Norton's mind at the moment. Once his Hind had been stored away properly, he grabbed a blanket and simply lay down on the cavern's floor underneath the helicopter— and instantly fell asleep.

And for the first time in years, he actually dreamed.

In his dream, he traveled to a small American Midwest town. A place where the fifties never ended. Here, at a grocery store, he met the wife of the gunship's co-pilot, Mrs. Pete Jones. She was cuter than her photo and hadn't aged a day since it had been taken. Norton had sought her out to ask her a question: How had her husband and the three other remaining crewmen of the ArcLight aircraft avoided getting shot in the back of the head? Mrs. Jones replied that Norton must have been mistaken. Her husband had died ten years before, during the Gulf War, and she barely thought about him anymore. So Norton took her back to her house and slept with her. But when he opened his eyes the next morning, he could not wake Mrs. Jones. She was dead herself, a bullet in the back of *her* skull. She had lain like that all night, bleeding slowly on the bed right next to Norton.

That was when someone began shaking him.

Norton opened his eyes for real and saw one of the SEAL doctors looking down at him.

He was saying: "You want to see this or not?"

Norton stumbled to his feet. He wasn't quite awake yet. The lights in the cave seemed to be flickering. Everyone he saw seemed pale and drawn, moving like shadows away from him. A rotten smell drifted into his nostrils. He stared at his watch. It read 2350 hours. Could that be right? Had he really slept more than *twelve* hours?

He shuffled to the rear of the cave, trying to keep up with the SEAL doctor who had roused him. The unpleasant smell grew more intense the deeper he walked into the cavern. Finally he reached an area where the SEAL doctors had one of the nine dead Americans up on a makeshift operating table. They had opened up the man's body like a side of beef and were performing an on-the-spot autopsy. Delaney, Smitz, and Chou were standing nearby, hands to their noses, eyes watering.

Norton nearly threw up.

"You woke me ... for *this*?" he barked at the SEALs.

"You're the senior military officer here," one replied. "There's something here you might want to know."

Norton had never seen a person gutted before, and it was not a pretty sight. The man was torn open from his groin up to the bottom of his rib cage. His stomach and large intestines had been removed and their contents placed inside plastic bags tied with string to the thighs just below his genitalia.

"This man was shot with an M-16," the doctor was saying, pointing to the man's slightly shattered skull. "The same type of weapon we were all carrying. Same ammo. Same bore. Same everything. All nine were killed that way."

Norton felt his stomach do a back flip.

"Now I'm not an expert at this," the SEAL continued. "But I believe I can tell you some of what this guy ate in the last eight hours or so."

Norton finally turned away. "I don't need to know that."

"Yes, you do," Smitz interjected.

The doctor had already started poking though the bag containing the contents of the dead man's stomach, trying to separate the bits of uneaten food from one another.

"Would you believe this guy had a steak about an hour before he died?" the doctor asked. "With some baked potato? Chocolate cake? And scotch?"

Norton gagged. But for the fact that he hadn't eaten

in twenty-four hours himself, he would have lost it right then and there.

"What are you trying to say?" Norton heard himself ask. "That the Gomers fed their prisoners real good before they shot them?"

Smitz just shook his head in disgust. "For Christ's sakes, Norton, get with the program, will you?" he said angrily. "This guy wasn't a prisoner."

Norton protested, "Of course he was! What are you talking about?"

Smitz dragged him away from the autopsy and to the place where the unit's video man had set up his equipment. Delaney and Chou followed close behind.

"Wake up, will you? Look at this," Smitz said.

He pushed a button, and the small video setup started a tape rolling. The footage showed the inside of the prison building shortly after the raid.

"Look real close," Smitz said.

Norton did. The battered insides of the building were clear of smoke when the tape was shot. And it was peculiar, because even though Norton had been there at the time the video camera was capturing these very images, he was seeing many things for the first time. Like a *lot* of wrecked TVs. And a wrecked Bose stereo system. And many wrecked CD players. And a bunch of busted X-rated videotapes. And several destroyed air conditioners. And many cartons of empty Budweiser cans tipped over.

Now Norton's head began a slow spin.

At that moment, the SEAL doctor was suddenly beside him again. He was holding a plastic spoon in his hand. It was covered with a black gooey substance, which in turn was covered by a ghastly bloody coating.

"You know what that is?" he asked Norton, not waiting for an answer. "It's caviar. Caviar! This guy had eaten about a half pound of it about one hour before getting iced."

Norton reeled back from the horrible stuff.

What was happening here?

His stomach began to flip again. His lungs seemed to collapse. His knees turned to water.

Suddenly Delaney grabbed him.

"Hey, pards, let's get some air," Delaney suggested.

With Smitz in silent protest, they walked to the front of the cave, picked up two M-16's, then passed through the fake foliage and quickly out into the hot night. It was past midnight by now, and the wind blowing across the desert below was kicking up dozens of little sandstorms. To the east, the moon was on the rise. Strange animal noises could be heard echoing nearby.

They walked to the edge of the cliff and beyond where the Marine pickets could see them. They were now facing due east. It seemed as if the entire country of Iraq was spread out before them.

Norton took in a couple of deep breaths. His head began to clear—slowly.

"Something is very, very wrong, Slick," he was finally able to blurt out to Delaney.

"A grand understatement as usual," Delaney replied. He was looking a bit pale himself—and worried. This was not a good sign.

"What do you think is going down?" Norton asked him directly. "Tell me."

Delaney just shrugged. "Well, let's review," he began. "They gather us together from the four corners of the earth—to train for a mission none of us is qualified for. Then they give us aircraft we can't fly. Then they bust our balls to get us over here. Then we spot the target in one recon flight instead of a dozen. We pick out the plane. We land. But it's not the right plane— and three quarters of the guys we're supposed to rescue have been freshly killed. With guns and ammo just like ours. *And* now it appears these guys haven't exactly been eating bread and water for the last ten years."

They went silent for a long moment. The hot wind blew in on their faces.

"Man, *none* of this computes," Norton murmured.

"Ever think that you're being set up?" a third voice asked.

Norton and Delaney whipped around, their rifles up in a flash.

They were startled to find a man standing right behind them. It was no one from the cave. This person was wearing an all-white flight suit, white boots, white gloves, and a white helmet. The helmet's mirrored visor was pulled down and despite the darkness, Norton and Delaney could see the reflections of their own stunned expressions staring back at them.

Delaney nearly shot the guy. He'd raised his gun, aimed it at the man's throat, and slipped off the safety, all in the span of one second. It was only Norton pushing the rifle barrel away at the last moment that prevented Delaney from pulling the trigger. There was an awkward, chilling span of several seconds. Finally the guy raised his helmet visor and showed his face. Both pilots nearly fell off the mountain with astonishment.

It was Angel. The mysterious Nordic-looking guy they'd seen several times hanging around Seven Ghosts Key.

"How the fuck did you get here?" Delaney hissed at him.

Angel just shook his head. "Can't tell you," he said with a relaxed smile. "If I did I'd have to kill you."

But Delaney was in no mood for such an old joke. He put his gun back up to the man's throat and asked him again.

Once more Norton intervened. "Hang on, Slick," he said, moving Delaney's gun again. "He's one of us. Or at least I think he is."

Another tense moment passed. Finally Delaney relaxed a bit. They both contemplated the man before them.

Obviously he had flown here—but how? And where was his aircraft? And why hadn't the Marine pickets seen his arrival?

But most important at the moment, *what* was he doing here?

"I don't want to see you guys get your asses hung out to dry," Angel replied, reading their minds.

"Is that right? Is that something that's going to happen?" Norton asked him.

"A distinct possibility," Angel said.

Norton finally lowered his rifle completely. Delaney did too.

"Really? Educate us then," Norton told him.

Angel just shrugged. "Well, look at the facts, like you were just doing," he said. "They send you over here to rescue a bunch of Americans who they said were being held prisoner. But those guys wind up dead ten minutes before you cruise in. What does that tell you?"

"Beats me," Delaney said. "What does it tell you?"

Angel just shrugged again. "If I had to guess, I'd say someone was making sure whatever those guys saw— or did—wouldn't get out."

Norton thought about this for a moment. "You mean like Iraqi atrocities, things like that?"

Angel laughed.

"Man, are you guys out of the loop!" he said. "You really still think those guys were imprisoned all this time?"

Both pilots looked back at him sternly.

"Are you saying they were . . . *in* on this?" Delaney asked him angrily.

But Angel just laughed again.

"You saw what they were eating, I assume? What they were entertaining themselves with?" he asked. "That sound like prison to you?"

"But that's insane," Norton said through gritted teeth. "There's got to be another explanation. Maybe the guards were plugged in to the TVs and CD players."

"And forcing gourmet meals down those guys' throats?" Angel asked. He paused a moment. A wild dog cried in the wilderness. A shooting star streaked overhead.

"Look," Angel went on. "Consider this: Suppose those nine dead guys *were* in on it, and the game was close to being up. What would happen? Maybe someone pulling the strings realizes there's a problem on just how to lose these people. Because people talk. Especially ones holding secrets. So they gather y'all together and send you in. But before you arrive they shoot nine of the crew, and make sure they do it with the same kind of guns you guys are carrying. In my mind that's setting you guys up. You wouldn't be the first patsies in the history of special ops. Or the last.''

Another pause. Another cry on the wind.

"And it all looks like a rescue mission gone wrong," Angel concluded. "Just like all rescue missions go wrong. Or most of them anyway.''

Norton and Delaney both collapsed, their rear ends hitting the hard cliff floor with two simultaneous thuds.

Norton was numb, his mind racing. By any stretch of the imagination, could this be true?

"But why?'' he finally mumbled. "Why would they do this? And who is *they* to begin with?''

Angel rested himself on one knee. "Look, I'm just a guy who is on hand to look for things. I'm the scout at the head of the cavalry column. I report what I see and leave it to others to sort it out. . . .''

"But . . . ?'' Norton prompted him.

"But from all my years in black ops, I've learned that it ain't just like the movies—it's *worse* than the movies. The layers go deeper than you can imagine. And I just think that someone somewhere is obviously pulling some strings here. I mean, they *knew* you were coming. You can't argue against that. Everyone back at Seven Ghosts was pissing their pants about security—so much so they didn't even tell you guys what was up until after you shipped. Yet the whole show was compromised somehow.''

Thirty seconds of absolute silence went by. There were no cries on the breeze now. No shooting stars. Even the wind stopped blowing.

"Bastards,'' Delaney finally whispered. "If this is

even half true, I'll kill anyone who put us in this position.''

Norton was just shaking his head. "But this still doesn't make sense," he said. "Why would they have to drag *us* all the way over here just to make it look like we killed those guys in a botched rescue attempt? I mean, we were at war with the Iraqis ten years ago— we're *still* at war with them in one sense. Why would they be so shy about icing a bunch of Americans? Or more to the point, icing them but shifting the blame?''

Angel just took a deep breath. "Maybe you're just assuming the people behind this are Iraqi," he said.

Those words hit Norton on the head like an anvil. He looked up at Angel.

"Well, damn it, we're *in* Iraq, and this fucking airplane has been operating *out* of Iraq, so how in hell can the Iraqis *not* be involved?" he asked.

"Oh, they're involved," Angel said. "But probably not the way we think. They're just hired hands in all this, I'll bet. Just like you. Just like me.''

At that moment they all heard an odd beeping sound. It quickly turned into a piercing shrill. Angel took a device out of his pocket. It looked like a TV remote control.

"I hope I've helped you two in some way," Angel said. "And if I just made things more confusing, I'm sorry. But one last piece of advice: Whatever you do, let's keep this little conversation just between us girls, OK?''

His device beeped again.

"Now I really gotta go," he concluded.

The two pilots just stared back at him.

"You gotta go?" Delaney said. "Go where? How?''

Angel smirked. "You guys can do one of two things," he said. "You can go back into the cave and not see what's about to happen. Or you can hang around out here, get the fright of your life—and then walk around for the next twenty years wondering if someone is going to pop you because you've seen something you shouldn't.''

Delaney was almost laughing now.

"Why do I have the feeling I'm in the middle of a bad spy novel?" he asked with frustration.

Angel smiled. "Because you are," he said.

With that he punched some buttons on his device and the beeping became more frequent.

Suddenly Norton became aware of a bright light over their heads. This was no shooting star. It was burning bright blue. Then he realized it was getting bigger. *Then* he realized it was actually descending towards them at a high rate of speed.

For one frightening moment he was sure this was a missile of some kind heading right for the cave. He instinctively threw Delaney and himself to the ground. There was a great rush of wind and dust—and maybe some laughter too. Norton just covered up and waited for the sound of the gut-wrenching explosion to come.

But it never did.

That was how Smitz found them not ten seconds later. Lying face-down, hands over their heads.

"What *the fuck* are you two doing?" he asked them with much exasperation.

"Getting some air," Delaney snapped back. They both scrambled to their feet, looking in every direction for any sign of Angel—and finding none.

"Mind telling me what's happening out here?" Smitz asked them. "You two going round the bend together?"

The two pilots stayed tight-lipped.

"You need us for something?" Norton finally asked him.

Smitz just stared back at them. "Yes, I do," he said. "Please get your asses back into the cave."

He started to walk away.

"What for?" Delaney challenged him.

Smitz stopped and slowly turned around.

"What for?" he asked bewildered. "We've got to help Ricco and Gillis—that's what for."

He began to walk away again.

"Help them with what?" Delaney called after him. Neither he or Norton had moved a muscle.

Smitz was not having a good day. He spun around this time, his face growing red.

"Do you remember what Contingency #2 is, Delaney?"

"Tell us again," Delaney said.

Smitz looked at them strangely.

"The Pumper?" he snapped. "Mutt and Jeff have to do their refuel rendezvous in one hour, remember?"

"Then what?" Delaney pressed him. "What are your immediate plans after that?"

Smitz was stumped. Why were they acting like this?

"I've decided our immediate plans are to get the hell out of here," he said. "If that's OK with you and your girlfriend here?"

Delaney looked over at Norton, who just shrugged.

"Yeah," Delaney finally said. "That's OK with us."

Ten minutes later, Norton and Delaney were part of a large team that was pushing the enormous Hook fuel chopper out of the cave opening.

It was not unlike pushing a tractor-trailer truck with a full cargo bay from a dead stop. Of course it would have been harder if the chopper was filled with fuel, but after the long flight to and from the raid site, plus the ingress journey itself, the copter's fuel bladders were nearly empty. Thus the rendezvous mission called for under Contingency #2.

If it was possible, Norton and Delaney were pushing the hardest on the huge bird. They had silently agreed not to mention to anyone the strange meeting they'd just had out on the cliff's edge. Who would believe them if they did? They had no clue how the guy called Angel had been able to find them, land on the mountain, and depart again so quickly, so silently. And as he himself had warned them, they didn't want to know.

Added to this the chilling message he left with them: that the operation had been compromised by either someone very high up or someone very close to it. After the day's tragic events, it was all getting just a little bit too much to bear.

So, at the moment, their combined frame of mind was focused on just one thing: to get the hell out of their present situation. The harder they pushed, the sooner Ricco and Gills could take off, make their rendezvous, come back with the fuel, and make that dream a reality. That was why Norton and Delaney were sweating like madmen.

It was also why, when the chopper was finally out on the huge ledge, Norton felt the urge to warn the tanker pilots not to delay in the performance of their mission.

"Don't waste any time up there, OK?" he yelled up to them.

Ricco looked out the cockpit window back down at him.

"What are you? An asshole?" he yelled to Norton.

With that, they began the process of getting their huge engines going.

Chou did a quick check of his picket line; an electronic sweep of the area said no one was around. He gave the Hook's pilots the signal and seconds later, the engines exploded and the rotor blades began spinning.

There were some last-minute checks, but finally the air techs gave Ricco the thumbs-up. The pilot hit the throttles and the huge beast started ascending, creating a great storm of dust and sand in its wake.

The Hook rose nearly straight up into the night sky. No nav lights, just the exhaust and the flare from the engines indicating its position. Very soon it was hardly visible at all.

Delaney was standing next to Norton, braving the dust storm and watching the chopper disappear into the starry night. Soon they couldn't even hear it anymore.

"You know something," Delaney said, resignation thick in his voice.

"What's that?"

"If those guys fuck up up there," he said, "then we're really fucked down here. No matter what Angel told us. No fuel. No way to get out. No way to even get down from this goddamn mountain. And if what Angel said *is* right, there's no way they'll ever send anyone out here to get us."

Norton shielded his eyes against the bright moonlight, trying in vain to see the last image of the Hook flying away.

"My thoughts exactly," he said.

23

On a playground near Rye, New Hampshire, nine-year-old Ryan Gillis was playing baseball all by himself.

It was early evening. A Friday. The sun was setting. It was still hot. Ryan was hitting the ball off the end of the bat, trying to get it to go straight up in the air. Whenever he was successful in doing this, he would hurriedly put on his glove and attempt to catch the ball as it was coming back down. In thirty minutes of trying, he'd accomplished this complicated feat exactly twice.

All this would have been easier if he had someone to play catch with—God knows he needed the practice. But these days, Ryan had been practicing mostly by himself.

Tomorrow was a big day for him. At noon, he would be playing in his first ever Little League game. He hadn't slept much just thinking about it. Ever since the coach told him Wednesday that for Saturday's game Ryan would be in right field for Susan Mantosh because she was getting fitted for braces, his heart hadn't stopped pounding. He'd made sure his mother had washed and pressed his unused uniform—*twice*. He'd bought new socks with his own paper route money, and had scrubbed his sneakers clean more than a half-dozen times in the past two days. He knew to play good, he had to look good. Or at least that was what his coach always told him.

Early Friday night was usually the time he and his father played catch. It was only that Dad had spent hours playing toss with him that he'd been good enough to make the Wickes Hardware Junior Tigers in the first place, even if it was as a benchwarmer. Now, Ryan would have given anything to have Dad see him start his first real game.

But Dad was not home these days.

Just around the time he'd gotten out of school for summer vacation, his mother told him Dad would be away for two weeks. At first Ryan thought no more about it. He knew his father was a big shot with the Air National Guard. He was away for two weeks a lot. But Dad had been away for more than a month now—and Mom told him the night before she wasn't sure now when he'd be coming home.

Where was he? Mom just didn't know. She guessed that maybe he was overseas, on a very special mission, picked especially by the President. How cool would that be? Ryan thought. But when he told the neighborhood kids this, they just laughed at him. Air National Guard guys never went on special missions, the kids said. They were just guys who cleaned up after the real soldiers.

And after a while, Ryan started to believe them.

The helicopter first began sputtering somewhere over the Shawar region of Iraq.

Ricco and Gillis groaned at the same time when they first heard the disturbing noise. They were ten minutes away from crossing over the coastline to the Persian Gulf. If trouble was coming, they would much rather be over solid ground—helicopters usually sank quicker than airplanes, and they certainly did not want to go down in the Gulf without the opportunity of sending out a distress call. But their orders said they had to maintain radio silence, no matter what. And this they would do.

The first real indication of trouble came about twenty minutes after taking off from the Bat Cave. The electrical output monitor had started fluctuating. Their control panel lights began blinking, with some losing function for as long as a minute or two. These were worrisome things—but not enough to force them to turn back.

But then, just as the coastline came into view north of Basra, their oil pressure gauge indicated a 20-percent drop. And the sputtering began.

Then they began to smell smoke.

"Damn," Gillis whispered, strangely. "My kid's playing Little League today."

Ricco didn't even hear him. He was pushing buttons and throwing switches—and making sure the copter's engines were still working right. They were. But they sounded awful.

"Shit, now what?" Ricco was saying more to himself than anything else. This was a real problem. Up to this point, the big Russian chopper had performed nearly flawlessly. Since that first flight from Seven Ghosts, through all the drilling, through the voyage here and the transit to the cliff cave, to the refueling after the raid, the Hook had not given them one whit of trouble.

But now, on their most important mission, the thing had decided to get cranky.

"We still have adequate pressure and adequate juice," Gillis reported, doing a quick diagnostic scan of their controls. "I say we continue."

Ricco just shook his head in disgust. "What other choice do we have? We got to pick up the gas just to get ourselves back to the cave. We ain't got enough to go back, fix this thing, then come out and meet the tanker again."

"Unless we just land near someplace friendly," Gillis said under his breath.

Ricco ignored him because he knew his partner didn't mean it. At least, he hoped he didn't.

They flew on, Ricco doing the piloting, Gillis watching the small laptop that was serving as their navigation system. In ten minutes they were over the deep waters of the Gulf and approaching the rendezvous point—five minutes too early.

This was not a good thing.

"Our gas is so low we must have a fuel leak somewhere," Ricco said, tapping the fuel gauge readout, hoping it would suddenly show more fuel.

Suddenly both of them knew just how valuable they'd been when they were out looking for lost and drained airplanes over the Atlantic. It was not a pleasant feeling to be on the other end.

"Christ," Ricco said, "We're at half reserves. If this keeps up, we might not have any choice but to get our feet wet."

"Not to worry," Gillis said, his voice suddenly calm. "Our friends are here."

Ricco looked up and sure enough, he could see the navigation lights of the refueling tanker. It was a Marine C-130, about a mile ahead and maybe a thousand feet above them, breaking out of a huge cumulous cloud. There were red lights all over it. They began blinking. It was a beautiful sight.

But now came the hard part. Ricco and Gillis had hooked up many times with C-130's during their night drills. But never under real conditions. Essentially, their most important role in the whole mission came down to what they would do in the next five minutes.

They began a series of blinking light signals with the C-130. Altitude, flight speed, and so on were transmitted between the two aircraft. Once all these things were out of the way, the refueling could begin in earnest.

The long snake-like hose began unreeling from the C-130's left wing. Ricco managed to twist the chopper to line up with the fuel hose.

"OK, I need your eyeballs now, Gilly," Ricco said. "Guide me in."

"OK," Gillis said, eyes glued on the hose as they drew closer to it. "Up a hair. Over . . . left. Good! Stay.

Whoops—go up. A little. Little more. There! That's it. You're golden.''

The fuel hose was now right above their heads. Their receptacle was four feet behind their line of sight, but it had a long spout on it and with a jerk of a controls, Ricco slammed the probe into the end of the hose.

"Contact!" Gillis yelled out. The series of green lights popping up on his control window confirmed they were hooked.

Ricco began flipping governor switches now. When they got a clear-flow situation-lamp light, they would know they were ready to take on gas. The light blinked on a second later. Ricco began flashing his nav lights madly. The C-130 pilots flashed theirs in return. A moment later gas began flowing through the C-130's hose into the Hook's receptacle, through the temporary piping, and into the fuel bladders in the back of the huge chopper.

That was when the chopper started sputtering again.

"Sheeeet!" Gillis cursed. "This is not good. . . ."

Suddenly the chopper was all over the sky.

"We're losing power in the left plant!" Gillis yelled to Ricco.

The chopper was now tipping out of balance.

"Damn! The left engine is failing!" Gillis yelled.

Ricco didn't reply. He was too busy trying to hold the chopper steady and hooked to the fuel hose.

"Can this thing fly on just one engine?" Gillis was asking.

They weren't sure.

Now another problem. They could both smell the stink of gas. This was enough to make Ricco take his eyes off the hose hookup and look over at Gillis. There was terror on his partner's face. Fumes were filling the cockpit very rapidly now. But where were they coming from?

"Either one of the fuel bladders is leaking," Gillis said, answering the question before it was asked, "or we got fuel coming out of the failing left-side engine."

"You gotta go check!" Ricco yelled back over to him.

Gillis was already unstrapping from his seat. With the slightest electrical spark, they'd both be blown to Kingdom Come—and probably take the C-130 tanker with them.

Gillis had to crawl back into the rear of the huge chopper on his hands and knees, so violently was the big Hook bouncing all over the sky. Using his penlight, he checked the bladders both front and back. They were slowly filling with the gas from the C-130, just as they were supposed to. The fumes were very thick back here, but he could see no leaks in either of the two huge gas bags.

This was not good. Gillis began crawling back to the cockpit. He'd wished the bags *were* leaking instead of the gas smell coming from the engines. If they had a fuel leak in the power plants, the possibility of an explosion increased about tenfold.

Gillis had trouble getting back into his seat, that was how much the big chopper was jumping all over the sky now. He looked at the fuel-take-on meter and saw they were only halfway through the refueling. The smell of gas was so bad, and the engines' power dropping so quickly, he couldn't imagine them surviving this flight.

"Should we disconnect?" Ricco yelled over to him.

"We've only taken on five hundred pounds," Gillis yelled back. "That's nowhere near enough. We've got to hang with it!"

So that was what they did. They stayed on course, took on gas for the unit, all the while waiting for the bright flash and the searing flames that would so horribly end their lives.

But it never came. The next two minutes passed like an eternity, but finally, the bladders had reached their full point. Now came the tricky part: disengaging. Ricco started easing the chopper away by reducing throttle. With the precision of a surgeon, he gently began extracting their receptacle probe from the fuel hose.

But then Gillis saw a bright flash off to their right. For a moment he thought he was seeing double. Suddenly he realized there was another plane next to the tanker. Another plane that looked just like it.

Another C-130 . . .

There was another flash. Then another. And another.

It was on that third flash that Gillis finally realized what was going on.

"Damn!" he yelled. "It's the freaking ArcLight!"

Ricco looked up and sure enough, saw the ghostly black gunship riding right next to the refueling tanker. Its guns were blazing away at it.

"Christ! *Disconnect!*" Gillis was yelling.

Purely on reaction, Ricco hit the full-disengage button. The Hook's receptacle opened up and the tanker's fuel hose came out, spraying aviation gas everywhere.

The tanker blew up an instant later.

The explosion was blinding. All Gillis could see were pieces of metal and wire and glass flying right at him, all of it on fire.

Somehow Ricco was able to pitch the big chopper away from the gigantic fireball. But it was a very violent maneuver. The fuel bags went one way and the chopper went another, and soon they were looking straight down at the Persian Gulf rushing up at them.

"This is not good!" Gillis was yelling out.

Ricco was battling the controls, but it was already hopeless. The Hook was falling way too fast and weighed too much to get under control.

They'd lost all sight of the ArcLight by now. The sky around them was filled with the burning debris of the C-130 tanker plane. And they were falling with it, very rapidly.

It was strange then, because Ricco just looked over at Gillis and extended his hand. Gillis took it and shook it heartily.

"Sorry, buddy," Ricco said. "I really am. . . ."

Gillis just shook his head as the Hook went nose-over.

"Not your fault, pal," he said calmly. "Not at all . . ."

24

If possible, things were even worse back at the Bat Cave.

It was now 0630 hours. The fuel chopper was so over-due, the unit had given up on it.

What had happened to the Pumper? There was no way of knowing. The unit had no means of getting the Hook on the radio or of getting a message sent by the fuel chopper back to them.

But an even larger problem had arisen.

By an incredible stroke of bad luck, there had been a traffic accident on the one section of the desolate high-way that ran closest to the mouth of the cave on Ka-el. It had happened about an hour after the fuel chopper left. A large truck carrying some kind of liquid had flipped over on the curve, completely blocking the road-way not a half mile from the base of the mountain.

The screech of the truck's brakes had nearly deafened the Marines monitoring the listening devices along the cliff's edge. Immediately turning their NightScopes on the wreck, they saw the driver stumble from his smashed cab and collapse on the side of the road. The Marines simply couldn't believe it. The first vehicle of any type to travel the highway since the unit reached the cave had crashed just a sneeze's length away from their hideout.

Smitz, Chou, Norton, and Delaney were immediately summoned to the ledge. Scanning the area with powerful NightScope binoculars, they could see the truck couldn't have wound up in a worse position: lengthwise, with its cab lodged firmly between two boulders on the north side of the highway and its trailer, twisted and split in two, dug deeply into the asphalt on the south side. The truck was also leaking something—maybe even gasoline, ironically enough. If that ignited, the glow would be seen for miles.

Norton and the others were appraising this sudden crisis when another ominous noise was picked up by the Marines' super-long-range eavesdropping devices. This was a low rumbling sound, mixed with the hum of generator-produced electrical energy. The Marines had heard this combination before. It was the sound of many heavy vehicles moving at once.

All NightScopes turned west, and sure enough, coming over the next hill were the lead elements of an Iraqi military column. With twenty-one T-72 tanks on flatbed trucks out front and dozens of troop trucks bringing up the rear, it was at least a battalion on the move. As the Americans watched helplessly, the column slowly approached the accident site. The lead truck nearly plowed into the wreck. This caused a series of bumper strikes and a storm of screeching brakes all along the convoy. In this manner, the column came to an abrupt stop.

That had been nearly thirty minutes ago, just as the sky was beginning to brighten. Now the highway was simply jammed with Iraqi military vehicles and their occupants, many of whom were out and walking around, trying to figure a way to dislodge the wrecked truck from the roadway.

But it was clear, even from a half mile away, that the Iraqis didn't have a clue what to do. The crashed truck's front half was wedged so firmly between the two rocks, no amount of pulling and pushing could budge it. The trailer itself was so deeply embedded into the macadam, even a hundred men could not move it either. And apparently there was no means to get one of the tanks off its flatbed to do the job.

So, short of turning the column around, the Iraqis were stuck.

All this put the Americans in a very precarious position. They had no fuel left in their choppers, and with no choppers they had no way to get off the cliff. If the Iraqis happened to spot them, it would be a bloodbath. Just the tanks alone carried enough firepower to take out the cave, the cliff, and everyone on it. And if that didn't work, the column's commanders could call in air strikes to finish the job.

What made the whole thing excruciating, though, was the fear that by some cruel miracle, Ricco and Gillis would finally show up. The irony of that possibility was as thick as the early morning mist now rising from the desert. If the tanker pilots didn't return, that meant something catastrophic had happened to them and the unit was stranded. But if by some act of God they *did* appear, the unit's position would undoubtedly be compromised— and they would be trapped and discovered.

Either way, it would be a disaster.

Of course, there was also the possibility of a third scenario.

"You know, those assholes Ricco and Gillis could have just cut out on us and landed somewhere friendly," Delaney hissed over to Norton as they remained crouched in a hidden position along the cliff's edge.

It was now nearly 0700 hours. The sun was almost up, it was even getting hot. The Hook was more than ninety minutes overdue. Norton was still scanning the highway. The Iraqis appeared to be getting a bit restless.

"If that's what those two did, I'd be lying if I said I didn't understand their temptation," he told Delaney finally. "A few hundred miles in any direction and they're out of this bad dream for good."

Delaney just shook his head. "Think they'd have the balls to do it, Jazz? To just to leave us here?" he wondered.

Norton lowered his electronic spyglasses.

"Match it up with what Angel told us," he said, his voice a whisper. "No one who cares knows where we are. If it all ends here for us, who will really give a fuck? In fact, it would be a big help for the people who put us in this wringer in the first place."

Delaney gritted his teeth as he mulled over Norton's grim words.

"I'll haunt those bastards if they turned tail," Delaney said finally. "Their families won't know a minute of peace. I'll be throwing pots around their kitchen; bleeding through their walls. I'll scare the shit out of their kids on a daily basis. I'll be one bad-ass ghost."

"Well, if they did run away, it would actually be better for us than if they showed up now," Norton said. "That looks like half the Iraqi Army out there."

No sooner were those words out of Norton's mouth when Chou ran up to their position, landing in a skid on his chest, knees, and stomach. He was out of breath, covered with dust, his face uncharacteristically dirty.

"My guys just spotted something on the big scope," he gasped. "Sixty degrees east, twenty south . . . below two hundred feet."

Norton put his glasses up and zeroed in on Chou's coordinates. And that was when he saw it. A pinprick of light coming out of the early dawn clouds, heading straight for them.

"Damn . . . is it *really* . . . ?" Norton breathed.

It was the Hook. Even head-on, the huge chopper's profile was unmistakable. But even from this distance it was obvious the chopper was in bad shape. It was trailing heavy smoke and barely flying no more than two hundred feet off the ground.

Even worse, it was heading right for the mountain in full view of the Iraqis on the highway.

Delaney grabbed the glasses and spotted the chopper as well.

"I'll be damned," he said. "*Now* those guys decide to be heroes?"

"Well, that's the end of this ballgame," Chou said. "You might as well get a neon sign and point it at us."

He looked around. "Anyone have any bright ideas?" he asked.

No one said a word. There was nothing they could do.

"We've got to let them land," Norton said finally. "If they don't crash first."

"Yeah, but if they set down here, we'll have a thousand Gomers on top of us before we know it," Delaney replied.

Chou lowered his glasses, turned, and yelled an order to his men. It sounded ominous, like "last-ditch defense posture," or words to that effect. The Marines immediately snapped to. They jumped from their various hiding spots and clustered together, visors down, weapons ready, in a forward trench they'd dug previously along the edge of the cliff. They looked like doughboys awaiting an attack across the fields of the Somme.

"Man, this is getting a bit too dramatic for me," Delaney whispered, checking his own M-16.

"Take notes then," Norton told him. "It will make good copy for your memoirs."

It took about another minute, but the Hook finally went right over the stalled Iraqi column, leaving behind a trail of sparks and very heavy smoke. It did a bone-charring turn to the right and fluttered its way towards the cliff.

While the others watched the stricken chopper, Norton kept his scope on the Iraqis on the highway. Those soldiers he could see looked absolutely baffled. To their eyes, they were looking at one of their own choppers in trouble. But how long would that incorrect assumption last?

When Norton looked up again, the Hook was only a

hundred feet out from the cliff's edge. It was obvious the refueler only had a few more seconds of flying left in it.

So in it came. One engine on fire, the other backfiring like a bad '55 Chevy. It went into a brief hover just above the far lip of the cliff. There was so much smoke pouring out of the chopper, it created a huge black smoke screen that was blowing down with great force on all those waiting below.

"NBW masks!" Chou yelled, and quickly his men were pulling down their gas masks. But Norton and Delaney had no such protection. They were soon engulfed by the maelstrom of exhaust and smoke.

"Jeesuz!" Delaney yelled. "They're *still* trying to kill us, those bastards!"

The Hook came crashing down a second later, not a hundred feet from the trench line. The entire mountain shook from the impact. Everyone hit the deck. The noise was unbearable. Screeching, grinding, the scream of metal twisting as the huge rotor buried itself deep into the hard rock of the cliff. This was all mixed with a bizarre sound similar to that of many huge waves hitting a beach in rapid succession. It was the gas inside the Hook's fuel bags, dangerously sloshing about. Now the cliff was suddenly thick with gas fumes as well as smoke and exhaust.

"Jeesuz!" Chou cried out. "They actually *got* the fuel?"

"Those guys are nuts flying that thing back here!" Delaney added to the din. "One spark and this whole fucking mountain will go up!"

The next thing he knew, Norton was on his feet, running towards the wreck. Air techs were scrambling out of the cave, many with fire extinguishers in hand. They quickly began hosing down the burning aircraft. But there was no sign of movement in the cockpit.

In seconds Norton was boosting himself up onto the twisted wing of the Hook, Delaney close behind. The lower side access door was crumpled. There would be no way of getting in from there. Smoke was pouring from the main cargo bay door. That way was blocked too. Norton only had one other choice. He climbed up to the top of the fuselage and crawled over to the cockpit window itself. He peered inside. He could see Ricco and Gillis, slumped over, still strapped in their seats. They looked dead. The fumes were nearly overwhelming.

Now Delaney was at his side, and together they began pounding on the cockpit glass with their rifle butts. But the strong panes would not budge. No surprise. They were bullet-proof just like the glass on the Hinds.

"What should we do?" Delaney was yelling over at Norton. "We can't shoot it out!"

Suddenly, a fire ax appeared between them. It hit one window with such force, the glass exploded into thousands of pieces. They looked down and saw Smitz standing on the twisted nose below. There was a fire in his eye they'd never seen before.

"C'mon!" he was yelling. "Get them out of there!"

Norton reached through the busted window and grabbed Ricco by the scruff of his neck. The window frame was just large enough to squeeze the injured pilot out, but it was like pulling deadweight. It took all of his strength, but somehow Norton managed to extract him.

Then Smitz hit the next window over with the ax; it too burst in a cloud of tiny pieces. Delaney reached in this hole and pulled Gillis's long lanky frame out. All around them, the air techs were dousing them and the chopper with mountains of foam. The heavy smoke was everywhere—which was a good thing. The haze was so thick it prevented the Iraqis on the highway from seeing the rescue efforts.

Yet no sooner had they lowered both pilots to the ground when Chou ran up. He was coughing from the fumes and smoke; so much, he couldn't talk. So he just pointed to the highway. Norton took one look and immediately felt his heart sink to his boots. A half-dozen trucks had split away from the Iraqi column and were racing for the cliff at full speed.

"We got about five minutes before they get here," Chou finally spat out. "Maybe another five before they realize we ain't towelheads and radio back to the column. Then we're fucked!"

Smitz took a few seconds to appraise the situation, and then nodded in grim agreement.

"There's only one thing we can do," he said.

He turned to the cluster of air techs surrounding the wrecked fuel chopper and yelled his next order at the top of his lungs.

"Start pumping this gas out—*now!*"

Lieutenant Ali Alida el-Sheesh had had a very long day.

He was the officer in charge of the engineering unit attached to the column that was now stalled on Highway 55.

The column had left Abu Ahl earlier the day before, and had been traveling for more than twenty hours when they came upon the jackknifed truck. It was a delay they could not afford. The column was already overdue for exercises in Dawrah, which was a suburb of Baghdad itself. Several troop trucks had already broken down, costing time and patience as the column's commanding officer, the hated Major Tariq Tziz, pondered over which trucks should be fixed and which ones simply pushed to the side of the road to be collected later. The decision on whether a truck was fixable actually came down to Lieutenant Ali and his men. They were called engineers, but in effect they were glorified mechanics. Whenever anything went wrong with the column's vehicles, Major Tziz would call on Ali's troop—and Allah help them if the work wasn't done quickly and efficiently.

So the radio call went back to Ali when the column came upon the overturned truck. Tziz was screaming in the microphone at him as usual, telling him to hurry up. But the top officer had no idea what it was like for Ali to get his men and equipment from the end of the convoy all the way up to the front. Engineers should always be placed at the front of the column, but Tziz considered them too low-class for such an exalted position.

When Ali finally reached the scene of the truck's accident, he was stumped. The truck was twisted in such a way that it could not be straightened out either mechanically or manually. Its gas tank was leaking fuel everywhere, and there was a great danger of fire. So the first thing Ali did was have his men cover the fuel on the roadway with sand. But how to move the huge eighteen-wheel beast? He didn't have a clue.

After studying the situation with Major Tziz and his bad breath breathing down his neck, Ali came to only one conclusion. They couldn't push the truck without significant damage to their own vehicles—even one of the tanks would have a hard time with it, even if they could get one down off its flatbed. They couldn't blow the truck up, as that might damage the road to the extent that the column could not pass at all. They couldn't radio back for a heavy towing vehicle from Abu Ahl, as that would take too long.

In Ali's opinion, then there was only one thing to do. Call ahead to Dawrah and ask that a heavy-lift helicopter be sent to the site. If the chopper's winch could be attached to the truck, it might be able to move it enough to allow the column to pass.

With much huffing and spitting, Major Tziz finally agreed to the plan.

But this was where it really got strange.

No sooner had Major Tziz made the request to Dawrah base, when a helicopter appeared in the sky. It was a heavy-lifter—a Russian-built Hook. Just the type that the column needed to move the disabled truck.

But something was wrong here. There was no way that the message for help could have been acted on so quickly. Secondly, the helicopter looked to be on fire and about to crash.

When the huge chopper flew right over them and continued north, toward the sheer mountain, Major Tziz cried out: "Why does he not land here, with us?"

"Perhaps he is afraid he'll injure us if he crashes," Ali replied.

A few moments later, the helicopter went right into the mountain.

Or so it appeared. Because when the smoke and fire cleared, it seemed as if the chopper might have actually crash-landed. It had not been destroyed—not completely anyway. But it had picked a very inopportune spot to come down on.

That was when Tziz began whacking Ali on the back of his head.

"Don't just stand there!" Tziz was screaming at him. "Go rescue those brave men!"

So now Ali was at the head of a small convoy of trucks filled with mechanics, racing towards the mountain, wondering what the hell he was going to do once he got there. The mountain's face was absolutely sheer, and climbing up to the cliff would be nearly impossible without extensive climbing gear such as ropes and cinches— and maybe not even then.

But Ali was smart enough to know that he would have to give it a try.

So when he and his six trucks arrived at the base of the mountain, he had his men line up. He selected the two smallest, lightest men and told them to start climbing.

Then he radioed back to Major Tziz and told him he had the situation well in hand.

The two climbers got higher than Ali ever thought they would. It was at least eight hundred feet up to the cliff where the helicopter lay burning, and his men reached a point about two hundred feet high, simply by using every rock and handhold possible to them. Ali was heartened for a moment—maybe there actually *was* a way to scale the rock face. He briefly theorized how big this would make him look in Major's Tziz's eyes.

But then his climbers found their climbing was being hampered by something falling on them from above. It was hot and sticky and in a very short time, they discovered it was aviation fuel, trickling down on them from the crash site.

This caused the climbers to quickly retreat back down the way they came. And Ali was back to where he started.

His next idea came when he spotted a substantial outcrop of rock located about one third of the way up the sheer face, and not in the current stream of hot liquid flowing down the mountainside. If he could get a chain up to the outcrop and secure it, his men could climb up and then possibly feel their way up from there.

He sent the two men climbing again, this time with orders just to reach the small ledge with the chain. This they did with remarkable ease. They attached the chain to huge boulder, and now a dozen of Ali's soldiers were scaling the chain. Not wanting to be left behind, Ali was the last one to make the ascent.

Now they were one third of the way up.

But the rocks here were very straight and they were not so good for climbing. However, there was another jagged outcrop about 150 feet above them. Could they get the chain to there?

He selected the strongest man among the twelve, and sure enough, with some lasso motion, and in three tries, this man got the chain to hook onto this new ledge. Now two of his men scampered up, and upon reaching this new high spot, helped the others, including Ali, up to the higher elevation.

Now they were more than two thirds of the way to their goal. Feeling very confident, Ali radioed back to Major Tziz and declared he and his men would gain the cliff within minutes. Tziz's reply was little more than a huff, but this did not dispel Ali's enthusiasm. If he reached the top in time and was able to rescue and give aid to the survivors of the crash, he would have to be recognized by Tziz's superiors, maybe even his unit commander, or the defense minister. Or maybe even Saddam himself.

So now Ali started barking orders, screaming at his men to find another place where they could place the climbing chain. But before these words were fully out of his mouth, the mountain started shaking. . . .

Ali was convinced that he'd had the bad fortune to climb a mountain during an earthquake—that was how violently the rocks beneath his feet were shaking. A storm of dust came down upon them, with smoke and rocks too.

Then he and his men saw an incredible sight—and a unexplainable one as well.

With much noise and exhaust, a helicopter lifted off from the cliff, now just two hundred feet away from Ali's position!

What was this? The chopper they'd seen crash into the cliff certainly was in no shape to take off again. Yet here it was, its engines roaring, its rotors spinning. Passing slowly right above their heads.

This seemed impossible in itself. But then, the mountain began shaking again. The vibrations increased and incredibly, *another* chopper appeared above them. It was as large as the one that had crashed, and was making twice as much noise. No sooner was this aircraft moving away when a *third* aircraft appeared. And then a *fourth*!

Ali was astonished. So were his men. What was going on here? Where were these choppers coming from? It made no sense.

They watched in stunned silence as the four choppers formed up and moved slowly towards the south, passing right over the stalled column again.

Ali's radio began belching, but he was not going to answer it. He didn't have to. He knew it was Tziz. And he was not going to talk to the major until he reached the top of the cliff—and that was what he began urging his men to do.

Somehow, his men got the chain to hook on a rock up on the cliff itself, and soon they were climbing up to the ledge. Ali was the third man to arrive on the cliff, and what he saw here made no more sense than seeing the four mysterious helicopters take off.

Up here the place was littered with shell casings, hoses, buckets, wires, empty chow packs, and puddles of gasoline everywhere. Sitting close to the edge was a helicopter—the one they'd seen crash. It was surrounded by pools of gasoline.

But there was something else. There was a small fire that had been left behind, and it was now following a trail of gasoline that reached about fifty feet into the largest pool of gas surrounding the badly damaged helicopter. Ali had just enough time to yell to his men to get down when the flame reached this pool of gas. A huge explosion shook the cliff once again. A ball of yellow and orange flame mushroomed straight up—taking much of the helicopter and the litter with it.

When it was over and the fire had died down, Ali finally had the courage to call back to Major Tziz.

"What is happening up there!" the major was screaming, so loud Ali imagined he could hear him all the way from the highway without the benefit of the radio.

"I don't not know, sir," Ali replied weakly. "We came up to aid one helicopter and four more appeared and took off. It does not make sense. Now everything is aflame. And if that is not the truth, sir, you may cut out my eyes and tongue."

"That might be just what we do," Tziz replied.

25

Zim had just completed his daily sponge bath when Major Qank came in on his knees.

The intelligence officer took a look at the mammoth Zim sitting atop the mountain of pillows, seven Japanese girls drying his enormous partially clad body, and nearly burst out laughing. This would have been a fatal mistake, of course—but it was hard not to laugh at the huge sultan-wannabe. He looked like a character from a bad science-fiction movie. Qank bit his tongue and waited until the girls had wrapped Zim into his expansive bathrobe. It was a job equivalent to setting up a circus tent.

"This is good news, I hope," Zim finally barked down at Qank.

The intelligence man took this as an opportunity to get off his knees and tiptoe over to the mound of pillows.

"It is, sir," Qank said, holding up the three-ring binder in his hand. "These are the final numbers for our . . . well, our pending sale."

"Of my beautiful gunship?" Zim asked him, sounding almost sincere in his sadness.

"Yes, sir," Qank replied. "And I must say the purchase price is substantial, considering everything involved. Your guest in Room 6 has really done well by us.''

Zim nodded to his squad of sponge girls, and the nubile teens quickly exited the chamber. Another wave from Zim and the two bodyguards left the room as well. Now it was just he and Qank—and the two dozen hidden microphones that recorded everything said inside the vast room.

''Read me the details,'' Zim told Qank with a yawn. ''I'm much too tired to do it myself.''

Qank excitedly opened the binder. ''With pleasure, sir . . .''

He quickly turned through the pages of handwritten notes—the man in Room 6 wrote down everything—and reached the last page.

''You will not be surprised that the gunship purchase is going to the highest bidder,'' Qank began. ''The offer begins with 20 F-14A Tomcat repair kits, complete with new carbon-hardened turbine blades and all-weather NACT weapons-radar retrofits.''

''Good,'' Zim pronounced. ''Continue . . .''

''Offer also includes delivery, over the next eighteen months, of twenty dozen TOW missiles, complete with new refit batteries.''

Qank paused and looked up at Zim, who looked uncharacteristically interested and engaged.

''Go on,'' Zim said. ''Get to the important part.''

Qank took in a deep breath.

''The remainder of the purchase price will be filled out in cash,'' he said.

Zim's left eyebrow arched a bit.

''How much?''

Qank wet his lips and began reading: ''Total cash payment for the gunship will be one hundred million, American, at the dollar-trading price on the Zurich Exchange on a day of your choosing within the next sixty days.''

Zim's eyebrow went up another half inch—a sign he was almost overjoyed.

"I hate to part with it," he finally said. "But we cannot turn down such an offer. The man in Room 6 has indeed served us well."

"He has, sir," Qank parroted.

Zim thought for a few moments.

"What about our camouflage?" he asked Qank.

The intelligence man was slightly confused. "Excuse me, sir."

"You know, for the media—in case word of this ever gets out."

Qank thought a moment—then it hit him.

"You mean the 'cover story,' sir?"

Zim just nodded. Qank had come dangerously close to correcting him.

Qank began flipping through the previous handwritten pages.

"Our friend says: 'If this transaction ever makes it into the public eye, our story will be that it was a secret third-party purchase of ten MiG-29 Fulcrums from an unnamed former Soviet republic.'"

Zim gave a little shrug. "Plausible, I guess," he said. "Now, what about the gunship's crew—the surviving ones anyway?"

Qank turned to another page. "They will be given a cash payment and then dispersed to the four winds."

Zim showed agreement with this also. "And these odd special operations people?" he asked. "The ones in the funny helicopters. The ones so easily fooled. What will happen to them?"

Qank hesitated a moment. It was true. The chopper-borne special operations troops had fallen for the fake-airplane ruse perfectly and completely, filling in several holes the man in Room 6 said had to be filled before the gunship could be sold off.

And although the present location of the American chopper unit was not known at the moment, finding them would not be much of a problem—again, accord-

ing to the man in Room 6. Indeed, since they had learned
the chopper unit was in-country, they had followed the
instructions of Zim's special hotel guest to the letter, and
so far his plans and information had been flawless. Why
would they doubt him now?

So Qank said: "The man in Room 6 has come up
with a rather creative solution as to what to do with these
helicopter people. I can tell you his idea now, sir, or
wait until it has been completed."

"I'll wait," Zim replied. "It will make more plea-
surable listening that way."

Now came several long minutes of complete silence.
All Qank could hear was Zim's labored breathing.

Finally the big man came back to life.

"All right, accept the offer," he declared. "I will
miss my lovely gunship. But it has made us substantial
sums in the past two years, and has served us well. Now,
even in getting rid of it, it is giving us a big return. I
think it's a good deal."

"I agree, sir," Qank toadied. "Shall I let the man in
Room 6 go ahead with the final arrangements then?"

Zim simply nodded. "Yes, and be sure to thank him
profusely for me. Send some nonalcoholic champagne
to his room. I know he just loves that stuff."

Qank did a deep bow. Time to get out.

"As you wish, sir," he said, backing up.

He was almost out the door when Zim cleared his
throat—a signal that Qank should freeze.

"One last thing," Zim said. "How is that cash payment going to be made?"

Qank began sifting madly through the handwritten
notes. He just hoped he could find the answer before
Zim lost his notoriously short temper.

He finally found the right page; it was covered with
scribbling, obscene doodles, and many, many numbers.
But at the bottom was the information Zim wanted to
know.

"The payment will be secured through a series of
wire transactions," he began reading. "Through the

usual avenues in the Cayman Islands, Hong Kong, and finally on to Zurich.''

To Qank's amazement, Zim actually laughed. A full, burst-out guffaw from the huge man was rather frightening.

''Do you realize how I was paid the first time by these people who are now buying the gunship?'' he asked Qank.

The intel man numbly shook his head. Was Zim actually going to reminisce with him?

''No, sir,'' Qank whispered.

''It was back in the late seventies,'' Zim began, looking at the ceiling. ''A minor transaction. An exchange of a SCUD missile for F-14 parts, coincidentally enough, with some money on the side. And those fools actually sent me a check! And a birthday cake! Can you believe it?''

Qank started laughing now for real—not so much that some government would make payment to Zim for a back-alley arms deal by check, but that they would send him a birthday cake along with it.

''I'm sure that won't happen this time,'' Qank told him. ''After all, they are just buying back what was once theirs in the first place. I have to believe they will want to cover their tracks better than that.''

Zim laughed again.

''Never underestimate the U.S. Government, Major,'' he said. ''You never know what they'll do next.''

26

Over central Iraq

Considering what it had been through, Truck One was flying just fine.

The troop-carrying Halo stank of aviation fuel—the entire unit had smelled of gas since the mad rush to refuel the four choppers on the cliff. But the chopper was cruising along without a hint of trouble now, and for that Gene Smitz was grateful.

He was shoehorned into a seat at the back of the chopper jammed up with half of the Team 66 Marines, most of the air techs, and two of the SEAL doctors. Most of his fellow passengers were asleep; the others were crowded around the chopper's windows, looking out for any trouble that might be following them.

Meanwhile, Smitz was trying like crazy to get his NoteBook to work.

They'd been airborne for about a half hour now, and it had been aces since their daring escape from the mountain. No one was following them. They'd received no SAM warnings or any warnings of hostile intent from the ground or the air.

But Smitz knew this was definitely a temporary situation. Thus the wrestling match with his laptop.

Since the mission began, he'd been receiving his orders directly from his office via the NoteBook. That was one of the beauties of the highly advanced machine. It had a remote modem and could connect him with his office no matter where he was in the world.

Of course, he didn't know who was on the other end of the pipeline. He never received any direct replies to his situation reports—and that was slightly troubling. But his missives were always followed by more orders. That was why Smitz was so anxious to get through to his office now. He had to apprise them of the new situation, and ask for immediate orders in extracting the unit—something he just didn't have the authorization to do himself. He'd been waiting for a small green light to start blinking in the upper left-hand corner of his screen, telling him a line to Langley was secure and clear. Yet in nearly thirty minutes of trying, that little light was still solid red.

He was distracted for a moment when he looked out the window to see Norton's Hind pull up in a protective position next to the Halo. Though they'd only been in-country two days, Smitz thought the Hind looked somewhat battered, used, as if it too was getting tired of this game. He also knew that its guns were nearly empty of ammo—the same with Delaney's machine. What's more, both Hinds were running on only half fuel. The rushed refueling job back on the mountain had given each of the four remaining choppers barely enough gas to get airborne and out of the immediate area, but not much more. Certainly not enough to reach friendly environs.

That was another reason why Smitz had to get new orders very quickly. There would be no more fuel to be had for them—not with the Hook gone. And they couldn't just fly around Iraq forever. They needed an extraction plan now.

So Smitz closed his eyes and for the first time in years, actually whispered a small prayer.

And when he looked down at his laptop screen again, the little green light was blinking.

He began typing madly, nearly forgetting to hit the scramble-mode button first. He quickly gave the unit's present position, then briefly reviewed what had happened. The raid on the Ranch, the empty prison, the dead Americans. He covered the details of their escape from the mountain in a few succinct words, and made no mention of his suspicions that the entire operation had been compromised. He concluded by asking for further instructions as soon as possible.

Then he hit the Send button.

Then he sat back to wait.

Smitz's message beamed up directly from his modem to a top-secret military satellite called the Red Door 3, some five hundred miles above the Earth. It was then bounced off no less than four other communications satellites, before being sent down to CIA headquarters in Langley, Virginia.

No human ever responded to Smitz's message, though. A computer had been awaiting a transmission—any transmission—from the unit, and now that it had arrived, the computer was sending back a response that had been entered into its hard drive several hours before.

The message told the unit to proceed to a point on the map known as El-Saad Men. This was an abandoned Iraqi Air Force base located in what was possibly the most barren part of the very barren central Iraqi desert.

Once there, the unit was to hide the choppers inside the most intact hangar on-site, and remain inside themselves until egress transportation arrived. The designated hangar would be easy to spot, as a large arrow was said to be painted on its roof.

This message made the return route up from Langley, to the four military bounce satellites, over to Red Door 3, and down to Smitz's NoteBook in less than one minute.

The CIA man was stunned when he looked down

sixty seconds later and saw his green light was blinking again. Nothing ever happened *that* fast. But when he read the message, he felt his heart lighten by a couple hundred pounds.

The words "egress transportation" were the most heartening part of the lone stark paragraph. It was official then. The unit was being pulled out of Iraq, a prospect that Smitz was sure would be greeted with much joy among the others. Had they accomplished their mission? No. Had they affected anything by coming deep into Iraq and raiding the Ranch? No. But would they be glad to get out of hostile territory after nearly forty-eight hours of pure nonstop anxiety?

Definitely.

Smitz shut down the laptop and began crawling through the sprawled Marines, telling them that things were looking up—unofficially, of course—and that they should get ready "for anything."

He finally made his way up to the cockpit and asked the Army pilots to pull close to Norton's Hind, now riding about 250 feet off the left nose.

The pilots nuzzled up to the chopper, and using a trouble light, Smitz sent a hasty Morse code message over to Norton. It took two attempts for the former fighter pilot to blink back that he understood. Then, in a burst of enthusiasm, he gunned the Hind and started wigwagging all over the sky. Obviously Norton was happy at the prospect of going home too.

Then Smitz blinked over the coordinates to the abandoned base at El Saad Men. A quick check of the aviation chart showed it was about twenty minutes of flying time away from their present location. Getting there would be a breeze compared to what they'd been through. Smitz asked Norton to fly ahead and scout out the location first.

Norton blinked back his reply, gunned the Hind's engines again, and was off like a shot.

Then Smitz returned to his cramped seat in the cargo bay, and for the first time in forty-eight hours, actually fell asleep.

27

El-Saad Men was an air base—or it used to be—located in the Tajji section of the central Iraqi desert, near the edge of Tharthar wadi.

Built a few months before the start of the Gulf War, it was little more than a pair of runways, a dozen support buildings, and three hangars. It had been designed for use as an alternative base for Iraqi fighters to transit to— a haven after a day of battle. But the base was knocked out the first night of the war by French fighters dropping Chaparral runway-busting bombs. Several times thereafter it was the target of follow-up Coalition air strikes.

Now El-Saad Men was a ghost town, literally. The runways were still cratered, and indeed only one hangar remained intact. The rest were just piles of rubble, victims of precision bombs dropped nearly a decade before.

This was the desolate scene Norton came upon when he reached the coordinates given to him by Smitz. At once he knew the base was the perfect place for the egress pickup. They could easily hide the choppers inside the last hangar standing—the one with the big ar-

row on top of it—and no one would know they were
there unless they came up and knocked on the front
door.

Still, he swept over the abandoned base several times,
making sure there was no unfriendlies around; making
sure there were no hidden weapons painting him. Once
he was certain of this, he turned back and met the rest
of the unit about fifteen miles east of the abandoned
base. He pulled up alongside Truck One and delivered
a nav light Morse code message.

"Looks good," he blinked. "Suggest we put down
ASAP."

Inside of fifteen minutes, they had done just that.

They landed with no problems, and the huge choppers
were pushed inside the last remaining hangar. It was a
tight fit, but with some creative angling, all four finally
squeezed in.

Now all they had to do was wait. And pray.

Ricco and Gillis were still in bad shape. The SEAL
doctors had treated them throughout the escape flight,
giving them oxygen and bandaging the multitude of
wounds both men had sustained in the crash landing on
the mountain. They had been taken out of their fuel-
drenched flight suits and put into spares rounded up from
others in the unit. Both pilots were now lying on makeshift stretchers, clad in Army T-shirts, Marine pants, and
Air Force underwear.

Only now were they able to tell their tale to Smitz,
Norton, Delaney, and Chou.

Though the Hook had developed engines problems en
route, their refueling went well, they said. But then the
ArcLight gunship showed up and blew the C-130 refueler out of the sky, taking the Hook down with it—or so
it must have appeared. The chopper *was* mortally
wounded and going down fast. But that was when Ricco
did a very strange thing: He *turned off* the Hook's one
good engine about five thousand feet from impact. Killing the engine allowed the rotor's kinetic motion to level

them out—an old chopper trick Ricco had somehow picked up. It saved their lives. Once the chopper was stable, he was able to restart the engine, and it gave them enough power to stay airborne—but just barely. It was all they could do to keep the chopper at two hundred feet altitude.

They made the dash back to the Bat Cave, flying perilously low over villages, highways, army encampments. Thus their rather spectacular arrival back at the not-so-hidden mountain base. Everything was rather foggy after that.

This tale took about twenty minutes to tell. Neither man could get out a complete sentence without requiring a fix from the SEALs' emergency oxygen tank. Ricco was especially woozy.

After hearing the story, Norton pulled Delaney away from the rest of the group.

"Well, what do you think?" he asked his partner.

"I think they're delirious," Delaney told him. "Do you really believe those two have all that in them?"

Norton shrugged and looked back at the two ailing pilots.

"They came down to the deck when we needed them that night during Desert Storm," he said. "And it would have been damn easy for them to have just plunked down someplace close to Kuwait and walked across the border."

Delaney took another look back at the pilots. They'd inhaled a lot of fumes and their skin had been drenched with aviation gas, not exactly a healthy situation.

"God, you mean I'm going to have to start admiring these guys now?" he asked.

"Someone has to be a hero in this big fat waste of time," Norton said, his tone turning bitter. "At least they might have a chance to keep flying. As for you and me, we'll be lucky if they let us shovel shit somewhere."

"I can handle that," Delaney replied.

But one aspect of the tanker pilots' story raised a very

disturbing question. Norton and Delaney were now joined by Chou and Smitz in the most isolated corner of the abandoned hangar to discuss it.

"Do you think these guys are hallucinating and just imagined the ArcLight killed their tanker?" Smitz asked under his breath. "Gas fumes can do that to you, I hear. Make you see things."

"That part of their story really doesn't make much sense," Chou said in a whisper. "I mean, how would the ArcLight know that the Hook was refueling and where to go to find it?"

The four men just stared at each other. Not liking what they were thinking.

"Turn it around, though," Smitz said. "Say it *was* true—why would the ArcLight go after the tanker?"

"Unless they were going after both the tanker *and* the Hook," Norton said grimly.

"Which means they really know what we've been up to," Chou said.

A dreadful silence fell among them.

Finally Delaney broke it.

"Listen, I've been trying to hold this in," he began. "But I think now is the time to speak my piece . . . any objections?"

Norton eyed him sternly. *Don't tell them about Angel*, he was trying to say.

"Go ahead, do it," Smitz told him.

"OK," Delaney began. "Let's look at the forest instead of the trees for a moment. I have a theory this program has been screwed up from the start. Anyone else thinking along those lines?"

"I thought you were going to tell us something we *don't* know," Chou said snidely.

"No—I mean screwed up *from the start*," Delaney said. "From day one."

Smitz wiped his tired eyes. Chou leaned back against a partially shattered wall. They knew this might take a while.

"OK," Smitz said. "Let's hear it."

Delaney took a deep breath and collected his thoughts.

"From the start," he repeated. "You got me and Jazz. We're fighter pilots—why have us come in, learn how to fly the choppers?"

"Because you scored high on the PS2," Smitz replied. "Your profiles said you could both adapt."

"Oh, that's bullshit!" Delaney shot back. "You're telling me that they couldn't find any *real-life* chopper pilots who could do the job as well as us?"

It *was* a good question.

"Apparently not," Smitz replied.

Delaney nodded over to the other side of the hangar, where the Army Aviation guys were sitting.

"Then what the hell are those guys doing here?"

The others just stared and let it sink in.

Delaney was on a roll.

"Point two," he began again, gathering steam. "We're in choppers here—but we've got a pack of Marines. Marines are usually good—and these Team 66 guys are great. But correct me if I'm wrong, don't Marines usually jump out of boats? Army guys are better at jumping out of choppers, right?"

The three others nodded. Again Delaney was making sense.

"Point three," he went on. "And no offense to Mutt and Jeff. But really, if you had a mission that was supposed to be this important, would you pick two National Guard guys to be your fill-up men? Two weekenders who have never flown choppers before?"

More nods.

"And SEAL doctors?" Delaney said. "I mean, don't you jarheads have your own corpsmen?"

Chou nodded. "We do," he said.

Delaney looked them all in the eye.

"Don't you get it?" he was imploring them. "This thing was fucked up from the start because it was *meant* to be fucked up. All these things we thought had some deep dark meaning behind them were actually roadblocks put in our path, so we wouldn't succeed. They probably thought we'd be at each others' throats more than actually drilling for the mission. That we were able to overcome everything they threw at us—well, I mean, what does that say about us?''

"That we should all get medals," Chou said.

"At the very least," Delaney said with disgust. "We've been set up, I'm convinced of it, but not just on the raid. From the first moment of this plan's existence. Someone knew this gunship was flying around and knew it had to be stopped. But for whatever reason, they didn't want it to be stopped. Yet they had to turn some wheel, had to push some button, to make it *look like* something was going to be done. So what do they do? They put together an interservice F-Troop—never in a million years thinking that we'd get as far as we have."

"Jesus Christ," Smitz swore softly. "I'm starting to believe him."

"I mean, let's really get back to ground zero," Delaney concluded. "If they really wanted this thing to go down, they would have done what we were all saying at the first briefing. Just send in some fighters and shoot the fucking thing out of the sky."

Now the silence was so thick it was like a veil had come down around them. Norton and Delaney looked at each other. Both were thinking the same thing: Was it time to come clean on Angel?

Delaney had one more thing to add, though. "I think now we have to go on the assumption that everything they've sent us has been skewered intentionally."

He paused.

"And if that is true, what was the last order they gave us?"

Now a wave of high anxiety washed through them. If every order had been compromised from the beginning, what did that say about their latest instructions?

But before anyone could say another word, something very strange happened: A knock came at the door.

It was such a surprise, Norton actually mouthed the

words: "Someone is knocking? At the door?"

It came again. Everyone tensed. Marines grabbed their weapons.

"Who the fuck is this?" Delaney asked. "The Mad Hatter?"

Chou barked a silent order, and in a snap the six Marines closest to the small access door had it covered, their rifles up and ready.

"Open it," Chou told them.

They did—and standing on the other side was a face familiar to all of them—most especially Norton and Delaney.

It was Angel.

"You've got to be kidding me," Smitz exclaimed. "How the *fuck* did *you* get here?"

"Never mind that," Angel said worriedly. "We've got to talk."

28

It was difficult but not impossible to operate the AC-130 gunship with only four people on board.

The plane could be flown by one person; two were required only for landings and takeoffs, and maybe not even then. And the plane's vital signs could be monitored on a periodic basis instead of having one person dedicated to that one job. And if the ECM suite was not in use, there was no reason to have a body praying over that either.

It was the aircraft's massive weaponry that needed the manpower.

The good thing was all three miniguns and the howitzer were computer-guided, computer-aimed, and computer-fired, as were their rearming systems. The bad thing was, the four remaining members of the Arc-Light's flight crew—the pilot, copilot, flight engineer, and loadmaster—were Air Force guys. Not one of them had the computer knowledge needed to fire the guns.

But together, the four of them had been able to cook up a way to get the weapons to fire semi-manually. In effect they had rigged a system whereby the guns would

fire on a timed command—and that command could be
sent by the pilot when he was able to get the plane into
position above their next target.

In order to do this, though, they had been forced to
erase a large portion of the weapon computer's original
firing commands, along with a ton of secondary and
backup commands.

But what difference did that make?

As far as they were concerned, this would be the last
time they would be operating the gunship.

At this time tomorrow, they would be gone—pockets
full of money—to places unknown.

They just had to hit this one last target.

That target was now just five minutes away.

It was ironic that they had been vectored to this part
of Iraq. Years before, the gunship had flown this sector
many times looking for SCUDs or other targets of opportunity. As they flew over these familiar parts once
again, it was almost as if the aircraft recognized its old
turf. There were the Tajji Mountains over there. The
Samarra dry river over there. The valley known as Ta-
wiq Cha was over there. And out on the horizon, coming
into range soon, was the air base, now abandoned,
known as El-Saad Men.

The main hangar stuck out like a sore thumb. It was
the only building standing in the ten-year-old rubble of
the base, the only structure that could be identified so
quickly from ten thousand feet.

Upon seeing it, the pilot lowered the gunship's altitude to 3,500 feet in a hurry, putting the ArcLight into
a dive so severe the other three crewmen had to hold on
for dear life. But it was a jovial plunge—one last time
on the Space Hog roller coaster.

Inside of sixty seconds, the airplane was in position
over the hangar. There was even a large arrow painted
on its rooftop. It couldn't have made a better bull's-eye.

"OK there's your mark," the pilot called back to his
"rookie" gunners. "Let's do a half-rotation, thirty-

second burst with the minis. Then we'll go around again and try the popgun.''

The three men in the rear weapons bay radioed ahead that they got the order. Now they had to see whether their jerry-rigged computer command would work. They felt the pilot dip the plane's left wing. Looking out the window, they could at last see the hangar themselves.

"OK, let's give it a shot," one said.

The second man did a mock sign of the cross and hit a button—just one of many on the firing panels connected to the three-minigun setup. There was a slight delay—almost too long. But then an amber light blinked on, indicating the pilot had punched in his timed-sequence command.

Five seconds later, to their great surprise, the three miniguns opened up full force.

The noise was sudden and the vibration so intense, it nearly knocked all three men on their rears. But they were laughing at the same time.

"It worked!" two yelled at once. "The fucking guns worked!"

"What did we need those other nine assholes for all this time!" the third joked.

Meanwhile, the miniguns were doing their deadly task. It was strange, but the worst vantage point to see how the target was faring was from the back of the gunship itself—especially in the first few seconds of a sequence. But as the airplane began to move around its semicircle and the three streams of fire combined into one and formed an arc, the rookie gunners could see at last the storm of lead tearing up the hangar with routinely chilling efficiency.

At the end of the thirty-second fusillade, the pilot twisted the airplane level again and called back for an assessment. The gunners looked out and saw that half the hangar was literally blown away and the other half was on fire. "Must have been a secondary within," one man yelled ahead to the cockpit.

The pilot laughed at this joke, and then brought the airplane down to 1500 feet.

"Let's fire up the popgun," he said, referring to the howitzer. "We'll use up whatever shells are left in the chamber feed and then get the hell out of here."

The gunners did as told. They hit a separate timed order for the howitzer, and soon it was firing away with its usual swooshing noise.

The streams of artillery shells made a longer arc than the miniguns. They exploded with great flare on impact, the result of their high-explosive warheads. It took but another twenty seconds—and 21 shells—to obliterate the rest of the hangar.

Then the pilot called back the cease-fire order. Then he straightened the airplane out again.

He looked out his side window and saw that where the huge hangar had stood just two minutes before, now was a raging fire encompassing a pile of rubble. Nothing inside, man or metal, could survive that, he knew.

Of course, he'd seen it all before.

"Good job, boys," he called back to the firing cabin. "Let's go home."

There was a sense of gaiety inside the cockpit of the AC-130 gunship now.

The aircraft had settled in at 5,500 feet in altitude and had reached its cruising speed of two hundred knots. The heavy plane was much easier to handle now because of all the ammunition just expended. In fact, the ride home was always smoother—and satisfying too. After a successful mission, it was always a pleasant feeling to go home with an empty belly.

All this was something they might eventually miss, the four crewmen had mused earlier. After ten years, the old habits would be hard to break. But they had little to complain about. Eight years of living in luxury at Zim's Hotel; another two fixing up and then flying the great gunship again. The money had been good. The food great; the booze better.

With just one day left, they only had one real regret. If only they had been able to score some women along the way . . .

But little did they know that this perverse tour of duty was coming to an end sooner than they thought.

The first indication that something was not right came from the crew's flight engineer. He'd been relaxing at his station, feet up, eyes closed, fighting off sleep.

Suddenly the radio in front of him burst to life with a howl of static. It jolted the engineer back to reality. His radio panel was lighting up like a Christmas tree. Red lights, green lights, blue ones too. All of them blinking madly.

"What the fuck?"

Then came some shouting. The loadmaster was trying to yell something up to the flight deck. The engineer took his eyes off his equipment, looked down into the weapons bay, and saw his colleague at the side window pointing at something off their left wing.

A moment later the engineer heard the copilot swear.

"Jeesuz . . . What the fuck is . . . ?"

That was when the airplane started bucking; it was so bad at first, the engineer had to hold on. The plane straightened out a bit a few seconds later, but the engineer could detect a wave of tension suddenly crackling through the ship.

He unstrapped, made his way back to the weapons bay window, and finally saw what all the commotion was about.

It was a helicopter, riding no more than twenty-five feet off their left wing. It was pale brown and red, with a strange bubble nose and long tail section. It was a two-man aircraft, but only one person could be seen on board. It was painted in Iraqi markings, but the pilot was definitely not an Iraqi. He clearly had red hair and a Caucasian complexion. In fact, he looked like an old-time cowboy. What kind of helicopter was it? The engineer didn't know one chopper from the other, but he believed this thing was a Russian-built Hind.

But what was it doing out there? It was so close to their wing, one wrong move and they would surely collide with it. And the way its pilot was flying seemed crazy. The chopper was all over the sky, going up and down, back and forth, flashing its nav lights wildly. The pilot himself was particularly animated. He was waving his arms, giving them the finger, and seemed to be shouting something at them. There was only one word describe his bizarre behavior: He was *taunting* them.

The engineer quickly climbed up to the flight deck, and now both pilots were looking out at the strange chopper.

"Who the hell is *this* guy?" the copilot was yelling. His name was Pete Jones.

"Beats me," the engineer replied. "But he skewered the comm set, he came up on us so fast."

Jones turned to the man riding in the AC-130's other control seat. This was Colonel Jeff Woods, the buzz-cut John Glenn lookalike.

"What'll we do, Woodsie?" Jones asked him.

Woods looked out at the chopper and then settled back into his seat.

"Well, let's see if you boys can shoot him down," he said calmly.

It took about a minute and a half to power up the three miniguns again; they'd all been shut down at the completion of the attack on the hangar at El-Saad Men air base.

Now the flight engineer and the loadmaster struggled to push the right panels and flip the right switches and reboot the right computers. Somehow, ninety seconds later, the weapons systems all came on-line.

The strange chopper had cooperated in this endeavor by not for a moment diverting from its strange behavior. It was still riding off the left wing, still flying in a weirdly provocative manner.

The ArcLight's makeshift gun crew was now facing an unusual situation. The orders from the flight deck said shoot the asshole down, so that was what they were going to try to do. But the miniguns were designed mainly to fuck up big targets on the ground. Hardened stuff, troops concentrations, general populations. Static stuff. Things that were standing still.

Shooting down another C-130 had taken some finesse. Could they really nail something relatively small and agile as a chopper?

They would soon find out. . . .

It was just fate that Colonel Woods was riding in the copilot's slot when all this happened.

He and Jones usually switched off and on for piloting missions. This particular day it had been Woods's time at the stick, but after the attack on El-Saad Men was through, they had switched seats.

So for this curious engagement, Woods was relegated to observer status. Jones would have to try and keep the gunship steady while the two men in back fired on the mysterious helicopter. For this, the copilot's seat had the worst vantage point. Woods couldn't see the chopper, nor would he be able to see the guns when they went off. He really could do little else but sit back and just listen to what was going on.

That was why it was so strange then that he happened to glance out at the right wing and saw someone staring back in at him.

He nearly crapped his pants. It was another helicopter—another Hind. It was flying so close to the right side of the airplane, Woods could see the pilot looking in at him, not twenty-five feet away. The guy was handsome—almost like a movie star.

Woods tried to cough out a warning or something, but everyone else on the plane was concerned with the wacky chopper off their left wing, the side where the miniguns were located. So Wood just sat there for an instant or two, gaping at the second helicopter and wondering whether he was seeing things.

And in this odd stupor he saw the chopper get even

closer. At the same time he watched as the chopper pilot opened the little side panel window on the Hind's cockpit. Then he saw the pilot sticking something out of the window.

Then he saw a tremendous burst of light—it was a muzzle flash from a gigantic pistol.

The huge bullet shattered the AC-130's right-side glass panel and struck Woods square on the temple. He felt the bullet enter his skull and explode his cranium outward. More shots were fired. The airplane's control panel was suddenly coming apart. Then Woods looked down and saw blood falling in great splats on his lap, on his knees, and all over the steering column.

Then he saw nothing but red.

Then nothing but black . . .

Zim was reading a copy of *The Wall Street Journal* when Major Qank showed up with the bad news.

The doors to the great chamber opened, but in a grand lapse of protocol, Qank did not come in on his knees. In fact he strode in, very quickly, and walked right up to Zim's mound of pillows. His teeth were clenched.

The Japanese girls saw his transgression and immediately scattered. They didn't want be around when Zim realized one of his many rules had been so flagrantly broken.

Qank stared up at Zim for a few moments and then clapped his hands twice, very hard.

It was enough to cause Zim to lower the newspaper. Still, it took a few seconds for him to figure out what was happening. He stared down at Qank, a blank expression on his face.

"Yes? What is going on here, Major?" he asked, regaining his composure.

"Bad news, sir," Qank said, quickly correcting himself: "I mean, *possibly* bad news."

Zim was mystified. "What is it?"

Qank took a deep breath.

"Sir, we've lost radio contact with the gunship."

Zim seemed even more perplexed. He folded the newspaper neatly on his lap.

"Has that ever happened before?" he asked.

Qank had to shake his head no. "They have always kept in touch, through either their passive or active radios," he said. "But now all four lines are dead."

Zim pulled his chin in thought, absentmindedly glancing at a story about Indonesian gas reserves.

"Do you think something might have happened to the airplane?" he asked. "Could it have crashed?"

Qank could only shrug. "Impossible to say, sir," he replied.

Zim went right on talking: "Because if it crashed, well, that would—how do you say it?—*queer* the deal we want to make. The one-hundred-million-dollar sellback? It would be *queered*?"

Qank almost laughed at the vast understatement.

"I would say that is an accurate assumption, sir," he replied.

Zim motioned for his two bodyguards to come forward. Qank did not notice the gesture.

"What do you suggest we do now then, Major?" he asked Qank.

Qank was prepared for this.

"I suggest we put all our security assets here on full alert, sir, until we re-establish radio contact with the gunship," he said.

"Full alert?" Zim asked. "Here? Why?"

Qank began shuffling his feet a bit.

"Just a precaution, sir," he replied. "The Americans have been unpredictable lately. You never know—they may even attack."

Zim was surprised to hear this word.

"Attack? Here?" he said. "I thought that was impossible."

Qank just shuffled his feet a little more. "Nothing is impossible sir." he said. "And I might add—nothing lasts forever."

Zim smiled a bit now. "That's for sure," he said.

He nodded to the guard who had silently placed a pistol at the back of Qank's head. The man pulled the trigger and Qank's throat exploded in a cloud of bone and red mist. The bodyguard then lowered the gun and put another bullet into the small of Qank's back. This round went through his lungs and demolished his heart. He was dead before he hit the floor.

Zim leaned back in his pillow and picked up *The Wall Street Journal* again.

"Clean that up," he ordered his guards. "And then prepare the compound for an attack. Whatever *that* means."

29

Norton was the first one on the scene after the ArcLight gunship went down.

He found it on the edge of a huge onion field inside a shallow valley about fifty kilometers north of El-Saad Men air base. It had come to rest at the edge of the long, narrow farming area, its extended nose barely touching a small road that ran into a small village nearby. It was rather amazing: Somehow the plane had found the softest piece of ground in a thousand square miles on which to land.

Norton roared low over the gunship. The pistol Delaney had given him had proved to be just enough weapon to finally bring down the flying monster. He was sure he'd killed at least one of the pilots, and that he'd wreaked havoc on the gunship's control board as well. Destroying the plane was never really his intention. That would have sealed forever a few secrets he was determined to uncover.

No—the plan all along was to disable the gunship, not kill it. Norton could tell now that the plan had worked. The plane had not crashed. Rather someone had landed it here, and had done a great job of it too.

And that meant someone was still alive on board.

The other choppers were soon on the scene.

Both Halos descended quickly; Norton followed them in. Delaney continued circling overhead watching for any unfriendlies.

No sooner had the Halos touched down when the Marines were jumping out of them and slowly enveloping the downed gunship. From ground level it was obvious that the plane was in remarkably good shape. A slight wisp of smoke was coming from its left outboard engine, and one of its tires had blown. But it had landed with its gear fully deployed and there was absolutely no damage to its propellers.

By the time Norton had climbed out of his Hind, Smitz and Chou were waiting for him.

"Look at the way they came in," Smitz said. "They thought they were going to take off again."

"The arrogant bastards," Chou cursed. "You can be sure that ain't going to happen."

Chou gave his men the signal to move in, and within seconds the plane was completely surrounded with heavily armed Marines. They were careful to avoid the left-side fuselage windows where the three miniguns and the howitzer were still in evidence.

"What do we do now?" Smitz asked Chou. "Yell, 'Come out with your hands up'?"

"No need," Chou replied. "Look."

The Marines had opened the rear left side door and three men were standing at it. They did indeed have their hands up.

The Marines pulled them out of the airplane, one by one, throwing them to the ground and frisking them. The trio was wearing U.S. Air Force flight suits. Not the modern multi-pocket space-suit type the chopper unit wore. No, these were of a design not seen in ten years or so.

"Jeesuz," Smitz said. "So they *are* Americans."

"They're three of the last four," Norton replied. "Just like Angel said."

Chou walked over to them.

"Name, rank, and serial number," he demanded of them.

The three men laughed at him. They were sitting up, legs crossed, by now.

"Who's working for the Agency here?" one man asked in a distinctive Southern drawl. Norton recognized him. He had dreamed about his wife. His name was Pete Jones.

"Name, rank, and serial number," Chou said again.

The men laughed again.

"Look, we're kind of tired here," Jones said. "And our boss, Colonel Woods, well, he's having a *really* bad hair day."

At this point Norton and two Marines climbed into the gunship and made their way up in to the cockpit. Sure enough, there was the guy named Woods, half his head blown off. There was extensive damage to the flight controls as well. Jones had landed the airplane here on the bare minimum.

They went back outside, and the three survivors were still joking around. They were making faces at the Marines, laughing at their own comments to each other, and asking for cigarettes. The Marines around them remained stone-faced and tight-lipped.

"OK, look," Jones said finally. "Just get us a phone or something and let us make a call. We'll straighten this whole thing out, then we'll let you guys buy us a beer."

But Chou was suddenly in his face.

"Straighten out killing more than a thousand innocent people? Straighten out sinking a U.S. Navy ship? And trying to kill us?"

Jones just laughed again. They all did.

"Well, damn, don't take it personally, man," he said. "We were just doing a job. Everyone at the Agency knew about it. Everyone who was high enough on the totem pole, that is . . .''

Suddenly three shots rang out.

Jones's face was blown away in an instant. The man next to him took a bullet behind his ear. The third man got it right between the eyes. Everyone spun around. The Marines all went down to one knee. Only one man was left standing in the onion field, a smoking M-16 in his hand.

It was Smitz.

"Fuck all three of you,'' he said, staring at the dead men. "No one told *me*. . . .''

Twenty minutes later, Norton, Delaney, Chou, and Smitz were huffing and puffing, climbing a steep hill about a quarter mile from the onion field.

Everything that had happened in the past hour had been Angel's doing. He had saved their lives by tipping them off about the pending gunship attack. They had had to scramble so quickly getting out of the hangar and into the sky, there had not been enough time for him to tell them all he knew or why he had decided to spill it to them in the first place.

So he told them he would met them on the highest piece of climbable ground nearest to where the C-130 came down, twenty minutes after the event.

And now, here they were, climbing up the steep, sandy hill just west of the onion field. They finally reached the top and sure enough, Angel was waiting for them.

"I've got about ten minutes,'' the mysterious man told them straight out. "Then I've got to be somewhere else.''

"Tell us everything you can in ten minutes then,'' Norton urged him. "And start with what you told me and Slick on the mountain the other night.''

Angel did just that, relating his suspicions to Chou and Smitz about the failed raid and why he thought the mission had been doomed from the start.

Then he elaborated further.

"But not only were you guys patsies," he went on.
"The genius behind it all was willing to kill you, simply
because you became an inconvenience. A holdup in a
business transaction."

"Business transaction?" Delaney asked. "What are
you talking about?"

"They were in the process of buying the gunship back
for the U.S.," Angel told them starkly. "Covering the
deal like they were actually buying some old Fulcrums
from Monrovia."

The four men were stunned.

"*Buying* it back?" Norton couldn't believe it.

Angel just shrugged.

"What better way to get it out of circulation?" he
asked. "The enemy you own isn't your enemy anymore."

"But buying it back?" Chou asked again. "After all
the misery it caused? Man, that's cold. . . ."

"True," Angel said. "But it's also business."

"How much were they going to pay for it?" Delaney
asked him.

Angel just shrugged again. "Hundred million," he
said simply. "Give or take. I mean, it's an old airplane.
Who knows if anyone would have ever used it again.
But that's why the people behind all this made sure it
was never shot down by our fighters. They knew it was
much too valuable for that."

"A hundred million dollars," Delaney said with a
whistle. "I guess it's good to know what my life is
worth these days. Me and a hundred and forty-six others."

There was a very long silence. Finally Chou said:
"So, what do we do now?"

"Well, that's up to you guys," Angel said. "You've
got two injured men. And all of you almost got killed
at least once before. There'd be no shame that I can
think of if you just split now. Fly over the next hill, get
back to the real world."

The four men didn't say a word. Delaney was looking at the lights over the hill. Norton was staring up at the stars. Chou was looking down at his men and the choppers.

And Smitz?

Smitz was looking east.

"But if it's revenge you want," Angel went on, "I can tell you where you have to go, how to get there, what you can expect on arrival."

He paused. A light wind blew across the hilltop.

"Now, I can't push you one way or the other," he warned them. "I've already overstepped my bounds."

Another pause. "But I know what I'd do if I were you."

They all looked up at him. "And that is?"

"I'd go after the bastards," he said quietly. "Why let them get away with it? Why should they sleep well at night? They'll just do it again. Somehow, some way. There will always be people on this Earth whose sole purpose in life is to fuck things up for everyone else. That's how these people are. Now you guys are in a position to do a little housecleaning, if you will. And do a big favor for the rest of us."

A very long silence now.

"And I have one more piece of evidence, something that might help you make up your minds."

"Show us," Delaney told him.

"Not all of you," Angel replied. "Just him."

He was pointing at Smitz.

The CIA man laughed out loud. "Me? Why me? If anyone is low man on the totem pole these days, it's me. That's pretty clear now. I'm the one who got everyone into this. I shouldn't have any say in any of it."

"Quite the contrary," Angel said. "It really will be up to you what to do next. Only you know the person who is behind the worst part of this."

Smitz just shook his head in bafflement. None of this made sense to him.

That was when Angel walked over to him and pulled

a small, computer-generated photograph from his flight suit pocket.

"This is a picture of the guy who started it all," he told Smitz. "He's the guy who set you up and nearly got you killed. You sure you want to see it?"

Smitz nodded, though timidly. "Yes . . ." he replied.

Angel held the photo up to eye level.

"Do you recognize this man?" he asked Smitz.

Smitz stared at the photo for a very long time. His face turned several shades of red. His eyes almost teared up in disbelief. Then his teeth clenched. Then his hands rolled into fists.

Then it all sunk in.

"Yeah, I know the *bastard*," Smitz said, his voice guttural, deep, sounding like something from a horror movie.

"Well, he's your boy," Angel said. "The guy who has been doing the dirty work. Playing both sides. Collecting a ton of dough for his trouble too."

That was enough for Smitz. He began walking very quickly back down the hill towards the choppers.

"Hey, Smitty!" Delaney called after him. "Where the hell you going, man?"

Smitz turned around. He was absolutely on fire now.

"I'm going to personally kill that son of a bitch," he said. "Even if I have to fly one of those fucking choppers and do it myself."

30

The mountain on which Zim's palace sat had three layers of defense.

The road leading up to it was about a half mile long,
and it was covered with motion sensors, remote-
controlled mines, and automatic-machine-gun nests. All
of this was watched by an umbrella of hidden TV cameras that left no part of the winding mountain passage
uncovered.

Anyone intending on getting to the palace without using this road would have to scale the sheer rock face
that led up to Zim's lair via the western side of the peak.
Even a military alpine unit would have a tough time
climbing this hazardous 2,500 feet.

But to make it even more unapproachable, Zim's defensive specialists had installed a variety of bizarre but
effective weapons up and down the rock face. Many of
these Zim's people had bought at bargain-basement
prices from various warring factions in central Africa.
Most were of homemade design but ingenious. Most
prevalent was an exploding glass bomb, a devious device that when set off by a trip wire, sprayed up to five

hundred shards of glass in a depressed 45-degree conical sphere. This was enough to shred anyone within fifteen feet. There were nearly two hundred of these mines hidden among the steep rocks.

There were also five remotely controlled gun emplacements tucked away in the cliffs, each one packing a 30-mm cannon. These guns had a full range of fire at anyone coming up the mountain's west side. They were worked by an operator stationed up above, using a fire-control system taken off an Iranian destroyer and sold lock, stock, and barrel to Zim.

The third and final line of Zim's defense protected the palace's east side. This had not cost Zim a thing. Rather this barrier came courtesy of a massive land shift eons ago that left a peak soaring about 750 feet above the highest point on Zim's domain. No mines were laid on this enormous, jagged piece of rock. No automatic guns or TV cameras watched over its approaches. There was no need to. The peak was absolutely impossible to scale.

Or so everyone thought.

The 150 mercenaries guarding the interior of Zim's palace were broken up into four squads, each with approximately three dozen members.

The so-called Red Squad was responsible for patrolling the high outer walls of the compound. Specialists within this group also operated and maintained the Rapier antiaircraft systems found in the palace's four minarets. Most of the Red Squad soldiers were white South Africans, veterans of many African conflicts.

Yellow Squad patrolled the interior of the compound itself. They were like the local police force. They responded to anything from a broken door lock to complaints of rowdy guests inside the "Hotel." Like Red Squad, they were mostly South Africans, and carried Uzis or elderly but effective Bren guns.

Green Squad was responsible for protecting the grounds outside the palace. They maintained the weapons imbedded in the roadway and on the cliff face. They frequently patrolled all the way down the mountain, to the flat desert valley beyond. They were a mix of former East German and Swiss mercs.

The fourth squad was called Black Squad, and they could usually be found lounging in their luxurious barracks located near the rear of Zim's main residence and hard up against the 750-foot peak that looked out over them all. Black Squad did not walk patrol or maintain weapons. Black Squad did only special ops. Favors for Zim, the orders for which came from his lips alone.

The people in Black Squad were all Muslim fighters, veterans from various wars, arrogant with power, and usually disparaging of the other mercenaries on-site. They were, however, the toughest of the bunch and the highest paid, simply because they had no qualms about doing the dirtiest jobs for Zim. In fact they enjoyed many of them.

Black Squad also functioned as Zim's personal bodyguards. It was they who stood watch over the doors leading into his chamber, they who stood guard outside his bedroom, his kitchen, his bathroom, his sauna, wherever he was at any given moment. All of Black Squad carried AK-47's and long Sherpa knives, usually honed to a razor-sharp edge.

There was not a red alert per se that could be called inside Zim's palace.

If an emergency arose, which had never happened, Zim's orders would filter down to Black Squad, who in turn would inform the other three squads of the situation and then instruct them what to do about it. But because the palace was deemed impregnable and since no enemies had ever dared come near, there had never been any drills or any rehearsals, not even a lengthy discussion about what to do should an adversary approach the compound in force.

That was why even though Zim had given the order for the compound to prepare for attack, no one among his security forces really knew what that meant. Usually in times like this, the squads would have looked to Major Qank, the intelligence chief, for guidance. But it was well known by now that Major Qank was not among them anymore.

So for what was about to happen, the mercs were on their own.

The first sign that things were not right came just before midnight.

There was a shift change on the outer parapets among the Red Squad members. Those soldiers charged with watching the Rapier radar-acquisition screens had spotted two dots out on the very fringe of their missile system's operational range.

This was not unusual. Iraq aircraft could be seen on their radar screens occasionally—Iranian aircraft too. But these two blips were acting very strangely.

They were moving back and forth, on the edge of the screen—appearing here, disappearing there, then reappearing way over there. The Rapier's electronics told the operators the blips were not airplanes. No, the way they were flying, they could only be one thing: helicopters.

Again, to see Iraqi military helicopters passing by the Qom-el-Zarz palace was no big deal. But these helicopters were not acting like typical Iraqis. Their pilots must have known they were being painted by the Rapier long-range radar system, this the first step in being shot down by the highly accurate SAM system. Even friendly airplanes were always reluctant to get tangled up inside their own SAM webs. Accidents happened, and Rapiers rarely missed their targets.

Why then were these helicopters playing such a dangerous game?

Things had been weird around the compound in the past couple of days; that was probably the only reason why the Red Squad commander was called to look at the radar screen just as the midnight shift change was about to take place.

His name was Bumpin Slakker; he was a former

South African military officer. Slakker understood Rapiers. He knew what they could do and that it was highly foolish for anyone to play tag by passing in and out of their fields of fire. Yet that was exactly what these two blips were doing.

At first, Slakker wasn't sure what to do. It was late, he was tired, and he certainly didn't want to go around yelling that the sky was falling just because of two weird radar blips. However, he was concerned enough to decide that he would pass this information on to the Black Squad. He would explain the helicopter situation as best he could to the Black Squad's CO, and let him decide whether or not to bring it to the attention of the Great Zim.

And because it was the end of the shift, and Slakker was due to go off duty anyway, he would deliver the message to the Black Squad CO himself.

It was exactly midnight when he started making his way across the vast compound. Down from the outer wall, through the inner perimeter, towards Zim's chamber itself. He nodded to a pair of Yellow guards on patrol near the inner gate, and finally reached the alley that led to the Black Squad's barracks. His immediate plans after passing on the information to the Black Squad were to inhale a plate of food, then drink a bottle of wine, and then go to sleep. He'd worked three shifts in a row and was dead-tired.

He deserved a little shut-eye.

Slakker reached the huge black ornamented door that led into the Black Squad's billet and pounded on it three times.

There was no answer.

He pounded three more times. Again, there was no reply.

There was a window next to the door, but it was made of thick yellow glass and only the barest of shadows could be seen through it from the outside. Slakker rapped on this window several times, but saw no movement inside.

Now this was odd. The Black Squad had little to do with the palace security, except to guard Zim himself, and they did this just two at a time. Even in a shift change, that would mean only four men could be out of pocket at any given moment. So where were the other thirty-two members of the squad? Asleep? Drunk? Both?

Slakker considered just forgetting the whole thing and simply retiring to his billet. Choppers out along the radar perimeter? What was the big deal?

But something was stuck in his craw about this one, and it wouldn't let go. So he decided to take one last step to pass the information along.

He began walking around the back of the small villa that housed Black Squad. Here, he knew, was a secret, emergency exit through which the Black Guards had been known to take delivery on drugs, booze, girls, and other very non-Muslim temptations usually supplied on the sly by the less-than-savory guests at the palace's Hotel.

Slakker figured that a knock at this hidden door was one the Black Guards would always answer.

But when he made his way to the back of the barracks, he was surprised to find this secret door unlocked and wide open.

Now this was getting *very* strange. He knew the Black Squad was very careful about this rear portal. He'd seen the myriad of locks on the door from the inside. Why now had it been left so carelessly ajar?

Slakker went through the door slowly, his hand on his pistol. The first thing he saw was a pool of blood gathered around the billet's refrigerator. He slowly pulled the pistol from its holster. He took one step forward, followed the stream of blood with his eyes, and made a shocking discovery.

Thirty-four members of the Black Squad were lying facedown on the floor of the barracks mess hall. They were lined up so neatly, it was obvious great care had been taken in leaving them just this way.

They were all dead.

Each one had been shot in the back of the head.

Slakker ran across the compound, out the inner gate and across the courtyard, reaching his squad's position in thirty seconds; it was a trip that would usually take about two minutes.

His mind was reeling. What he'd just seen in the Black Squad billet had not yet registered fully in his brain. But he was relying on instincts. He was a soldier, he'd been in combat before. The Black Squad was dead—their killers unknown. His job now was to get to his own position and make sure it was secure.

That was why he made it back to the first minaret in one quarter of the normal time.

But another nightmare was waiting for him there. He burst into the Rapier control hut only to see yet another pool of blood. Two of his men were still in their seats, heads hanging back, throats slit from ear to ear.

Slakker lost his poise at this point. A bunch of guys from Black Squad getting killed was one thing. He'd just talked to the men in front of him not five minutes before. Now their heads were hanging off their bodies in the most ghastly fashion. Slakker threw up in the corner and then staggered outside.

The compound was eerily quiet. He could see no one moving about. This was not all that unusual. The palace was usually sedate, especially at night. Yet amidst this deathly silence, three dozen men had been very quietly killed.

Slakker was convinced the bloodbath was the work of Zim—a coup pulled off by the palace king himself. But then Slakker heard a low growl coming from off in the distance. Suddenly his mind switched back to the matter at hand: the mysterious helicopters orbiting just beyond the Rapier's missile's range.

He looked to the west and heard the noise again, and

saw two helicopters flying very low and heading right
at him.

He stood, stunned, as they went over his head, so low
he could see the faces of the men at the open loading
door staring down at him. In the next instant, he felt a
cold sensation below his right ear. Then he heard a horrible slitting sound. Then he felt strange hands grabbing
his chest and a foot kicking his legs out from underneath
him. Then he hit the hard wooden floor of the parapet
and saw yet another pool of blood gathering. This blood
was his own. His neck had been sliced, from ear to ear,
with no noise, no muss, no fuss.

As Slakker's life ebbed away, he became aware of
two things. The helicopters were almost right above him
now. And many feet were rushing by him—and still
there was so little noise. Who were these silent warriors?

Two pairs of boots stopped right next to where he lay
dying. One boot was so close to him, he could actually
read the serial numbers on its heel: 97846304991. Beneath these numbers it read: MADE IN THE UNITED
STATES OF AMERICA.

Americans? Slakker thought in his last instant of life.
How did the Americans ever find us here?

Unlike the four color-coordinated squads of mercenaries
protecting the outer and inner walls of the palace, a
hodgepodge of paid soldiers guarded the Hotel, many
from black African nations, wearing nothing more elaborate than plain green camo battle fatigues and bush
hats.

What these men lacked in aplomb and style, they
made up for with numbers. Indeed, there were a hundred
of them watching over the Hotel alone. They all carried
AK-47 assault rifles and prided themselves in seeing
who could carry the most ammunition on his person. It
was not unusual to see men in this so-called Z-Squad
walking about with five or six ammo bandoliers hanging
around their necks.

A dozen men were on duty in the lobby of the Hotel

this night. Six were actually standing guard duty next to the Hotel's expansive sliding door. Six more were playing cards on a long table inside what doubled as the Hotel's lounge area.

The men near the doors saw the two helicopters fly over the main wall, and at first thought nothing of it. Helicopters were constantly going in and out of the palace area—it was the easiest means to access the place. They watched the two choppers split up. One flew over the inner walls, heading toward Zim's main chamber. The other landed in the courtyard right in front of the Hotel itself.

Before the guards could react, the doors of the huge chopper burst open and men began pouring out. They were wearing what appeared to be Iraqi uniforms, but these men were not Iraqi. These were white soldiers, tall, powerful-looking, clean-shaven.

Terrifying . . .

They started shooting the moment they left the helicopter. The Hotel guards hardly had time to raise their weapons before being cut down in the brutal fusillade.

While the helicopter's landing barely upset the card game going on inside the hotel lobby, the sound of gunfire did. But before these interior men could even reach for their weapons, the Marines had broken through the plate-glass windows and were spraying the lobby with high-powered tracer fire. The cardplayers were dropped where they sat, their blood mixing in with the cards and piles of crumpled-up money.

The Marines quickly spread out. Twelve men took the lobby, then three dozen more began flooding up the stairs. Smitz was at the head of this contingent.

It would have been easier by far to simply call in the Hinds and have them decimate the Hotel—but that would not have allowed Smitz to get another peaceful night's sleep ever again.

There was a question burning in his brain; it was a fire so hot, it would not be soothed until he confirmed

what Angel claimed was true. The man who had set
them up, who had a hand in pulling the strings of this
whole bizarre affair, that man was in this building, Angel said.

In Room 6 . . .

But Smitz had to see it for himself. So now he was
running full tilt down the Hotel's long first-floor corridor, firing his M-16 at anything that moved in front of
him, usually a fleeing member of the Z-Squad.

At the same time, he could hear the gunfire intensi-
fying outside. A quick peek out a window revealed a
huge battle erupting between the troops left on the parapets and Marines firing from the second Halo, which
was moving very slowly back and forth over the palace
compound.

Time was now becoming a factor. The first group of
Marines had infiltrated the palace thirty minutes ago.
They had come in through the back door—literally.
Over the jagged mountain peak, over the only unguarded
wall in the palace, and through the rear door of the Black
Squad's barracks, quickly eliminating the most dangerous threat within the compound with their silencer-
equipped rifles—all on the advice and directions of the
guy named Angel.

But there was still danger about, as the growing gunfight outside the walls revealed.

This brought one thought to Smitz's mind. "We can't
stay very long," he whispered. This made him run even
faster.

He and the Marines finally reached the far side of the
Hotel's expansive first floor. Leaving some men behind
to watch critical passageways, Smitz and six Team 66
members moved swiftly down the last corridor.

Finally Smitz found what he was looking for: the door
to Room 6.

The Marines automatically lined up three on each side
and got ready to do a standard kick-in-and-start-firing
entry. But at the last moment, Smitz held up his hand.

"No," he said "This one is just me. . . ."

The Marine squad leader began to protest, but after a

month of being around Smitz, he knew better.

"Put three men at that end," Smitz told him, indicating the far end of the hallway. "You and the other two watch the near staircase. If I'm not out in five minutes, *then* you can kick the door in. . . ."

The Marines grudgingly acknowledged his orders and made their way to their positions. Once Smitz got the OK sign from both ends of the hallway, he took a deep breath, raised his rifle, opened the unlocked door, and stepped inside.

It looked like a Presidential suite within. It was enormous, with a big window looking out on the starkly beautiful scenery beyond. Smitz took a deep sniff—he smelled cigar smoke and alcohol.

He reached over and clicked on the light. A dim bulb popped on in the corner of the huge room; another flickered to life inside a hallway that Smitz assumed led to the bedroom. He walked slowly into the main living area, heel to toe, his gun up and ready for anything.

The room was empty, though. It was covered with newspapers, empty scotch bottles, and hundreds of pieces of scrap paper, scattered everywhere, with endless writing and doodling on them. The neatest part of the room was the kitchen area, where he found no less than a hundred bottles of nonalcoholic champagne stacked neatly into one otherwise dusty corner.

Smitz stepped into the hallway, which led to the bedroom, all the while realizing the gunfire outside was getting even more intense.

He didn't have much more time for this.

He raise the gun a bit more, walked into the bedroom, and flicked on the light. And there in front of him, he saw huddled beneath the bedclothes the man who had been living here in Room 6.

"Well, this is certainly ironic," Smitz said, stepping one foot closer to the huge bed. "Hiding under the covers, just like the last time I saw you."

With that he reached over with his snout of his rifle

and snagged the bedspread. He gave it a yank and un-covered the partially clad man beneath.

Smitz just looked down at him and spat in his face.

"What kind of man are you?" he asked, his voice filled with rage.

George Jacobs looked up at him and said: "What kind of man are *you*, spitting at an old man?"

The question gave Smitz no pause. His anger only intensified.

"I respected you," Smitz said, standing over his very healthy-looking former boss. "I thought you were the only guy with a head on his shoulders and some ethics in his pocket in the whole fucking Agency. But you turned out to be just like everyone else at that place."

Smitz just shook his head. Jacobs was looking up at him the way a man looks at his executioner.

"And not even a classy way to go out either," Smitz went on. "I mean, faking your death? Running into the arms of the puke that owns this place—and actually helping him pick targets for the gunship?"

Smitz was nearly in tears. "What kind of an American does that? I came all the way up here just to get an answer to that question."

Jacobs just shrugged—the smell of scotch was strong around him.

"Well, it's an easy question to answer," he finally replied. "Certainly not worth the trip."

Smitz raised his M-16 so it was nose-high to Jacob's face.

"Talk," he told Jacobs. "Educate me."

Jacobs just shrugged again. "Sure, I knew what the gunship was doing was despicable—I knew it a year before I even made the arrangements to come here. Just like the guys flying the damn thing knew before *they* came here. But thousands of despicable things happen around the world every goddamn day. In deepest Africa. In China. On the subcontinent. Where the hell is the great USA then? They are nowhere near the situation. Not because they can't do anything, but because they couldn't be bothered. If the person that's getting butchered is black or yellow, they certainly don't care. And if he's brown they might help out—but only if he happens to live in a country where the oil just oozes out of the ground.

"So where the fuck do you get off being so high-and-mighty, Smitty? Don't wave that flag in my face, sonny boy. I served it for forty years."

But Smitz was just shaking his head. He wasn't buying any of this.

"You still think you're so fucking clever," he growled at Jacobs. "And even when you're about to die—you're trying the same old Spook games. What do you call it? Distraction? Disinformation? Whatever it is—it ain't working. For one minute do you expect me to believe that just because a lot of immoral stuff happens around the world, it was OK for *you* to join in?"

He reached over and slapped Jacobs hard across the face.

"You're scum!" Smitz screamed at him. "Because I can see right through you. You told me that day in the hospital room why you did this—I remember now. All this—faking your death, coming here, directing the gunship, and tipping everyone we were coming—it was all for one reason."

He paused.

"Money . . ." The word dripped out of his mouth.

Jacobs began to say something, but couldn't. Smitz was right—and he knew it.

"Fucking government," Jacobs began mumbling. "Paying me a lousy eighty grand a year!"

Smitz slapped him again.

"Don't you dare bitch to me about your shitty paycheck being justification for what you've done. You were *greedy*. That's the bottom line here."

Jacobs just looked up at him and smiled. "That's the bottom line everywhere, Smitty."

The next thing Smitz knew, Jacobs's chest exploded in two bursts of blood. The old man looked down at his sudden wound and then at Smitz's rifle, as if the shots had come from there.

But they hadn't. . . .

Then a third shot hit Jacobs in the neck. His throat began gurgling. Then a fourth and a fifth shot got him right in the heart. With these, he finally slumped over, dead.

Smitz spun around and saw Chou standing at the door.

"Jeesuz, man," he screamed at the Marine officer. "We were supposed to take this guy back!"

Chou didn't say a word. He just walked forward and pulled the rest of the covers off Jacobs to reveal an Uzi in the man's right hand, his cold fingers still on the trigger. The way it was pointing, it would have blown off Smitz's genitals and sawed his lower torso in half.

"Never go into a hostile environment alone," Chou finally told him calmly. "That's the number-one rule of special ops."

By this time the Great Zim was nearing a state of complete panic.

He'd heard the first round of gunfire and when he couldn't get hold of the Black Squad members in their barracks, he knew that catastrophe had struck.

Now he only had two bodyguards with him, and they were both looking very concerned. The Japanese girls had left long ago, fleeing to parts unknown. The lights were flickering inside the palace for the first time anyone could ever remember, which made things even worse. Zim was extremely afraid of the dark.

Yet even in this moment of calamity, Zim wanted to do something very strange: He wanted to climb up to the roof of his chamber, to see what was happening for himself.

It took much grunting and pushing, but somehow the two bodyguards managed to move him up the long staircase that led out to the top of the compound's main building.

Up here, the view of the ongoing battle was intense.

There was a massive helicopter sitting just outside the gate leading to the inner compound. There were dead bodies all along the parapets and littering the outer courtyard. All four of the Rapier positions were aflame.

Zim looked down and saw the mysterious gunmen running through the building containing his precious cars—they were shooting everything to pieces. His house containing his vault of splendid art had already been dynamited. Nearly one third of his compound was on fire. Surely these soldiers would come for him next.

But then something very weird happened.

Just as it seemed the raiding soldiers would break into the main part of the palace itself, they began running back towards the waiting helicopter instead. And all the while, another huge helicopter was picking up even more of the raiders outside the main wall near the Hotel.

From all appearances, it looked like a very hasty retreat.

Zim was instantly delighted.

"See!" he began screaming to the guards. "They run at the sight of me!"

The guards shrank back a bit, but Zim seemed to have a point. They were the only two people with guns standing between the raiders and the Great Zim himself, and yet the soldiers did seem to be running away.

Why?

"Because they are afraid of me!" Zim was yelping.

It was hard to argue with him. The two huge helicopters were now taking off, their engines straining mightily as their pilots attempted to perform an almost true vertical ascent. Both helicopters finally did get off the ground, but just barely.

Zim was so excited with this turn of events, he actually began waving good-bye to the departing soldiers. The helicopters flew right over their heads, the guards cowering, again thinking someone was going to take a shot at them. But no one did. The pair of aircraft swung up and over the mountain and slowly moved away to the southwest.

Zim was beside himself now. He was absolutely astounded that he was still alive.

"Lose the battle, win the war!" he was yelling.

He turned back to his two guards.

"Together, the three of us will build another palace, bigger and better than this place. And for your loyalty, you two will be my four-star generals. What do you say to that?"

But the guards weren't really listening to him anymore. They had detected something over the shrill tones of Zim's boasts. It was a very low rumbling, so deep it seemed to be shaking the air itself.

And right away, they knew what it was.

"Up there!" one guard yelled. "See it?"

It came out of the dark sky as always, looking like some kind of monstrous bird, its engines droning, its ghostly, unmistakable camouflage visible even in the night, four huge guns sticking out of one side.

It was the AC-130 gunship. Coming home to roost.

The guards fled and Zim tried to, but it was tough to beat the speed of a bullet. The airplane went into a left-hand arc about a hundred feet above the palace and opened up with all four of its guns at once.

It was like a hailstorm of fire and metal as the awesome barrage tore into what remained of the compound. The Hotel was decimated first. Then the remains of the car hall, the art vault, the power station, and the waterworks.

The plane dipped its left wing even lower, and this served to focus its firepower. Like a massive ocean wave, the cascade of bullets walked through the front gate of the inner sanctum, over the minarets, through the thick walls themselves. The tracers looked like a solid sheet of flame as they hit the pale blue dome of Zim's inner chamber. Everywhere was smoke, fire. The sound of things blowing up.

Three revolutions around the palace and the guns finally snapped off. There was really nothing left to fire at by then. The palace and every building within it had been leveled.

Nothing over twelve inches high remained standing.

Inside the C-130, Delaney crawled back up to the flight deck and settled into the copilot's seat beside Norton.

The plane was handling like a breeze, so much so, Norton could hardly believe it had just cracked up a few hours before. But the C-130 was known for surviving rough landings and making scary takeoffs. As it turned out, the onion field had proved to be a reasonable runway.

"How'd we do?" Delaney asked Norton, whose eyes were still glued on the burning palace. "It's hard to see from back there."

"The weaponry performed as advertised," was how Norton replied.

Deep down, though, even he was shocked at the destruction he and Delaney had managed to inflict. The palace looked like it had been carpet-bombed by a squadron of B-52's. Yet they'd been over it for less than two minutes.

"This plane is too powerful," Norton heard himself whisper. "Too dangerous . . ."

At last, Delaney got his first good view of the demolished palace.

"Muthafucker," he whispered. "That's a lot of hurt for just the two of us!"

"Well, whoever ran this bird before helped by rigging the software to fire on command," Norton said. "That's what made it so easy."

"Yeah, lucky us," Delaney mumbled.

Norton finally turned the big plane southwest and gunned its engines, anxious to leave the burning mountaintop behind. They would now meet the others back at the onion field, where they would abandon the helicopters and head for greener pastures. And not a moment too soon.

It was a weird place to end a story that had started

just off the Florida coast so many twists and turns ago. Norton and Delaney weren't even sure who owned the palace they'd just destroyed or what this person's position on the planet was. All they knew was this: He was the man behind the gunship—and now he'd just tasted its wrath big-time.

"So, fuck you," Delaney said, taking one long last look at the flames lighting up the horizon. "Whoever you were . . ."

31

Western Saudi Arabia

Colonel Larry S. Howard was the commanding officer of the secret American air base in the Saudi desert known as Al-Khalid.

It had been a long, busy day at the base. An unusual amount of military activity had been reported in the northeast regions of Iraq in the past forty-eight hours, and no less than fourteen U-2 spy planes had dropped in on Al-Khalid since the previous evening, needing gas-ups and fresh film for their cameras.

The last one had departed just thirty minutes ago. Once it had reported from its first radio checkpoint that all was OK, Howard dragged himself back to his quarters and collapsed on the bed. He hadn't slept for more than ten minutes at a time in the past two days. Now he was hoping for at least six undisturbed hours of down time, maybe even more.

Yet no sooner had he drifted off when his phone rang.

It was the security officer for the base.

"Sorry to bother you, sir," he said. "But we have a Green-Zulu-Six situation. . . ."

It took a moment for these code words to sink into Howard's sleepy brain.

"Are you sure?" he asked the security officer. "Green-Zulu-Six?"

"That's confirmed, sir," was the reply. "We're looking at something happening inside of fifteen minutes."

Howard checked the time. It was 0130 hours—one-thirty in the morning. It was raining outside.

"OK," Howard told the security officer wearily. "Call a Code Three alert. I'll meet you on the flight line in five minutes."

Four minutes and thirty seconds later, Howard was roaring along the base's main runway. Up ahead he could see six vehicles gathered near the auxiliary taxiway. He tapped his HumVee driver on the shoulder, and the man brought them to a skidding stop right in front of the base security officer's vehicle.

Howard got out and pulled his rain slicker up around his neck. It was a fallacy that it was always hot and dry in the desert. Many times it was cold, wet, and miserable. This was one of those times.

The security officer approached. Even through his slicker, Howard could see his face looked rather troubled.

"Green-Zulu-Six?" Howard asked him again. "You're certain?"

"Yes, sir," the security officer replied. "We got the message about oh-one-thirty hours. Confirmed it two minutes ago."

Green-Zulu-Six was code for an unauthorized flight requesting permission to land at the secret base. Usually this meant some kind of defection was about to take place, usually Iraqi pilots bugging out and taking their fighter jets or helicopters with them. Of course, the U.S. military greeted such people with open arms, especially if they brought additional valuables like code books along with them.

"Is the translator at the ready?" Howard asked the security man.

But the man did not reply right away. Howard looked at him closely; he could tell the officer had something further to tell him.

"Well, spit it out," Howard told him. "What is it?"

"This is not an Iraqi defection situation, sir," the security man finally said.

"What do you mean? You said Green-Zulu-Six."

"We *do* have an unauthorized flight coming in," the security man replied. "But the call sign matches an aircraft that once flew from this very base. An *American* aircraft."

Howard just stared at him. "What are you talking about? Why would an American airplane be requesting a Green-Zulu landing?"

The security officer had anticipated this question. He had with him a prime operations log. It was a record of all takeoffs and landings made at the base in any given year. This book was for 1991.

He opened the page to February 9. He pointed to an entry. It read: *ArcLight 4.*

Howard scanned the page and looked at the security man.

"Is this a joke?" he asked, not in the mood.

"I . . . don't know, sir," the security man replied.

He pointed to the page again.

"This aircraft, U.S. Air Force AC-130 . . . code-named ArcLight 4 . . . has asked for permission to land here, sir."

Howard was suddenly trembling slightly, though he didn't know why. He'd heard about ArcLight 4, of course. The special ops plane took off from Al-Khalid nearly ten years ago and simply disappeared.

Now it was coming back?

"That's what it says," the security man replied. "The person we talked to on the plane knows all the old security codes, as well as the current ones."

Howard just shook his head. This didn't make sense. He didn't want it to make sense.

"OK, call command," he told the man finally. "And get your security detail up here."

The security officer pointed to the four troop trucks parked nearby.

"Already on hand, sir," he said. "And no other flights are due in."

"Damn," Howard whispered to himself. "Am I still asleep?"

"I'm asking myself the same thing, sir," the security man replied.

Fifteen minutes later, there were twenty-two heavily armed troops lining the end of the main runway at Al-Khalid.

It was still raining, but some fog had moved in and now visibility was down to almost zero.

Howard was there, leaning against his HumVee, with a video man as well as the base chaplain. Four emergency vehicles were parked nearby. The rest of Al-Khalid was on lockdown.

Howard had no idea what to expect. He was closely watching the time. The plane was supposed to have landed ten minutes ago. Yet absolutely nothing had happened.

He finally turned to the security man. "This is a bust," he said. "Must have been a security test or something."

That was when they heard a deep groaning sound. It seemed very far away and oddly echoing. It startled them all.

"Jeesuz," Howard whispered. "What the fuck was that?"

The chaplain shifted his weight from one foot to the other, but Howard didn't care. He'd been around airplanes all his career. He was a pilot as well. He knew their different sounds. And what he heard now—eerily so—was the distinctive sound of a C-130 Hercules on final approach.

He turned to the video man and said: "Start taping and don't miss a thing or your ass is in Thule."

The sound got louder. Deeper.

Then through the fog they saw a light. It was very faint at first. But slowly it grew brighter and brighter, until it was sending a thin beam piercing through the rain and mist. It seemed like a monster flying right at them.

Suddenly it burst through the fog. It looked huge, ghostly—and it was going way too fast.

"Damn!" Howard heard a few people cry.

The C-130 roared by them at tremendous speed and way too high for a successful landing. It was trailing smoke and exhaust, and was moving through the fog in such a way that it looked like a blurry photo.

As quickly as it came, it was gone, enveloped by the fog again. In all, they'd seen it for only two or three seconds, no more.

"Dear Jesus, what the *fuck* was that!" the chaplain cried out.

No one was sure. It was quiet again for a few seconds. Then they heard the deep rumbling again.

They all looked to the right, as if the airplane had turned around and was coming in again. But then it roared by—from the opposite direction.

This time it was a little lower, but it was still going very, very fast.

The noise didn't go away, though. The airplane made an impossibly tight turn and came in a third time. This time it was still going fast, but it was very low.

And its wheels were down.

"Shit! He's going to crash!" Howard yelled.

The plane slammed into the runway an instant later. It came down hard, bounced, came down again, scraped its right wing along the asphalt, causing a brilliant cascade of sparks, bounced again, and then finally came down for good about eight hundred feet from Howard's position.

In seconds, the base's emergency vehicles were screaming down the runway after it, as were the trucks filled with security troops. Howard found himself running towards the near-wreck, the chaplain on one side, the video man on the other.

When they arrived, the rescue team had already reached the aircraft and had yanked one of the rear doors open.

And that was when they all saw a very haunting sight.

A troop of soldiers came marching out of the airplane. They looked ghostly. Their uniforms were covered with white dust, as were their faces. Some were also covered with dried blood. Two were on stretchers. But they were in order and in step, and they marched out like a company of spirits, right past everyone and coming to a stop in a single line beside the burning airplane.

Howard felt a chill go right through him. The chaplain made the sign of the cross. The video man stopped taping; he was too stunned.

Three men came crawling out of the heavily damaged cockpit. The rescue forces were on hand to help, but the trio did not want any assistance. It seemed important to them that they walk away from the demolished airplane under their own power.

These men looked as bad as the frightful soldiers. Two of them Howard tagged as pilots. The third man looked particularly agitated. He walked right up to Howard and flashed a burned and broken ID badge. It was CIA. It identified the man as Gene Smitz.

"My men need a hot meal and a place to sleep," he told Howard. "Then we want transport out to a commercial airport."

"And who *the hell* are you?" Howard demanded.

"You have a cell phone?" Smitz asked in reply.

Howard didn't, but the chaplain did. Howard snapped his fingers, and Smitz was soon punching a series of numbers into the phone. Smitz waited for the phone to ring twice. Someone on the other end finally answered. Smitz threw the phone back to Howard.

"Ask *them* who we are," he said.

Howard had a brief conversation and read out the numbers on Smitz's ID card. Then he counted the number of men lined up beside the airplane.

Then he turned back to Smitz.

"They want to know what happened to the helicopters," he said.

Smitz looked as if he was about to burst. The two men behind him shared this feeling.

"Tell them," Smitz said in measured angry words, "that our mission was to return the ArcLight 4 and its crew. There's the airplane—and there are thirteen body bags inside. You can bury them as far out in the desert as you want. I suggest in unmarked graves. . . ."

Howard repeated these words to the person at the other end of the phone.

Then one of the pilots broke through and had another thing to say. It was Norton.

"And tell them they can cancel their buddy Jacobs' pension payments," he said angrily. "He won't be needing them anymore."

Howard said these words too. There was a long pause. Then he shut off the phone and called up his security officer.

"Give all these men a hot meal and a place to sleep," he snapped. Then he looked at the ragged bunch and the burning airplane.

"In fact, give them anything they want. . . ."

32

It was already hot this Saturday morning when Ryan Gillis arrived at the empty ballpark.

He took his ball from his glove and rubbed dirt on it. Then he picked up his bat and rubbed dirt on it too. Next he put dirt on his hands—he wasn't sure why. He'd seen a lot of real ballplayers do this, so he thought he should do it too. After his disastrous oh-for-four, three-error debut a week earlier, he figured he needed all the help he could get.

The park seemed bigger this early morning—big and empty. Ryan just sighed, picked up his ball, and hit it straight up. As soon as the ball left his bat, he slipped his glove on, planted himself under the ball, and caught it. At least he was getting good at this routine.

He picked up the ball again, adjusted his glove, threw the ball in the air, and hit it again. Again, it went straight up, he pulled his glove back on, and got under the pop-up just in time to catch it.

Two for two . . .

He repeated the process again, but this time he some-how managed to hit the ball very high behind him. He quickly yanked on his glove and started backpedaling, trying to keep his balance and his eye on the ball at the same time.

The ball seemed to hang up forever, but when it came down Ryan finally got himself right under it. He lifted his glove, closed his eyes, and . . . nothing happened.

He stood there waiting for the ball to hit him some-where—on the head was usually where he got plunked. But this did not happen.

So finally he opened his eyes.

And that was when he realized someone else had caught the ball. Someone who was standing right over him—an adult. The ball was firmly in his hand. Ryan spun around and looked up.

And that was when he saw the hand belonged to his father.

"Dad!" he yelled, dropping bat and glove and hug-ging his father for the first time in many years.

"Hey, kid," Gillis said. "Looking good with that glove these days."

Ryan held on tight.

"Geesh, Dad," he said, looking up at his father's weary eyes. "Where have your been all this time?"

Gillis laughed. "I can't tell you, son," he said. "If I did, then I'd have to . . . well, never mind."

Ryan's eyes widened. "Wow! You mean you really *were* on a secret mission?"

Gillis picked up the bat, and handed Ryan his glove.

"I promise I'll tell you all about it someday," he said.

He threw the ball in the air and hit a high pop-up. His back hurt from the swing, and his burned legs still twinged, but he didn't really feel the pain.

"In the meantime," Gillis said, "let's see what you've learned since I've been away."

Ryan ran and caught the ball and began to hand it back to Gillis—but then stopped and took a deep sniff.

"Hey, Dad," he said. "How come you smell so much like gasoline?"

Gillis managed another smile, and took the ball from Ryan's glove again.

"I'll tell you all about that someday too," he said.

The waters were unusually calm in the Straits of Florida this hazy Sunday afternoon.

The chartered game-fishing boat was heading south, at high speed, having left Key West about a half hour before.

The boat cost $150 an hour to rent, bait and tackle included, but the two passengers had no interest in fishing. This was a covert ride.

Neither one had even touched the free beer provided them by the boat's owner. From this, he knew something was up with them, so he just let them be. Sitting on the rear deck, staring out at the wake of the vessel, they looked like two soldiers suffering from shell shock. The boat owner knew it was best he leave them alone.

They had given him a strange destination—and would pay him $100 extra if he found it too. This was odd because he knew the place they wanted to go to very well. He'd brought many people there in the past two weeks. In fact, he'd been enjoying a real boom in transporting sports fishermen out there lately.

So this was another reason why the boat owner kept his mouth shut.

The trip took less than ninety minutes. The only thing that slowed them down really was the gaggle of surface traffic surrounding the location where the two mysterious guys wanted to go.

So crowded was this place, it took fifteen extra minutes and many calls to the marina before the boat owner was finally able to find them an open berth at the dock.

Only then did he pull into the south bay of Seven Ghosts Key.

*   *   *

Norton and Delaney climbed off the boat in a state of shock. Actually, they were suffering from a state of shock *on top of* the state of shock they'd been in for the past week or so.

Seven Ghosts was simply crawling with people. Small private planes flying in and out. Hundreds of fishing boats tied up or anchored offshore. The south beach full of sunbathers.

The restaurant was especially packed. There had to be at least a couple thousand people—men, women, and kids—crowded onto the previously isolated island.

The two pilots just stood and stared at it all.

"Have I finally gone crazy?" Norton asked.

It had been that kind of week.

They stayed at Al-Khalid only a few hours. The thought of getting caught on the ground, exposed again, still haunted all of them.

So somehow Smitz arranged for two buses to carry them out of the secret air base and on to Riyadh. Once there, he gave each man a credit card, the source of which was unknown. Then they all boarded commercial flights—seventeen different ones—and flew in different directions.

Norton and Delaney went east, through Islamabad, to Delhi, to Sydney, Hong Kong, and finally Anchorage. They lay low there for two days before flying to San Diego and finally on to Miami.

They moved like dead men, with ease but caution. The bad guys in the CIA probably didn't know where they were or if they were dead or alive, and they wanted to keep it that way. They were both still carrying for protection the huge pistols they had used to shoot down the AC-130 gunship. And anytime they were stopped by airport security, they simply flashed their Level Six security passes and were let through.

They really felt like lost men, though. Like ghosts doomed to wander the earth, with nowhere to go. So they'd decided early on that the one place they could seek answers and revenge was back where it all started: Seven Ghosts Key.

But now, the place looked as crowded as Disneyworld.

"Man, just when you think things can't get any nuttier," Delaney said. "They do!"

They started walking slowly down the runway, wondering if this was like a CIA family outing or something. It didn't seem to be, though. Everyone they passed appeared very normal, very touristy. Very un-CIA.

They finally reached the restaurant, and it was absolutely jammed. And next door, gone were the shuttered-tight buildings that had housed their simulators. The structures were now open and housing dozens of small private airplanes. And the places where the Marines had attacked and billeted were now overnight motels.

They elbowed their way into the restaurant, and found the big briefing room filled with happy drunks and ravenous diners. Yet everything, including the wall murals, was the same.

They made their way over to the bar, Delaney bringing up the possibility that maybe the CIA had fed them LSD somewhere along the line—and all of this was just a hallucination. Norton replied that they just weren't that lucky.

The bar was crowded with fishermen and bathers, sucking down martinis like they were water. Both Norton and Delaney needed a drink—if just to convince themselves they were indeed still among the living. So they finally hailed the burly bartender. He turned and looked at both of them and smiled.

It was Rooney.

The CIA man who used to run Seven Ghosts Key.

Delaney reached over and grabbed the man by the collar.

"Whose side are you on, asshole!" Delaney growled at him.

Norton quickly intervened and pulled his partner off the CIA man. The place was so loose, none of the other patrons had noticed a thing.

"Relax," Rooney said, barely ruffled. "Fistfights are bad for business."

"So are bullet-riddled bodies," Delaney snapped back. "Which you are going to be . . ."

Norton restrained Delaney from pulling his massive handgun. Then he turned back to Rooney.

"OK, tell us," he said wearily. "What the fuck is going on here?"

Rooney just shrugged. "You must appreciate the concept of protecting one's cover," he said matter-of-factly. "Can you think of a better way?"

Delaney went for his gun again. Norton froze his hand.

"We were set up over there," Norton continued through gritted teeth. "Or are you not familiar with that concept?"

Rooney served a few more drinks. Then he came back to Norton and Delaney.

"Look," he said, his voice lower now. "You guys don't realize it, but you're heroes. You uncovered, shall we say, 'a major internal dispute' within the Agency, and you applied the remedy. A permanent one. Plus, you did a hell of a job getting that airplane back."

Delaney was still furious. "Think that was easy, asshole?"

Rooney just shook his head. "Think I haven't been in the same spot?"

For some reason, that silenced all three of them. Rooney poured a couple of martinis from a pitcher and pushed them towards Norton and Delaney.

"You see, you guys think you're still in the military. Still in the real world," Rooney said, his voice sounding like a grandfather gently scolding his grandsons. "Well, you're not. And you haven't been since you set foot on this place. You're in Dreamland now, baby. You're

Spooks. Spooks in deep. Nothing makes sense. Nothing ever will.''

Norton thought about this for a moment, then reached for the martini and downed it in one gulp.

"Give me another," he gasped as the liquor burned its way down to his stomach.

"Now you're talking," Rooney said, pushing Delaney's drink a bit more towards him.

Delaney finally relented, and downed his drink in one swallow as well.

"Very good, gentlemen," Rooney said, refilling their glasses and expertly popping two olives into each. "Now my advice to you is to just relax. Spend a few days here fishing, on the beach. Eat good. Rest up. Get ready for your next assignment."

Delaney started to go for his gun again.

"Next assignment!" he growled. "You *must* be insane."

"Well, that is a concept I'm familiar with," Rooney said. "But take a look around you. A good look."

Norton did—and slowly he realized just who was crowded into the restaurant with them. Over in the corner was Chou, having a beer, surrounded by many of his noncoms. In the next corner were the four Army Aviation guys. Beside them were the SEAL medics. Sprinkled throughout the crowd, mixing with regular citizens, were the rest of Chou's men. They were blending in perfectly.

Norton looked at Delaney, and both men drained their martinis again, this time much more slowly.

"You see," Rooney explained, "most everyone who went with you to Oz came back to Kansas eventually. They always do."

He poured them two more drinks. They were finally catching on. They were in this strange business to stay.

"That's it, guys," Rooney said. "Lighten up. I hear the fishing off south beach has been really good in the past couple of days."

Delaney began sipping his third martini. He was slowly getting stoned.

"It better be," he said, his speech slurring. "They better be catching fucking whales."

Norton slumped in his seat, and he too felt the world slowly lift off his shoulders.

"Or mermaids," he added.

Rooney smiled and winked.

"Well," he said. "That can be arranged too."

Somewhere in the Nevada desert

In a sky filled with billions of stars, the greenish-bluish object moved very quickly across the horizon.

Atop a mountain known only as H-13, a small observatory was tracking the oddly illuminated flying object. Inside this tiny station, two technicians were watching a huge screen that, at the push of a button, could depict any part of the earth via real-time television transmission.

Once the bluish object appeared on their screens, several sensor lights went off.

"OK, finally, there he is," one technician said.

"Let's get him over and down and then we can all go home," the other replied.

Now came an orgy of button pushing and computer keyboard clacking. The object was over Utah and heading right toward them. It was 650 miles away. Then 550. Then 450. Then 350. All in just a matter of seconds.

"His inertia dampener is overloading a bit," one tech said. "We'll have to check it."

"Sure we can check it—*tomorrow*," the second one replied. "I feel like I've been here a month."

"Same here," the first tech agreed.

They watched the object cross over the Nevada border.

It was now 225 miles away. Then 175. Then 125.

"That gyro buffer is getting crazy too," the first tech

said, reading the constant flow of diagnostic numbers on one of the many screens facing him.

"That's the fucking sand," the second man said. "If anyone ever finds out he actually set down in that thing three times near blowing sand, for Christ's sake—they'll shoot us all. You, me, *and* him!"

"That's why no one will ever know," the first man responded.

The object was now on their primary screen and they could see it up close for the first time in a while. It was a very plain but odd-looking thing. A kind of pancake with winglets, triangular in shape, the size of a utility sports vehicle, flattened out. Like a bad flying saucer from a bad science-fiction movie was how someone once put it.

But it could move very *very* fast.

The aircraft was twenty-five miles away—and then, a few seconds later, it was right above the observatory. It had made the transit over the desert in less than two minutes.

One tech hit a button, and the roof of the station slid open. Both men looked straight up, and saw the blue object hovering absolutely still about a hundred feet above them.

The second tech keyed his microphone.

"OK, bring it down before the whole world sees you."

With that, the aircraft began to slowly descend. It took about ten seconds before it was inside the observatory itself. Then buttons were pushed and the roof closed back up again.

The aircraft made absolutely no sound; there was no outward sign of any propulsion. Up close it really looked more purple than blue, and its hull was still sparkling slightly from its high-speed trip back home.

Once it was down on its special receiving platform, a seamless door opened on its top. Next to it was the only identification that could be found on the strange aircraft. In very small gold-leaf letters it read: *Aurora-6/ h-M.*

The door finally opened all the way. Inside, the pilot stood up, stretched, and stepped out.

He took off his helmet, shook his hair out, and then took a baseball cap offered by one of the two technicians. The cap said, "Angels Last Longer than Eternity," on the brim. It was his second-favorite hat.

"Change the oil, check the tires, and put some water in the radiator, OK, guys?" he said as he put on the hat.

One tech took a huge pod from the behind the vehicle's front landing strut. It contained thousands of minutes of videotape. In reality, this strange airplane was supposed to be a recon vehicle. Nothing else.

"They want you downstairs ASAP," one tech told the pilot. "If you broke anything, don't blame it on us, OK?"

The pilot walked to a small elevator, pushed a button, and the doors opened. He stepped in, pushed another button, the doors closed, and he was soon hurtling straight down through the mountain.

After fifteen seconds, the elevator stopped with a hiss of air and the pilot walked out. Before him was a dark chamber with a huge gleaming table.

Seven men sat around it. They were all elderly, with either long flowing gray hair or no hair at all. Each one was dressed in a Western shirt with blue jeans and cowboy boots.

The pilot took an empty seat at the head of the table. Someone passed him a Coke, his favorite beverage.

"We watched just about the entire episode on the big TV," one of the men told him. "Those chopper guys were never at a loss at getting their asses in a ringer."

The pilot nodded. "Yeah, but they got good at getting out of them as well."

"Only because you were there," one said. "Without you, they'd all be dust by now."

"Yes, maybe so," the pilot said. "But you're the ones who were really watching over them, feeding them the right orders when they needed it. And telling me what to do and when to do it. I realize it was risky, but without you guys, they wouldn't have even made it over to Iraq alive. The only difference is, they saw me. They think I'm the one who saved them. For all they know, you guys aren't even alive.''

The pilot slurped his Coke, shrugged, and added: ''I guess that's another reason they call me Angel.''

The seven men all laughed at once.

Then one said: ''And that's the reason they call us ghosts.''